A
WISH FOR
CHRISTMAS

A
WISH FOR
CHRISTMAS

A Novel

COURTNEY
COLE

AVON

An Imprint of HarperCollins*Publishers*

A WISH FOR CHRISTMAS. Copyright © 2023 by Lakehouse Press. All rights reserved. Printed in the United States of America. No part of this book may be used or reproduced in any manner whatsoever without written permission except in the case of brief quotations embodied in critical articles and reviews. For information, address HarperCollins Publishers, 195 Broadway, New York, NY 10007.

HarperCollins books may be purchased for educational, business, or sales promotional use. For information, please email the Special Markets Department at SPsales@harpercollins.com.

FIRST EDITION

Designed by Diahann Sturge

Garland image throughout © Yellowj / Shutterstock

Library of Congress Cataloging-in-Publication Data has been applied for.

ISBN 978-0-06-329639-8

23 24 25 26 27 LBC 5 4 3 2 1

To everyone who believes in Christmas magic

A
WISH FOR
CHRISTMAS

CHAPTER ONE

The undisturbed snow in Central Park glitters like diamonds in the night, catching Nora's eye as she chases her runaway dog. Elliott drags his leash over the icy walking paths, and every once in a while, Nora swears he turns around and laughs at her.

"You are a mangy mutt!" she calls out. In response, Elliott makes a sharp turn to the left, plowing through a pristine powdery snowbank and emerging on the other side, back into civilization. With snow on his massive snout, he heads toward the nearest sidewalk, oblivious of traffic and pedestrians.

"Adopt a mastiff, they said," she mutters breathlessly. "It'll be fun, they said." She glances over her shoulder, hunting for her husband.

"Jack!" she calls when she doesn't see him. "He's headed toward Mercy Street."

She breaks a left and leaps onto the sidewalk, her snow boot sliding just a bit on landing. She rights herself and sprints after her dog, who in spite of her grumbling, she loves more than life itself.

Ahead, through the sparkle of festive Christmas lights adorning the street, Elliott lopes through the shoppers peering into store windows. Some look at him curiously, and some step back in horror when they see the two-hundred-pound canine lumbering in their direction.

"He won't hurt you!" Nora calls out. "He's a giant baby."

Elliott emits a deep bark, as if to argue.

"I'm going to kill you!" she hollers.

She can tell he's finally slowing down. He pants a bit more, and gallops down the sidewalk, as people part to allow him through. No one has the courage to step on the giant dog's leash and bring him to a stop.

He pauses in front of a dimly lit store at the end of the street, sniffs at the door, and then nudges his way in. The door, apparently, hadn't fully latched, but it does so now after he walks through.

"Got ya," Nora crows as she races to trap him inside.

The old door has brass bells overhead that tinkle when she pushes it open. The smell of cinnamon and orange hits her nose, and she comes to a stop. Soft Christmas carols come from an old record player in the corner, and as Bing Crosby croons, Nora scans her surroundings. Antiques of all sorts are crammed into every inch of available space. Vintage Christmas decor is out on display; dark old wood surrounds her at every turn.

"Hello?" she calls.

She takes a few more steps and comes eye to eye with a Victorian doll dressed in caroler's garb, complete with a mink muff. The doll unfortunately has only one eye, which does give

Nora pause before she continues poking her way through the cluttered shop.

"Hello!" a deep voice calls. Nora looks up and spots an elderly man emerging from the back. He's got a lion's mane of white hair and bushy white eyebrows. He's so large that he dwarfs her traitor of a dog, who trails closely on the man's heels, happily munching on something. "I assume this hungry boy is yours?"

Nora nods. "I'm so sorry for intruding. I was walking him, and his leash slipped out of my hand. He thinks this is a great game to play." She eyes her dog, who has crumbs on his muzzle. "I assure you, no matter what he told you, he's not hungry," she adds wryly.

The door opens at that moment, and her husband bounds through, panting and tired.

"Oh, good," he manages to say. "I thought I saw you come in here." He looks around, his hazelnut hair hidden beneath his stocking cap. "Oh, no. Did he break anything?"

The old man chuckles. "Not a thing." He eyes the two of them. "I was just getting ready to make a nice cup of hot cocoa. Would you folks be interested?"

"Oh, we couldn't," Jack says at the exact same time as Nora answers, "That would be amazing!" She's rubbing her cold hands together.

The old man laughs again. "I think we'd better get the lady some chocolate."

Jack winces. "I don't want to spoil the fun, but I've got a conference call at nine. I barely had time to walk the dog with you tonight."

Nora shoots him a look.

"But sure." Jack sighs. "Of course we'd love to join you. It's the least we can do—you caught our dog. If I have to, I can take the call from my phone."

"I didn't so much catch your dog as he caught *me*," the old man says as he leads them to a quaint sitting space on the side of the store. "I was just getting ready to have some cookies, and I'm supposed to be avoiding sugar." He gestures for them to sit on the antique settee and then turns his attention to a small portable stove.

"My name is Padraig; you can call me Pad. I'm afraid I don't have much gingerbread left to offer you," he says apologetically. "Elliott here sure liked it, though."

He motions toward an empty plate, where crumbs line the bottom. They match the crumbs on Elliott's muzzle, and he shows no remorse whatsoever as he wags his tail at Pad.

"Oh my word," Nora breathes. "I'm so sorry. He has no manners when it comes to food. You'd think he's starving, but he is the best fed dog you've ever seen, I promise."

"He's not wanting for groceries," Pad agrees, staring at Elliott's stout frame. "But there were just a few out on the plate. I thought it was only going to be me, after all. Having company is a nice surprise. Christmas isn't meant to be spent alone, after all."

Nora shoots another glance at her husband. *Humor the old man*, her eyes say. *He's lonely.*

"You've still got a few days left to shop," Nora reminds him. "Do you have any family coming?"

He shakes his large head. "No family *to* come," he tells them as he stirs the milk. "My wife died years ago, and we didn't have any children. You?"

Both Nora and Jack visibly flinch.

"We don't have children," Jack answers him, almost stiffly, taking the pressure from Nora. "But we do have family. We're actually not from the city. We both grew up in a small Wyoming town. Our parents want us to come visit, but this year, our schedules are just too crazy."

"Work?" the old man guesses.

"Always." Nora sighs. "Jack works on Wall Street. It's dog-eat-dog, and he never has any free time." Her tone is slightly sharp and a bit resentful, even to Pad's untrained ear.

"Your schedule isn't much better," Jack mutters. He glances at Pad. "She's an editor for a publishing company here in the city. It was supposed to just be an easy breezy job to occupy her after college until we started a family, but it grew a life of its own, and now she's on track to be the editor in chief within a few years."

"Well, now," Pad drawls, spooning heaps of chocolate powder into red mugs. "That surely sounds impressive."

"It is," Jack agrees. "She'll be the youngest editor in chief Parker-Hamilton has ever had." His tone is also a bit resentful, and his wife shakes her head a little.

"Thirty-seven is young to be an editor in chief, but old to have a baby," she explains to Pad. It's clearly a sensitive topic, and both she and Jack hate that they're talking about it in front of Pad. "I got sucked into building a career. Jack doesn't think it's possible to do both."

She grimaces, and they try to change the subject, but as Pad hands them their hot cocoa a few minutes later and sits down across from them, he brings it back up.

"These days, plenty of women in their older thirties have babies," he offers. "Or so I've read."

"We barely have time for our *dog*," Jack tells him. "We have to hire someone to come check on him twice during the day and to walk him during the week. You've seen how he behaves. If we can't make time to appropriately care for a dog, how can we make time for a baby?"

"I reckon priorities change after little ones come," Pad says easily, sipping his frothy brew.

"Or they *don't*, and we'll end up paying lifelong therapy bills for our kid," Jack answers.

"Choices are always within our control," Pad reminds him. "If you want to make time for something, you can."

"Not so easily done if your spouse doesn't agree," Jack answers.

Nora's head snaps up. "I'm not the only culprit here. I'm quite positive I can have a worthwhile career and still be a great mother. You're the one who can't even take an hour every evening to walk our dog together."

"I'm here, aren't I?" Jack mutters back.

It's a sore subject, and Pad finally steers away from it.

"Marriage is funny, isn't it?" he muses. His blue eyes study the couple in front of him. They're a beautiful pair, tall and slender, near the same age. By all appearances, they're perfectly matched, yet they aren't touching now and, in fact, practically lean away from each other on the couch.

Jack absently strokes Elliott's head, with his other hand balled up and tucked beneath his leg.

"They say that after a while, married folks even start looking alike. Thank goodness that wasn't the case with my Maria." He laughs, his bulbous nose red. They laugh with him as he runs a hand through his thick unruly hair. "But you two—you're a perfect pair. How long have you been married?"

"Since college," Jack answers. "We got married the summer of our sophomore year."

"Our parents thought we were too young," Nora adds. "We'd known each other our whole lives, though, and we knew what we wanted. We thought."

Pad eyes her now. "You thought?"

"Things change, I guess."

Her tone is sad, almost hollow.

"Things do change," Pad agrees. "Changes can even be made backward, if you do it just right. But whatever the case, things can change. Sometimes, you're just too close to something to see what needs to be done."

Changes can be made backward? His words seem nonsensical. Jack and Nora exchange a covert glance.

"Do you live here alone?" Nora asks him, trying not to be intrusive but suddenly a bit concerned.

"I do," he tells them. "Having an apartment behind the shop saves on money, and everyone knows that Social Security isn't what it used to be. I putter around here all day, and I work on my story. I'm writing a book, you see. Or trying to."

Nora suddenly tenses and hopes it's not apparent. The worst

part about being an editor is that whenever someone finds out, they inevitably try to pitch her a book.

Padraig doesn't, though. Instead, he turns to Jack. "It's nearing nine o'clock. Would you like to use one of the back rooms to take your call?"

Jack glances at Nora. Even though they clearly resent each other, he still wordlessly checks with his wife. Pad notices.

"Nora will be fine here with me," he tells Jack. "I'll keep her entertained with stories of my Maria."

Nora nods slightly and smiles. "Go ahead, Jack. I'll be fine."

When Jack stands up, Elliott sprawls onto the floor, taking up all available space. He makes sure, however, to keep one paw touching Nora's foot.

"He had a bad upbringing," Nora tells Pad. "He was used as a bait dog for dogfighters. See the scars?" She points to various scars on Elliott's head, neck, and torso. "It took him some time to get used to normal life when we first adopted him. He's come a long way, but he definitely likes to stay near us."

"How does he get along during the day when you're gone?" Pad asks.

"That's why we have to hire a dog sitter," she answers. "He doesn't like to be alone."

"Poor ol' boy," Pad croons. Elliott's tail thumps the ground, even though he doesn't open his eyes.

"His shenanigans have exhausted him," Pad announces.

Nora laughs. "You've certainly got his number. He's got a good heart but an eye for antics."

Pad laughs with her. "That's the only way to be," he answers. His own blue eyes sparkle merrily.

"I can tell that you're familiar with that particular trait." Nora grins. "Jack used to be that way, too."

Pad raises an eyebrow.

"I think Wall Street changes a person," she finally answers. "It's so high-pressure, it's so cutthroat . . . he's forgotten who he is outside of that."

"That's too bad," Pad says, clucking his tongue a bit. "Maybe you should try to remind him."

"I have." She sighs. "He pushes my buttons, I push his. Our lives haven't turned out the way I thought they would. I wanted a family, Jack wanted a career. When I started getting promotions, Jack was so supportive. He loved that I was building a career, and I loved that it made him happy. But I always thought that eventually, I'd have a baby. Now that I'm pushing for it, he's using my career as an excuse. I'm resentful, and so is he. I guess we're just not in a good place right now."

"Have you acknowledged that out loud to each other?" Pad asks. "That's an important thing to do. If you identify something, you can fix it."

"Not really," she admits. "But we both know it. I'm sorry for oversharing with you—we aren't usually like this."

"Sometimes, a situation simmers and simmers until it comes to a point where it's about to boil over," he says. "Would you say you're about at the boiling point?"

She hesitates, then nods. "I'm afraid of that, yes."

"What do you think the answer is?"

She thinks on that. "I don't know. But I wish I did. We need to remember who we used to be and why we love each other, I guess. It's too easy to focus on being mad. I guess that's the simpler thing to do."

Pad respects her frankness and tells her so.

"I was married for a long time," he says. "Would you like some advice?"

She nods. "I'd love some."

"Nothing matters but each other," he tells her solemnly. "In the end, nothing else matters."

"In a perfect world, maybe," Nora replies respectfully. "Nowadays, everyone has work and no time and responsibilities—"

"We've always had work and responsibilities," Pad interrupts. "You just have to narrow down what's important to you and focus on that."

"It sounds so simple to say," Nora says.

"Sometimes not so simple to do, though," Pad agrees.

"Because everything is important. Our jobs. Our dog. Our families."

"You said 'our jobs' first," Pad points out.

"I meant them in no particular order," she replies, but her cheeks flare.

"What specifically is keeping you from visiting your families this Christmas?" Pad asks bluntly.

"I . . . well, we . . ." Nora stutters. "Jack has conference calls and pressing things. I have edits due on four different manuscripts by January 1, and I'm only partway through. We don't have time to travel to Wyoming. Sitting in airports, having our luggage lost, sedating Elliott for the trip . . ."

"Too much trouble?" Pad asks, a strange tone in his voice.

"No. Just . . ."

"Not enough time," Pad says.

"Yes. And Jack really doesn't like Christmas. It's a long story."

"Well, time *is* finite," he says. "But some things are worth stretching it for, Nora. Your folks won't be around forever."

"No, they won't," she agrees, feeling her chest get a bit heavy. "I know."

"If I had my folks or my Maria back, I'd move heaven and earth to see them for Christmas," Pad says, his voice wistful.

Nora's chest gets even heavier.

"I bet so," she says, her voice small. "Jack and I . . . we don't celebrate Christmas in a big way. But we *do* love each other."

Before Padraig can reply, Jack emerges from the back.

"All done," he reports, and then he notices the serious looks on their faces. "What did I miss?"

"Pad was just telling me how much he misses his wife and his parents," Nora tells him. Her husband glances at her.

"I'm sorry, Pad," Jack says. "The holidays must be difficult."

"Oh, I'm used to it now." Pad waves his large hand. "And visiting with nice kids like you makes it bearable."

He smiles.

Jack stares down at his wife. "We should probably be getting home, Nora," he hints. Pad gets to his feet, taking Nora's cup.

"If you'll bear with me a moment, I'd like to give you something. I have just the thing."

He leaves them staring after him as he wanders up and down his shop, hunting through shelves. "Nope, not that," he mutters, pushing aside a crystal candlestick shaped like a reindeer. "Although that is certainly timeless."

He pokes around for several more minutes until he crows in delight.

"Eureka!" he says, emerging from the aisles, a slightly dusty snow globe in his hands.

The scene inside is that of a quaint glass family gathered around a fireplace decorated for Christmas.

He shakes it and hands it to Jack.

"This is the gift for you to give to your wife this year, Jack."

Jack startles, and for a minute, it almost seems like he hadn't considered what he was going to give her, and Christmas is in less than a week.

Nora pretends not to notice, but her stomach sinks.

"Like I was saying . . . we don't really celebrate Christmas," she begins to say, but Jack is already thanking the elderly man.

Pad glances at Nora as he pulls out paper to wrap the globe. "I think you might be my friend Beth's editor. I was her critique partner for a while. Beth Jacobs?"

"Oh!" Nora's head snaps up. "Yes. I'm her editor. She's an amazing human! What a small world!"

"Isn't it?" Padraig agrees.

Jack tries to pay for the snow globe, but Pad won't hear of it.

Instead, he touches his nose. "How about this: someday, if I ever finish it, Nora agrees to read my manuscript." He finishes wrapping up the globe, puts it into a small brown sack, and offers it to her. "Whattaya say?"

"I say that you are more creative than most at pitching me your book," she replies with a smile, taking the sack from him.

He smiles. "Well, writers are creative," he says. "But editors are, too. Editors revise worlds until they're absolutely just so, and that takes creativity."

She seems unconvinced.

"You refuse to believe that there's nothing a good red pen can't fix. Right?"

Jack nudges her. "He's not wrong," her husband points out. She glares at him.

"You know that if you work hard enough, and study the sentence from every angle, you'll convey the situation in a way that makes the scene real to the reader. You'll pull the reader past the point of no return, a place where they're your ride or die. Right?"

"How does he know what *ride or die* means?" Jack mutters quietly to Nora.

"You're right," she announces, surprising Jack, but not Padraig. "I do revise sentences to be better. But I never get to create. That lies in the blue pen, not the red. That is in the writer, not the eraser."

"Oh, pish. That's nonsense," Pad tells her. "The slightest revision, and a world is changed. You know that, Nora. The editor fine-tunes the details until the world becomes better than the author ever thought possible. Without you, the world would be flat and one-dimensional, told from only one perspective. The editor offers a layer of enrichment, an outside perspective, that the author wouldn't have had alone."

"That's . . . so insightful," Nora says softly. "I've never considered it that way before," she admits.

Pad nods knowingly. "So, with that in mind, Nora, what would you do if you could create your own world?"

Nora considers both his question and his original request.

"Okay, I'll read it," she finally tells him. "If the synopsis holds together."

"It's a deal," he says with a grin. "And maybe I can come up with something more creative than a synopsis. But you're avoiding the big question." He looks at them both and points at the brown gift bag. "If you could shake that snow globe and make a wish, creating the world you'd want . . . what would it be? Think on that, both of you," he tells them, then pats Elliott's big head. "Be a good boy, Elliott," he says to the dog. "Come back and see me anytime."

He nods at the couple. "You have a merry Christmas. This old man has gingerbread to bake."

With that, he disappears into his back rooms without a backward glance.

They walk home in near silence, each lost in thought as their boots crunch in the snow. They're almost to their condo building when Jack turns to his wife.

"I didn't tell him Elliott's name," he says. "Did you?"

Nora thinks on that. "I don't remember. But I must've, because it's not on his collar."

The door of their building opens, and the doorman greets them.

"Good evening, Mr. and Mrs. Blake," he says. He bends slightly to Elliott. "Good evening, young sir," he adds to the dog. He looks at them. "Can he have a treat this evening?"

"Of course, Matthew." Nora smiles.

He reaches into his pocket and pulls out a treat that he carries specifically for Elliott. Elliott wolfs it down in half a second, licks his chops, and then promptly drools on Matthew's shoe. The doorman doesn't miss a beat. He simply pulls out a tissue and wipes it off, something he's done a hundred times before.

"Have a good evening," Nora tells him with a chuckle.

The couple makes their way to the twenty-second floor and emerges into their condo. Many would call it luxurious, but both Nora and Jack find it a bit empty and cold tonight.

Nora pulls the snow globe from the bag and sets it on a bookshelf in their bedroom. They brush their teeth in silence, turn off the lights, and fall into bed.

They manage to do all this without touching.

Elliott jumps onto the bed and sprawls between them. They both fall asleep snuggling with the dog instead of each other as they ponder the question that the kind but strange old man in the antique shop had left them with.

What would you do if you could create your own world?

Moonlight shines into the window, falling upon the snow globe.

The glittery snow stirs, lifting into the liquid, surrounding the glass family in a flurry that lasts several minutes before once again settling into motionless silence.

CHAPTER TWO

Noel

Sunlight hits me square in the eyes, and I groan, scrambling to find my phone and turn off my wretched alarm.

Wait. My alarm.

I haven't slept until my alarm sounded in years.

I open my eyes. The sun is midway through the white winter sky. I snatch up my phone and look at the time.

9:43 A.M.

I have a slew of texts, emails, and phone notifications. I blink, then blink again, trying to clear my head.

How in the world did I oversleep?

I gaze around the room as I try to remember what I'd done last night. My champagne silk robe is strewn across the white chair. My matching slippers are next to the bed, where they belong. I'm nothing if not a creature of habit.

Did I have too much wine? That can't be it. Wine gives me a headache. I rarely drink it.

For the life of me, I can't remember my evening. And worse, I don't have time to think about it because I'm late.

I launch into action, racing from my bed into the bathroom, taking the fastest shower in history. I pull my hair into a wet bun, then yank on a pencil skirt and a fitted red-and-gray cashmere argyle sweater.

I don't even take time to make coffee. I just scoop up my laptop and notes, cram them into my satchel, and then rush past the empty kitchen with my phone already held to my ear.

I jab the button for the elevator as I listen to voice mails from my assistant, Emily. I watch the lights on the wall signaling the elevator's descent. It's on the thirty-first floor now. It's a minute or two until it reaches the twenty-first floor and the doors slide open.

A man in a suit is inside with a woman in a cocktail dress. *Last night's* cocktail dress, I realize as I notice her smudged makeup.

The man is crisp and clean, obviously showered for work. He's on the phone, talking to someone quickly and decisively. They're speaking the language of stockbrokers, and my eyes glaze over.

I turn back to my own voice mails. I listen to agents, junior editors, and a writer, all telling me what they need from me.

An extension.

Cover mock-up approval.

A manuscript review.

Approval to use a cover model. That last one snags my attention, and I dial quickly. Emily picks up.

"*Fabio?* Really?" I demand. "Why Fabio? He's a hundred and twelve."

"OMG, Noel!" She laughs. "He is not. It's for Casey Clark. She grew up sneaking her grandmother's romance novels, and to her, having Fabio on her cover would be the epitome of success."

"We can't spend that on this project," I say. "You know that. This is only her second book. She didn't earn out on the first one."

"She almost did," Emily interjects. "Gen Z is loving her—they found her on TikTok, and she's blowing up. I think this book is going to be the sleeper hit of the summer, honestly."

"Fine." I sigh. "Get a quote from art and come back to me."

Emily crows and hangs up. The woman in the day-old makeup stares at me.

"*The* Fabio?" she asks.

"I think there's just the one," I answer with a small smile.

She's visibly impressed. Her companion, the guy in the suit, is not.

"My college roommate's mom used to read cheesy books with him on the cover," he says. "I agree with you. He's too old. And cheesy."

"I didn't say he was cheesy," I correct.

But he shakes his head. "*Far* too cheesy."

"Jonah," the woman says. "That's mean."

The man, *Jonah*, is dressed in a thousand-dollar suit, gleaming Oxfords, and a ten-thousand-dollar watch and smells like a winter day in the forest. He reeks of money. I'm betting that he *is* a bit mean. Successful people often have to be.

"You should respect your elders," I tell him as the elevator settles to a stop at the lobby. "He's a hundred and twelve."

Jonah's mouth twitches, and I notice now that his lips are full, and his jaw is chiseled and clean-shaven.

"That's mean," he tells me, smiling slightly.

I shrug. "When in Rome."

I step out of the elevator and head out the door, but I *feel* him smiling behind me.

I wait while the doorman, Matthew, hails me a cab. Out of the corner of my eye, I see Jonah deposit the woman into a car and then close the door. He doesn't kiss her. He walks away, his breath forming white clouds in the winter air.

As the morning light shrouds him, for a moment, a sense of déjà vu envelops me, a sense of familiarity, like I've stared at this man before. Have I watched him walk in and out of this building and never paid attention?

"Have a good day, Ms. Turner," Matthew says, bringing me out of the moment.

"Thank you," I reply. "Matthew?"

He pauses before closing the cab door for me.

"That man I just walked out of the building with. Does he live here?"

Matthew nods. "Yes, ma'am. That's Mr. Blake."

Jonah Blake. I make a mental note to google him later. "Thanks."

Matthew smiles and closes the door.

"Parker-Hamilton Publishing," I tell the driver. "On Broadway."

The driver nods and pulls away from the curb. I spend the

drive sorting through the notes in my bag and preparing to spring into action the moment I step from the car.

I do that very thing.

And then promptly slip on the ice.

I skid like a scene in a cartoon, my legs scrambling, seemingly hovering in the air.

My assistant appears from nowhere, grabbing my arms and saving me from breaking my neck.

"I was waiting for you," she says, thrusting a cup of coffee into my hand. "You're never late."

"I know." I sigh, readjusting the bag on my shoulder and taking a big gulp of caffeine.

"You missed the marketing meeting for Elias Gray's book."

"Dang it," I mutter as we enter the building. Emily fills me in on everything I missed as we make our way up to our floor. Tasteful Christmas decorations adorn the halls, and someone in a cubicle somewhere is playing Christmas music.

Emily follows me into my office and closes the door behind us.

I eye her suspiciously.

She beams.

"You have a date for New Year's Eve," she announces proudly.

"I do?" I ask, relaxing ever so slightly as I drop my bag onto an empty chair. "How so?"

"Remember when I was showing you pictures of my Italian cousin on my dad's side? Michel—the model?"

My shoulders tighten again. I do remember. He'd been posing on a yacht with the slightest slip of fabric covering his . . . business. He'd been gorgeous.

"He's way too young," I tell her. "He's like, what . . . twenty-five? I'm thirty-seven."

"He's twenty-six," Emily corrects. "And age is just a number. He's not the sharpest tack in the box, but he's good-hearted. And beautiful. He'll look perfect with you at the party."

"I'm only going to that party because you RSVP'd for me." I'm growing annoyed again. "New Year's Eve was a night for me to relax, curl up in sweats, and ponder the status of my life."

"Not happening," she says firmly. "You're going to the party at Stitch."

"We'll see," I mutter, sitting down at my desk.

"If you want to be editor in chief, you'll have to start doing things like this," she reminds me. "You know that. You have to go."

"I don't," I answer calmly. "And I don't understand why you've been riding me so hard about becoming EIC."

"Because I want your job." Emily sighs. "Keep up, woman. Once you level up, that will open up your current role. Brittany will be promoted for that, then Jess will become associate editor, which leaves her role as junior editor open."

"You know, when I brought you on here, I didn't realize you were so enterprising."

"You did, too." Emily scoffs. "Don't plead ignorance. But back to the party. You're still my favorite cousin, but you have to go."

"No."

"You have to," Emily says, actually concerned now. "We RSVP'd. You can't cancel on Lillianna Cox."

"*We* didn't RSVP," I tell her sweetly. "*You* did. So you can un-RSVP me. Or maybe you can go in my place, since you want to climb the ranks so badly."

Emily stares at me, her mouth opening then closing.

My phone rings, and I reach to answer it.

"We'll talk about this later," Emily promises before she leaves the room.

"Don't count on it," I say to the closed door.

I bury myself in work for the rest of the day, reviewing contracts, approving manuscripts, and returning emails.

Contrary to popular opinion, my days don't contain much actual reading of books. Any manuscript reading I do has to be crammed into my off-hours or read in the back seat of a taxi. I've fallen asleep with a printed manuscript on my chest in the wee hours of the morning more times than I'd like to remember.

Reading used to be my passion, and while I still do love it, things change when you turn your hobby into your job: a little bit of the passion subsides, and it's replaced with the hard edge of business.

I love the voice in this MS, but unfortunately, it's not right for our list at this time.

The main character is engaging, and the story line is robust, but the secondary characters fall flat. Revise and resend.

While I love the idea of this author's story line, it's not executed smoothly enough. If you don't get the offer you're looking for elsewhere, come back to me and we can discuss a revise and resubmit.

Every rejection letter I've sent over the past fifteen years as I've climbed the ranks from editorial assistant to assistant editor, then through associate editor and editor to senior editor to executive editor, where I am now, has killed my soul ever so slightly. I know writers pour their hearts into the words they write, and I don't take the responsibility of crushing dreams lightly.

Midafternoon, I find myself searching for Fabio's most recent photos online. The man *might* be 112, but who actually knows? He's ageless.

It *would* be a fantastic PR hook. Casey Clark's story line features someone who falls in love with her childhood celebrity crush.

I press the intercom to Emily. "I'm on board for Fabio, if the art department is."

I can hear her squeal through the closed door.

What Emily lacks in poise, she makes up for in character.

My finger twitches, and then I type into my search bar: *Jonah Blake, New York City*. I'm surprised by how many results pop up.

Just turned forty. Wunderkind. Genius financier. He was a wild child in his thirties but has seemingly calmed down just a bit.

There's no shortage of photos of him, with plenty of different women on his arm.

I stare at his face.

His eyes are surprisingly kind. His face is unmistakably handsome. His grin is undeniably deadly.

Emily walks in with an armload of mail, and I close my laptop. I feel my face flush.

She looks at me curiously, setting the stack on my desk.

"Were you looking at porn?" she jokes, raising her eyebrows. But then she narrows her eyes. "Or was it a dating site?"

She rushes for my computer, but I block her with my shoulder in a deft move that would make any linebacker jealous.

"It's none of your business," I tell her primly. She rolls her eyes and steps back.

"Fine. If you want to rob me of whatever joy I can glean from this life as I toil for you night and day, giving up my youth for you, wasting away to nothing for you"—she pauses, her healthy hip bumping into my shoulder—"then fine. So be it."

I stare at her, deadpan.

"Are you done?" I ask.

She rolls her eyes.

"Here," she says, thrusting a piece of paper toward me. "Michel's socials and his phone number. Start a conversation. He's your date for New Year's Eve. You don't want it to be awkward."

She tries to disappear before I can argue, but I catch sight of a package wrapped in brown paper and tied with white string sitting on my mail stack.

"What's this?" I ask her, stretching to pick it up.

"I don't know. I thought it might be a gift, so I didn't want to open it for you." She pauses. "Do you think it's a bomb? Or anthrax?"

"You've read too many manuscripts."

Nonetheless, she lingers almost eagerly as I open the wrapping and pull out a printed manuscript.

I sigh.

"Speak of the devil. A manuscript."

Emily seems disappointed. But then she perks up. "There could technically still be anthrax."

"There is something wrong with you," I tell her.

She's unaffected. "Do you need anything else before I go home?"

"Is it that time already?" I glance at the clock. It's six P.M. "My word, where did the time go?"

"It's literally dark outside." Emily gestures toward the floor-to-ceiling windows behind me, where the lights of the city brighten the dark horizon. "Are you okay?" she asks. "You've seemed a little off all day long."

"I'm fine," I assure her. "I overslept, and it just threw me off."

"You never oversleep," she says.

"And now you see the problem," I tell her patiently. "It's why I seem off, I'm sure."

"Hmm. Well, I hope you have a good weekend," she says. "If you need anything, text me."

"I won't," I tell her. "Enjoy your time off."

She seems suspicious again.

"Are you getting into the Christmas spirit?"

I don't blink.

"You usually text me at least ten times over the weekend."

"I do? That doesn't seem like me," I say.

She rolls her eyes. "Okay, weirdo. You know where to find me."

After she's gone and I'm gathering my things, I pause when my fingers slide over the manuscript. There's a card tucked inside the string.

I pull the card from the envelope.

Dear Ms. Turner,

Please forgive my presumptuousness in sending you this unsolicited manuscript. I'm an old man, and social correctness escapes me at times. We share an acquaintance, Beth Jacobs, and she encouraged me to contact you. I hope it isn't a misstep.

I've lived what feels like a hundred lives, although that might be because I've written about a hundred lives, and as you know, characters can take on lives of their own, enmeshing with ours in ways we'd never imagined.

I was compelled to write this story because sometimes relationships need an outside influence to examine them under the appropriate lens. I chose you to send it to because the main character reminds me of you.

I don't want to waste your time, so I'm only enclosing the first chapter. If you like it, you can let me know, and I'll send more. This is a story that needs to be told, and I hope, after you read my humble chapter, you agree.

Sincerely,
Padraig Sinclair

The main character reminds him of me?
Padraig Sinclair.
I pull out my phone and text Emily.

> The manuscript is from a Padraig Sinclair, who says Beth Jacobs gave him my info. Do we know him?

Three bubbles pop up, then a reply.

> You lasted five minutes! Nice! And no, I don't think we know a Padraig Sinclair. Although Beth shouldn't be giving your info out without checking first. That's rude.

> True. But don't forget, Beth chose to go with us in auction, even though Random House outbid us.

> Only because she wanted to work with YOU.

Still, I answer. One good turn deserves another. You've got to remember that if you want my job, little grasshopper.

I slide the manuscript and my phone into my bag and head out the door.

I choose to walk for a few blocks before I grab a taxi. The night air feels good against my face, and the Christmas lights add a festive flair to the streets. I rub my hands together, since I'd forgotten my gloves. I glance at the traffic light, waiting for the walk signal to appear.

From somewhere in the night, I hear a man's voice holler. "Dangnabbit! Come back here!"

I turn to find a moose barreling down the street toward me. Startled, I take a step back and peer into the darkness.

It's not a moose. It's a giant dog with flopping jowls and ears, and paws bigger than my hands.

An older man with a wild head of white hair and a beard trails behind him.

"He won't hurt you!" he calls out to anyone who will listen. "He's a big baby."

The dog's massive paws are hitting the pavement so hard, I can practically feel the ground shake, and if I'm not mistaken, the giant animal is aiming straight for me.

My arm shoots into the sky, hailing a cab. Luckily, one pulls up, and I drop inside while the dog is still half a block away.

Whew.

I press my forehead to the glass and watch the forlorn expression on the dog's massive face as it skids to a stop. The man reaches him and picks up the leash that had been dragging behind the animal.

"People really need to better control their animals," the cabdriver says, clucking his tongue.

I nod in agreement. "Especially with an animal like that. What is he . . . part Clydesdale? Part grizzly?"

The driver chuckles, and I look back, watching the old man patting the dog's massive head and giving him a treat.

The man looks up at me, and our eyes meet.

His seem to twinkle, and he touches his nose.

Then he and the dog turn and walk back the direction they'd come from.

CHAPTER THREE

Jonah

M r. Blake?"

I blink, bringing the junior executive in front of me back into focus. I'd been thinking of the woman from the elevator this morning. Again.

"Yes," I answer finally. "This path forward works for me. Thank you, Tim."

He nods, pleased with himself, without realizing that I truly don't know what he even pitched to me.

"Get the details to Millie," I tell him as he gathers his things from the conference room table.

"Will do. Thank you, Mr. Blake."

"Anytime."

Without waiting for him to exit, I walk out and return to my office, a mere twenty feet away. My secretary, Millie, follows me inside, her purse in one hand and my messages in the other.

"Thanks, Millie." I take them from her.

"Chelsey called twice," she says.

"Who?"

"Your date from last night." The older woman hides her disapproval, a frequent occurrence in our ten-year relationship.

"Oh." I try not to feel disappointed. Chelsey was great, perfectly nice.

But the woman in the elevator . . . her wit was quick, and her eyes were such a deep blue. They'd sparkled a little devilishly . . . which is basically my kryptonite.

"I've called for your car," Millie tells me. "Do you need anything else?"

"No, thank you."

"I've already placed the Bell report and the Kinsington numbers in your briefcase."

I smile. "You know me so well," I tell her.

She continues. "Also, you sent your father a new pair of thermal hip waders for Christmas. The last pair you sent him was five years ago, so I'm guessing they're about due for replacement."

I glance at the photo of my dad that Millie had framed for me behind my desk.

My father, standing hip-deep in the Colorado River, proudly holds up a trout as big as my head.

"That's a perfect gift for him, Millie," I tell her. "Thank you for thinking of it."

She nods, her face softening.

"How's he doing?" she asks me. "I know Christmas is hard for him every year."

"He's . . . well, he's Judd Blake," I tell her. "He doesn't complain, he doesn't whine, he doesn't feel."

"He feels, Jonah," she tells me in a rare instance of using my first name. "He just doesn't want anyone to know it."

"Kinda like you," I point out. "You like to hide your big heart."

"I do not have a big heart," she announces. "I will deny that to my dying day. I just have to take care of you. Of course, if you'd finally get married, your wife could do these things, and I wouldn't have to."

Score: Millie, 1. Jonah, 0.

"Don't pretend you don't like it," I tell her, unfazed. "You take care of me because you don't trust anyone else to do it, and I appreciate you for it."

Red blotches form on Millie's face, so I move smoothly along, pretending not to notice.

"Millie, have a beautiful weekend," I tell her. "Get your Christmas shopping done, relax, rejuvenate. In fact, book yourself a spa weekend on me. I need you well rested for next year."

She sniffs. "That's already been done, sir."

I grin. "Of course it has. On my credit card, I assume?"

"Naturally. You cause the stress. You can pay for the cure."

"I completely agree," I concur. "In fact, add in a facial. I've heard frowning causes wrinkles, and you do frown at me a lot."

Millie doesn't miss a beat. "Consider it done. Anything else, Your Majesty?"

Only Millie could get away with that, and she knows it.

"Not now, but if I think of anything, I'll let you know," I promise.

She nods. "Beautiful. Have a good weekend, Jonah. And do try to get some fresh air. You're looking peaky."

She turns and leaves me alone with the remnants of her powdery perfume.

As I gather my things into my briefcase, I see that Millie also included a stack of Christmas cards for our most important clients. Already addressed, already inscribed. All I have to do is sign my name. I smile. I definitely don't deserve Millie. The day she decides to retire will be a dark, dark day.

I don't even need to look up from my phone as I make my way to the ground floor. Every door is opened for me, elevator buttons are pushed, people nod in deference. I've found that if I don't look up from my phone, everyone assumes I'm too busy to bother, and thus, I don't get stuck making small talk.

Instead, I read emails as the elevator descends to the lobby.

I answer a few texts from my senior staff after I'm settled into the black car that had been waiting for me. Once the tinted windows hide me from the world, I relax and put my phone back in my pocket.

It's not that I don't like people. I do.

But when an entire building . . . an entire company . . . depends on you to be brilliant and to execute flawlessly at all times, and their financial well-being depends on it, it makes for a bit of pressure. It's a pressure I try not to focus on, and so I ignore it. It's not healthy, but it's effective.

Tonight, my driver glides effortlessly through the New York streets, and I lean my forehead tiredly against the cold glass.

Once upon a time, I'd relished the pressure, the stress, the excitement. It meant that I was on the way up. It meant I was accomplishing things, that I was chasing that brass ring.

And boy, had I loved the chase. Of women, of the finance game, of everything. Every day, I'd known that something bigger and better was on the horizon.

But now . . . I don't know how things can get bigger or better. I'm at the top of my game and have been for quite a while.

I've traveled—a lot. Hong Kong, Tokyo, London. Sydney. I've dated. A lot. I've made money. A lot of it.

More and more, I've been finding myself sitting with a big question.

Now what?

"Here you are, Mr. Blake," Thomas says, interrupting my thoughts and sliding the glass partition down. "Have a good evening, sir."

"Thanks, Thomas."

I step from the car and stride into the building, the doorman holding the door.

"Good evening, Matthew," I greet him.

"Hello, Mr. Blake." He starts to say something, then hesitates. I pause.

"Yes?"

"I might have messed up, sir."

"We've discussed this. You don't need to call me sir."

The kid smiles. "Thank you, si— Thank you."

"How did you mess up? Did you slam the door in the president's face or something?"

Matthew smiles again and shakes his head.

"No, nothing like that. This morning, when you left for work, you were walking with a woman from the building. She asked me if you lived here, and I told her you did."

I wait to hear the mistake while simultaneously my pulse surges.

The woman from the elevator asked about me.

Matthew stares at me. "I violated your privacy, Mr. Blake. I'm sorry. That wasn't my intention."

Ohhh.

"That's not a problem," I assure him. "I'm sure she's not a serial killer." I pause and lift an eyebrow. "Is she?"

"Oh, no, sir. She's a really nice lady that lives on the twenty-first floor." He flushes. "And I did it again. I shouldn't have said that."

"I won't tell anyone." I glance at him. "Do you have a piece of paper?"

Matthew nods. "Sure."

He digs behind his podium and pulls out a notepad. "Here you go."

I scrawl on the paper.

If you have any further questions, I'm in 3112.

I fold it in half and hand it to Matthew. "When she comes in tonight, will you give this to her?"

Matthew nods. "Of course, sir." I glare at him. He backtracks. "Of course, Mr. Blake."

"Thank you." I tip him and wish him a great night. I'd let him use my first name if the building allowed it. They, unfortunately, have rather strict rules about that kind of thing. Some of the other residents like it that way.

I'm alone in the elevator as it makes its way to the thirty-first floor, and a moment later, I step into my penthouse suite. The lights inside are on a timer that turns them on at six P.M. so that my home seems inviting when I arrive. The black marble floors gleam, and my footprints echo. My style is sparse, minimalist, and masculine. I don't like clutter, I don't like mess.

Dropping my briefcase on a chair, I slip my shoes off and head for the kitchen, knowing what I'll find.

Like every other night that I don't have a previous engagement, Millie orders my dinner and arranges for it to be waiting.

Tonight, it's beef Wellington, steamed broccoli, a dinner roll, and herbed rice garnished with lemon. A glass of ice water accompanies the meal.

"Ever the optimist, Millie," I mutter.

I pour a scotch instead.

I eat in blessed silence and then move to my quiet living room, where I sit with my legs crossed at the ankle as I stare into the night.

Lights from the city sparkle below, through the expansive windows in front of me. It's interesting how Christmas trees seem from up here . . . so small, but still festive.

My own apartment doesn't reflect the season at all. It's a decision that Millie long ago stopped arguing with.

A pleasant voice emanates from the surround sound speakers.

"Incoming call, Judd Blake."

"Answer," I instruct.

I take another long draw from my scotch.

"Pop?" I say.

"Jonesy," my dad says. Am I imagining it, or does his voice sound thin? "Whatcha up to, son?"

"Just got home from work. Had a bit of dinner, and now I'm resting. How about you?"

"I was out mending the fence earlier but ran out of supplies. I'm gonna have to go into town tomorrow."

I sigh. "Pop, don't drive if the roads are icy. It can wait."

"For what? For you to come home and do it? I'll be waiting until next spring." His tone is resentful, and he's got every right to be.

"I know, Dad," I tell him. "I'm sorry. I promise you, I'll get home this year. Soon."

My dad pauses.

"About that. Rich Turner seems to think that I'm too old to work effectively anymore. He's petitioning the city council to have me replaced."

"What?" That captures my attention, and I sit up straighter. "What do you mean? You've been mayor of Winter Falls for longer than I can remember."

My dad chuckles. "That I have."

"Then what's the problem?"

"Rich would very much like to be mayor, obviously. He's wanted it for years."

"So he can run against you like anyone else," I tell him.

"He doesn't want to wait."

"Why? What difference does it make at this point?"

My father sighs. "Same old argument. Says I'm killing the Christmas tourist commerce."

I pause. "Well, I mean . . ."

"Son, I don't like Christmas. Everyone knows I don't like

Christmas. I have *reason* to not like Christmas. Liking Christmas is not a requirement of being mayor."

"No, it isn't," I agree. "But perhaps you should listen to citizens on what they want Winter Falls to feature at the holidays. There used to be a party in the town square, for instance. When I was little. I still remember it."

It had stopped the year after my mom had died.

"Those lights stopped working, and I haven't had the budget to replace them."

"I'm sure that someone would donate replacement lights," I point out. "And I bet you could've found the budget if you'd tried."

"Rich and Susan think that I've deliberately squashed their business by not allowing them to offer sleigh rides and a bunch of other Christmassy tourist crap."

"Why didn't you allow it?" I ask.

"Well, there's the zoning, for one thing," my father sputters. "They can't have reindeer in the city limits, Jonah."

"It's not like Winter Falls is a bustling metropolis, Dad," I remind him. "It's rural."

"Yes, Jonah, I'm aware that you live in the big city now." My father sighs. "You don't need to keep reminding me."

"That wasn't what I was doing," I mutter. "I've lived in the city a long time. I assume you know it by now."

"I well know," my father confirms.

"Okay." I sigh, recognizing his offended tone. We're not going to get far today. "How can I help?"

"Oh, I don't know why I called you in the first place," he grouses. "It's not like you're going to come."

"What do you need me to do, Dad?" I ask as patiently as possible.

"It would be nice if you'd come here so we can be a united front over Christmas," he finally says.

"A united front?"

"You know. Just show folks that you're home for the holidays."

"You want me to come celebrate Christmas?" I ask, confused. "We haven't celebrated Christmas in thirty-three years."

My dad is silent.

"Not *celebrate* per se," he finally replies. "But maybe we could *look* like we are."

"You mean lie?"

My father isn't one to lie. Ever. He's uncomfortable now.

"No. I just want them to see that a family can come together for Christmas and not have to hang gaudy lights up everywhere or put tacky inflatable Santas in their yards."

"Or sell sleigh rides," I add.

"Perhaps." He pauses. "Listen. I'm a good mayor. You know that. The town doesn't need to be turned into a tourist trap—Christmas or not. I'm not against Christmas. I'm against tourist traps."

"Tourism is good for commerce," I remind him.

"I know that. But we don't need to turn our town into a flashing neon Christmas light, Jonah."

"I'm not arguing that," I clarify. "I'm just saying . . . you might need to loosen your iron grip a little bit and come to a compromise."

"Compromise is the same as defeat," my old-fashioned father mutters.

"Compromise is usually necessary," I tell him.

"Can you come here or not?" he asks, impatient now.

I sigh, long and loud.

"I haven't seen you in months, son," my dad adds. "I'm seventy years old."

"Don't try the guilt trip," I advise him. "I know it doesn't actually bother you."

"That's not true—" he begins indignantly.

"I'll come," I interrupt. "For a few days. I don't know what it will accomplish, but if it'll stop this conversation, I'll come."

"Perfect," my father says, completely chipper now. "I'll expect you tomorrow. This is important, son."

He hangs up without another word, and I get the distinct impression that I've been had.

"Son of a buck," I mutter. But I'm nothing if not a man of my word. I pull my phone out and text Millie.

> I'm going to Winter Falls for the holiday after all.

She calls me immediately.

"Oh my word, this is wonderful! I'll get everything booked. You'll take the jet, I assume?"

"No. This is personal, not business. Just book me commercial, please."

"You could use the jet, if you like," she says. "You're the CEO."

"I don't want that kind of fuss," I tell her. "Commercial is fine."

"Whatever you wish," she concedes.

"Remember that phrase," I tell her. "I like it."

"Don't get used to it," she answers with a laugh. "And I'll book commercial if they have a decent flight. If not, you'll get the jet." She hangs up.

I start to refill my scotch when I receive another call, this one from my COO.

"Tyler," I greet him. "What's up?"

"I just wanted to thank you for your patience with the Newberry deal," he tells me. "I appreciate you, and we've found the perfect way to show it."

"We?"

"Me and the team," he clarifies. "We appreciate you, man." There's a lisp in his voice, and I narrow my eyes.

"Too much eggnog?" I ask.

"Never," he answers. "Just enjoy, man."

"Enjoy what?"

But he's already gone.

Shaking my head, I attempt to refill my scotch glass one more time. This time, the doorbell interrupts me.

Giving up, I set the glass down. I'm just not meant for a second drink this evening.

I'm not prepared for what I see when I open the door.

A beautiful young woman stands in front of me in a skimpy Mrs. Claus outfit.

"Are you Jonah Blake?" she asks. I don't think quickly enough to say no.

She sees the answer on my face and reaches up to grab my tie.

CHAPTER FOUR

Noel

My building is aglow when the taxi pulls up in front of it. Matthew opens my door before I can even grab the handle.

"Good evening, Ms. Turner," he greets me, offering me his hand.

I take it, and he helps me from the car.

He accompanies me to the building, and as he opens the door, he dips his head. "I have something for you, ma'am," he tells me, handing me a piece of folded paper. "It's from Mr. Blake."

"Did he seriously pass me a note through you?" I ask, trying not to smile.

Matthew looks sheepish. "It's my fault, ma'am. I told him that I'd talked to you about him because I felt guilty, you see, and then he wrote this. I'm sorry, ma'am."

"No harm done, Matthew," I tell him briskly, unfolding the paper. "Surely he wasn't offended that I asked."

"No, ma'am, he was not," Matthew says, relieved.

I read the heavy slanted writing.

If you have any further questions, I'm in 3112.

My heartbeat explodes into tiny patters.

I look up at Matthew. "He wasn't agitated?"

Matthew shakes his head.

"Then he must be flirting," I decide.

Matthew looks pleased.

"*Is* he flirting?" I ask him.

"Uh," he stammers. "I don't know, ma'am."

I pat his hand. "No matter. There's only one way to find out."

He nods, happy that I'm leaving him be.

"Thank you, Matthew."

I leave him behind and board the elevator, punching the thirty-first-floor button before I lose my nerve.

I haven't had the time to meet anyone in years. Jonah Blake is a handsome, successful man who is flirting with me. He clearly wants to know more about me.

I picture his eyes from this morning, crinkled as he'd smiled at me.

Of course, let's not forget that he was with someone. Although their vibe was that of two people who weren't that into each other. He didn't even kiss her goodbye.

The elevator passes the twenty-first floor.

Past the point of no return, I decide dramatically.

The elevator comes to a stop. The doors open.

Something I didn't know . . . there is only one condo on this floor: Jonah Blake's.

I know this now because his condo is directly in front of me, and it is the only door around. His door is open, and he's standing in it with a very scantily dressed young woman in a red velvet costume, fishnet stockings, and six-inch fur-trimmed heels.

The woman clings to Jonah, and her rump isn't covered by the ruffles on her short, short Mrs. Claus dress.

I freeze, not knowing what to do or where to look.

Jonah's eyes meet mine, and we're suddenly connected.

I hold up the note in two fingers.

"I had another question," I say limply. "But I can see now isn't a good time."

Trying to appear as nonchalant as possible, I turn around and punch the elevator button, feeling his eyes burn into my shoulder blades.

The doors open.

"Wait," he says, but I'm already inside, and I push the close-door button.

My cheeks are so hot, I think they'll explode. I don't look up again until the doors have closed. Then, and only then, I exhale raggedly.

Well, *that* was humiliating.

I should've known better. More than half of the photos of him online had a woman or two hanging on him. He's clearly a womanizer, just like the articles said. Whatever I'd seen in his eyes was just fanciful thinking.

I swallow my disappointment, go back into my own condo, and pour a glass of ice water, pressing it against my still-hot cheeks. I don't know why I'm so embarrassed. I didn't do anything wrong. It wasn't even a rejection, really. He was just . . . occupied. And clearly not as infatuated with me as I was with him.

Was. I've learned my lesson now.

I busy myself answering texts from Emily in front of the fire.

> Have you seen Edgar's email from production?
> There's an issue with the cover.

> Eloise St. James needs an extension.
> She said 30 days ought to do it.

> Padraig Sinclair somehow got my direct email—
> he says he needs to speak to you about the
> chapter he sent, and Elliott. Who is Elliott?

I wrinkle my forehead and answer.

> I have no idea. Forward me the email.

It comes through a scant moment later, and I scroll through it.

Dear Ms. Monroe,

I'm writing you on this snowy evening to inquire about the chapter I sent to Ms. Turner. I know she is very busy, but this story is somewhat urgent. It needs to be told, and once

Ms. Turner reads the chapter, I feel confident she'll agree. Then there's the issue of Elliott. If I'm to finish this book in time for a Christmas release next year, I can't take care of Elliott. He's proving to be a handful. A delightful handful, but a handful nonetheless.

Sincerely,
Padraig Sinclair

He also listed his phone number.

I stare at my phone, at the words, and I'm no less confused than I was before I'd read them.

We get pushy writers sometimes, particularly writers who are dying to have their debut published. They get passionate and that's okay. But he's acting like I know him. It's weird.

I scroll through my contacts, find Beth Jacobs, and push the phone icon.

I'm glancing at my watch when she picks up on the second ring.

"Bethany the Great!" I greet her. "I didn't realize how late it's getting. Am I bothering you?"

"Of course not," Beth answers with a laugh. "My muse just kicked me in the pants, and I'll be up writing all night."

"Oooh—can't wait to see!"

"You'll be the first, of course," she assures me.

"Hey, what I'm calling about tonight . . . Padraig Sinclair. Do you know him? He submitted a manuscript."

She crows. "It's about time! I've been pushing him for months."

"So you recommend him?"

"By all means, in every way. He's a beautiful person, Noel. He writes just as beautifully, and in fact, he was my critique partner for *Love Never Fails*. He really impacted my life."

"Really?"

"Yes. He just has a sense for what the story needs," she answers. "It's a gift."

"Thank you for the heads-up," I tell her. "Truly. I trust your insight."

"And I'm sorry for not checking with you first. I should've. Emily pinged me about that. It won't happen again. I just know that you'll be ecstatic with him. He'll be your next blockbuster, if you give him enough time to grow his base."

"Don't worry about it," I assure her. "It's fine. I appreciate good talent. Thank you for pointing him in my direction."

"He's quirky," she adds, "so prepare yourself. But *so* worth it. Trust me."

We hang up, and I cross the room and riffle through my workbag, pulling out the manuscript. It's neatly typed on what looks like an old-fashioned typewriter rather than a computer.

"Oh, boy." I sigh.

I can't deny, however, that I'm intrigued. *Who uses a typewriter these days?*

Curled up in a chair, I turn to the first page of the manuscript. In front of me, the fire roars.

The undisturbed snow in Central Park glitters like diamonds in the night, catching Nora's eye as she chases her runaway dog. Elliott drags his leash over the icy sidewalks, and every once in a while, Nora swears he turns around and laughs at her.

"You are a mangy mutt!" she calls out. In response, Elliott makes a sharp turn to the left, plowing through a pristine powdery snow bank and emerging on the other side. With snow on his massive snout, he heads for the nearest sidewalk . . .

Before I know it, I'm sucked into the story of two unhappily married people, Nora and Jack. The words leap from the page, filled with authenticity and emotion. By the time I read the entire chapter, I feel as though I know them. I feel as though they could be friends of mine, and I sympathize with both of them.

Also, Elliott is a dog.

"Why is he telling me he can't take care of his dog?" I wonder aloud, shaking my head.

I pause, and then in a move that is uncharacteristic for me, I email the writer myself.

From: <n.turner@parkerhamiltonpublishing.com>
To: <Padraig.Sinclair@sleighmail.com>
Subject: Request for full manuscript

Dear Padraig,

I must admit, though your methods are not conventional, I'm intrigued. Please send the full manuscript at your earliest convenience, as well as a synopsis and outline. Also, do you have an agent?

Thank you,
Noel Turner
Executive Editor
She/Her/Hers
Parker-Hamilton Publishing

I lay my phone down and stretch with a big yawn.

Glancing at my watch, I see that it's somehow after nine P.M., and I haven't eaten dinner yet. When I open my fridge, I study the contents. Four-day-old leftover Cantonese dim sum, four packets of ketchup, a shriveled-up cucumber, and a case of Acqua Panna.

I'm examining a questionable apple lying next to my sink when my mother calls.

I answer immediately, because if there is one thing about Susan Turner, she never calls someone after nine P.M. unless there's an emergency.

"Mom, what's wrong?"

"Nothing," she answers. "Or everything."

"Well, that seems dramatic," I say slowly. "Do you want to elaborate?"

"It's Judd Blake again," she answers wearily. "I swear to you, he's trying to ruin my life."

"That seems even more dramatic," I point out. "What's he doing?"

"He keeps denying our business permit. You know we want

to create a Christmas village in Winter Falls. We have the perfect town for it, the perfect town name. I want to expand my Etsy Christmas store into a real community. I want to have sleigh rides, and reindeer, I want to have several Christmas shops . . . I want it to be a holiday destination."

"Why does he keep rejecting your permits?" I ask.

My mom's voice raises an octave and lands in the screech-owl zone. My dad takes the phone away.

"Hey, honey," he says calmly. "I'm sure you remember . . . Judd doesn't like Christmas."

"Yes, I remember that," I tell him. "But he's the mayor. Ever since Ridgemont Outerwear went out of business last year, I'd think he'd be up for any solution that replaces revenue for the town."

"That's the problem. He can't imagine anyone loving the holidays enough to travel to Winter Falls to celebrate and shop. He just doesn't get it, and I think he's so closed-minded about it, he'll never get it. So I'm going to do something about it."

I wait. "And what will that be?"

"I'm appealing to the town council to get him removed, and I'll be mayor instead. I won't stand in the way of commerce, no matter what my personal views are."

"You're going to run for mayor," I repeat. "And oust Judd Blake."

"Yes."

"He's been mayor for as long as I remember," I tell him.

"I know. It's time for someone new."

"But—and I'm just playing devil's advocate here—you don't know anything about politics or city government," I point out.

"I mean, you can do anything you set your mind to, but there will be a learning curve, Dad."

"I know, honey," he answers patiently. "But sometimes, if you believe in something, you have to be willing to do whatever it takes to make it happen. Don't you agree?"

"Of course I do. You taught me that."

"Good. It's an important lesson. Now, in the interest of doing whatever it takes, are you willing to come home a few days earlier than you'd planned? The city council has agreed to hear my petition in a special session on December 24. I know that was the day you were planning on coming, but it would help an old man out if you could get here earlier. To help me prepare."

"Yikes. It's already the fourteenth."

"I know. That's why I'm asking you for help," he says slowly, as though talking to a child.

"I don't know how soon I can get there, Dad. I have to wrap up budget planning, and . . ."

"If you can't find the time, it's okay," Dad says now, and his voice is purposely thin.

I sigh.

"Okay. I'll get there as soon as I can. As long as I have Wi-Fi there, I can work."

"Perfect!" he crows, any trace of frailty gone. "See you soon, punkin."

He hangs up, and I drop the bruised apple into the wastebasket.

"Looks like I'm headed to Wyoming," I mutter.

I text Emily, which prompts an avalanche of questions that

I answer as I check out my laundry situation. Luckily, I picked up my laundry a couple of days ago and have plenty I can pack.

> Yes, book the ticket ASAP.

> Yes, cancel any meeting that I can't take remotely.

I ignore the phone ringing as she tries to call.
Then I receive a slew of more texts.

> You HAVE TO be back for NYE.

> You MUST go to the Stitch party with Michel.

> I don't even know what I'm going to do about your schedule.

Three dots appear, then disappear.
Finally, a last text comes through.

> You know what? It's my job to figure this out. My job is to make yours easier. I'm happy you're seeing your parents during the holidays. I'll figure things out here.

I knew she would. She just needed to be dramatic first.
I brush my teeth, then collapse into my vast, ballet-pink,

satin-covered bed. I'd better stretch out while I can. I'll be in the twin bed with the Pepto-pink canopy that I slept in my entire childhood soon. I do a quick snow angel on the satin, enjoying the way I can stretch from fingertip to fingertip and not touch the sides of the bed.

I'm asleep before I know it.

When I wake, I stretch in the early-morning light. The light is dark gray, too early. I glance at my phone and see that it's silently ringing.

The buzzing must be what woke me.

"Hello?" I say after I fumble for the buttons.

"Ms. Turner," Matthew, the doorman, greets me. "You have a delivery. You really must come get it right away, please."

He has a slightly panicked tone that startles me.

"Be right there," I tell him. I wrap myself in a plush robe and stick my feet into feathery white slippers before I head out the door and into the elevator.

It's only six A.M. There's absolutely no reason *any*one should be delivering *any*thing at this ungodly hour.

The doors slide open at the lobby, and I march out.

Then stop in my tracks as I take in the scene in front of me.

A massive, slobbery beast is trying to root through Matthew's pockets, snorting and snotting all over, as Matthew yelps helplessly. The dog surely weighs two hundred pounds—significantly more than Matthew.

"Come get it, please," he croaks as politely as he can.

"Me?" I'm stunned. "No, he's not . . ."

But Matthew is holding out a note with my name on it.

With my belly sinking, I quickly read it.

Ms. Turner,

I received your email with great delight! I will continue work-ing on the rest of the book, and I'll send you the chapters as I complete them. I know that's not standard practice, but I do hope you'll humor this old man. I want to make sure I get it right.

About the synopsis, I have the story in my head, but it's hard to say what my characters will do. I have a vision for them, but Ol' Bess, my typewriter, might have other ideas. We'll have to see what happens.

Thank you for being willing to care for Elliott while I write. I love him, he's got a heart of gold, but he's a bit mischievous and I need to concentrate. If necessary, I'll pick him up after I send you the last chapter.

Sincerely,
Pad

I blink.

At the bottom of the page, there's a postscript.

P.S.
Watch your feet.

"Ow!" Matthew yelps pathetically as Elliott stamps a mas-sive front paw on Matthew's shiny loafer.

I rush to help, but Matthew, Elliott, and I manage to get tangled in the leash and tumble to the floor. I'm not oblivious to the fact that I'm wearing a robe as I wind up with one leg thrown over Matthew, one slipper off, and wet jowls against the side of my face.

Self-consciously, I try to keep my robe closed as I untangle myself, find my slipper, and climb to my feet. In the debacle, Elliott has slurped the side of my head, leaving my ear soaked and my hair standing up in a gooey mess.

"Do you have a tissue?" I ask calmly, trying not to shudder. Matthew hands me one, eyeing the damage. I swipe at it, but it's no match for the slime in my hair, which will require a shower.

"Thank you," I say, taking the leash as primly as possible. I've no sooner looped it over my hand when Elliott bolts with all his might, and I fly along behind him, my feet barely on the ground.

"Be careful, Ms. Turner!" Matthew calls out. I dig in my feet and pull as hard as I can and manage to slow the animal down enough that I can punch the elevator button.

The doors open, and I tumble inside with Elliott on my heels. Literally.

Mournfully, I stare at the muddy paw prints on my white slippers. I call Beth.

"He left a giant dog for me to take care of," I tell her without a greeting.

She laughs.

"You must be talking about Padraig, and that sounds right. I told you he's quirky. Just bear with him . . . I promise, he's worth it. I'm telling you, I've never met anyone like him."

I sigh and stare the dog in the eye as I hang up.

"What will I do with you, though?"

He's not overly concerned and sits abruptly. On my foot.

I call Emily.

"I have a companion now. I need a pet sitter for a dog the size of a Clydesdale. ASAP. Don't ask."

I hang up and look into the dog's face.

He's got a sleek brindle coat, massive muscle striations, and jowls that wave when he moves, throwing speckles of slobber into the near vicinity. His ears are practically as big and floppy as an elephant's, and his eyes are soulful as he stares back at me.

"You've got a face only a mother could love, you know that?" I ask. If I didn't know better, I'd think this was the dog I saw running down the street yesterday.

He licks his wrinkly chops, and I swear . . . he winks.

CHAPTER FIVE

Jonah

"Why are we meeting at the airport?" Jace asks as he claps my back and winks at the bartender.

"Because I'm leaving in thirty minutes, and you said you wanted to see me *tonight*," I remind him.

"Good point." My best friend orders a scotch on the rocks and turns back to me. His face is suddenly serious.

"I need your help, Jones," he says softly.

"Anything," I answer immediately.

He smiles. "You don't know what I'm going to ask."

"Does it really matter?" I sigh dramatically. "You know I'll help if I can. I've been cleaning up your messes since college."

"Like when?" he demands, his blond eyebrows knitted. "I can only think of the one time. When my mom showed up to visit, and Maggie Rollins was in our dorm room at seven A.M."

"She was in your bed," I correct. "Not just our room."

"Mistakes were made," he acknowledges. "But I still owe you for covering for me, and jumping in bed with Maggie."

"Yes, you do," I agree. "Maggie seemed too startled to be believable, but I think your mom is still disappointed in me for 'tomcatting around.'"

"Hardly." Jace chuckles. "She thinks you walk on water. She's getting worse, though, Jonah. That's why I'm here."

This gets my attention. "How long's it been since her diagnosis?" I ask, trying to add up the time in my head.

"Four years. She forgot how to use her cell phone yesterday."

I flinch. "What are you going to do? Is it time for a . . . home?"

"I can't put her in a facility." Jace runs his hand over his face and through his hair. "I just can't. I want to build something, Jonah. And I need your help to get financing in place."

Over the next ten minutes, Jace tells me about a town in Norway where the residents are all dementia/Alzheimer's patients.

"They can buy ice cream, go to the store, wander around, all in safety. The 'workers' in the shops are all trained staff. They get to feel like they're living their lives without feeling like they're in an institution. There are no cars allowed in the main streets, so they can wander without fear of getting hit."

"It sounds amazing," I tell him. "And expensive. Where do you want to build it?"

"I don't know yet," he says. "I'm still doing the research."

"There are regulations you'll have to follow, licensing, et cetera."

"I know. It'll be complicated, but the best things always are."

"Well, you know I love your mom. If this will help her, and other people like her, I'm happy to help however I can. Get your research done, and bring me a business plan. We'll see what we can do."

Jace exhales. "I was hoping you'd say that."

"You knew I would," I tell him. "All you had to do was mention your mom."

"You're a peach," he answers. "Truly."

"I know." I put some bills on the bar. "I'm a peach that has to fly to Wyoming now, though."

I stand up and grab my bag. Jace grasps me in a tight hug.

"Merry Christ—er, I love you, man."

"I love you, too. Go home and give your mom a hug for me."

He salutes, clicks his heels, and heads out.

I skirt the tables and emerge into the busy airport corridor. Taking a sharp right, I pass the shops and head toward the private terminal.

I'm weaving through people, preparing to circumvent the TSA lines, when I see a commotion.

Or . . . I see *something*.

I turn to look just in time to see a blur of long red hair, arms and legs, and a massive dog bursts wildly around the corner, tearing down the hall in my direction.

"Holy crap," I exclaim, unsure what to do.

"He's harmless!" the woman's voice calls to me. She's being yanked along like a rag doll, and out of instinct, I take a step to block the dog's path, praying that he doesn't maul me to death.

He rams me in the groin instead.

I drop my bag and cling to the wall so that I don't fall to my knees from the pain.

"Oh my gosh, I'm so sorry," the woman is saying, and I can't see her through my watering eyes. The pain has literally turned my vision blurry, and something is leaning heavily into me.

"It's"—my voice is a croak—"okay."

I blink a few times, and when I'm finally able to breathe again, I look up.

The dog is leaning on me, staring into my eyes. His are friendly, even if they seem to sparkle impishly.

"I've never seen such a big dog," I tell the woman, glancing up.

I meet the gaze of the woman from my building.

My head snaps up. I suck in a breath.

She'd met my gaze just like that yesterday, when she stepped out of the elevator and saw the stripper-gram on my doorstep.

I could swear she was disappointed then, just as she is right now when she recognizes *me*.

"I know," she says a bit coolly. "He doesn't seem to know his own size, either. I'm sorry about your shirt . . . and pants, and your, um . . ."

I look down to find a swath of dog saliva a mile wide across my chest and groin.

I exhale.

"It's okay," I say again, with less conviction than the first time. I could almost swear the corner of her mouth twitches, but she masks it.

"I'll be happy to pay for your dry cleaning," she offers, and she hands me her card. "My assistant will take care of it."

It seems that she mentioned that last bit on purpose, as a message. *I don't want to talk to you, but my assistant will.*

"Thanks," I tell her. "But it's not necessary."

"Of course it is," she answers. "It's the least I can do."

Her phone rings, and she snatches it up. "I'm sorry—I've been waiting for this call. Excuse me."

She begins to turn away, but the dog has other plans. His eyes widen when he sees a man down the corridor preparing to eat a big cheeseburger. I can almost see the plan in his eyes as he takes a giant leap in that direction.

I deftly grab the leash as it yanks out of her hand.

Thank you, she mouths.

"Hey, Emily," she says into the phone. "What flight am I on?"

Meanwhile, it takes all my strength to hold the dog back from sprinting to the cheeseburger. It makes my biceps strain trying to control his strength, and I have no idea how this woman thinks she can do it. She's half my size.

"What do you mean, he can't fly?" Noel asks now, dumbfounded. "Emily, I'm at the airport. On the way to the counter to check in. I need to be in Cheyenne today. There's got to be something we can do. Tell them he's a support animal. Something. *Anything*."

Cheyenne? She's going to Cheyenne? What are the odds of that?

She listens, and the massive, massive animal finally gives up trying to pull my arms off. He sits at our feet now, staring calmly at the chaos around him. A fleck of saliva drips onto Noel's shoe. She doesn't notice.

"You are *not* allergic to dogs," she says dubiously. "Whenever Angelica Aimes brings Dash to the office, you hold him for the entire meeting."

She rolls her eyes, and I hide a grin.

"You can't *only* be allergic to giant dogs. It doesn't work that way."

I have to cough now to hide my laugh. Clearly whoever she's talking to doesn't want to dog-sit.

She sighs. "Just pay for all the seats in the row or something. I don't care what you have to do. Just get us on that plane. Please."

She hangs up and stares down at the animal.

"I know this isn't your fault," she tells him, "but you're making my life very difficult right now."

The dog thumps his long, whiplike tail in response, unconcerned.

"Hey, I couldn't help overhearing . . . while your moose here was trying to pull my arms out of the socket, that you're going to Cheyenne."

"I'm sorry about your arms," she tells me, and I think she's sincere now. She subconsciously rubs her own shoulder, and I know she empathizes. "Yes, I'm supposed to be on a plane right now, actually. But apparently, they don't have to let Elliott fly."

That seems like something she should've known, as a dog owner, but I don't say that. Instead, I make a suggestion.

"I very likely will regret this, Elliott," I tell the dog. "But you are welcome to join me on my flight. It's your lucky day. I'm headed to Cheyenne, too. It's my company's jet." I look up at Noel. "You can come along, too."

She's uncertain.

"Are you sure he'd be allowed?"

"Pretty sure." I nod. "I know the guy in charge."

"I was always taught not to take rides from strangers, but I don't know if an airplane counts."

"Under normal circumstances, it should. But it sounds like you're in dire straits. And I only bite upon request. I promise."

She rolls her eyes. "Well, I do have a rather large body-guard," she finally says.

Her bodyguard is currently licking his nethers.

"And he's certainly diligent," I agree.

She chuckles. "If you truly mean it . . . you're right. I'm desperate."

"I don't know how any gentleman could refuse such a flat-tering plea," I tell her. "So, yes, you're absolutely welcome as my guest." I grip the leash. "Let's go, Rover." I reach for her rolling bag.

"You don't need to," she protests. "I've got it. He's a handful."

"Then it's a good thing I've got two hands," I answer, depos-iting my duffel on top of her bag and pulling the handle.

"Well, okay then, Hercules," she says.

"Men have to show off just a little," I tell her. "It's important for our self-confidence and sense of well-being."

"Do they teach you that in junior high?" she asks, keeping pace with me as I keep pace with Elliott, trying my best not to let him pull me out the nearest window.

"In a roundabout way," I confirm with a wink.

She rolls her eyes again, and I can't help but notice what an interesting shade of blue they are: the color of a stormy sea, dark and layered.

"This way." I lead her down a private corridor.

The sounds of the crowd fade away now, and I can almost see her physically relax.

I lift my eyebrow, and she sighs.

"Elliott wouldn't hurt anyone on purpose," she explains. "But he's so strong. I was afraid he'd get away from me and trample someone."

The flight attendant waiting to greet us overhears that, and her eyes widen.

"Don't worry, Daphne," I tell her. "He's friendly." I wink, and she smiles.

"If you say so, Mr. Blake."

"Daphne, we'll need to add two people to the manifest. Well, one animal that weighs more than the average person, and his owner."

"I'm not his owner," Noel interjects. "I'm just . . . his temporary owner."

"That makes more sense," I agree.

"Is that the plane?" Noel asks, gazing through the windows at the Gulfstream jet on the tarmac.

"Yes, it is," I tell her, expecting her to be impressed.

Her eyes widen as she eyes the steps leading up to the door.

"I have no idea how we'll get this dog up those stairs," she says instead.

"It's a valid concern," I agree. The dog stares up at me, unbothered.

"Food always works for my German shepherd," Daphne tells us. "Do you have any dog treats?"

We both look at Noel, and she shakes her head.

"I just got him today," she says defensively. "You were the one showing off your muscles. Maybe you could carry him."

My mouth drops open. "You want me to sling him over my shoulders and carry something that weighs as much as I do up a flight of stairs only minimally less steep than a ladder?"

"I mean, it would be impressive." She shrugs, baiting me.

"Daphne, do you have any meat at all in the galley?" I ask.

"Yes. Be right back." She races away and returns a few minutes later, out of breath, but holding a fistful of ham. A forbidden treat is enough to tempt any dog, and this one is no exception.

Elliott smells it before he sees it and lumbers to his feet, eagerly following his nose.

"I didn't think this through!" Daphne calls as she spins and runs back in the direction she'd come from. Before I can grab him, Elliott takes off like lightning, chasing Daphne to the plane.

I've never seen a dog scale a flight of steps so fast in my life.

CHAPTER SIX

Noel

D aphne, I'm so sorry," I tell the flight attendant again. And again. And again.

She smiles as she smooths her rumpled hair. "It's fine. I won't need to do cardio today now. He did me a favor, didn't you, buddy?" She bends and fluffs Elliott's massive ears.

He leans into her leg, probably hoping for more ham, but also maybe apologizing. I can't be sure. He does seem contrite.

"Can I get either of you a drink?" she asks when she straightens. "Gin and tonic, Mr. Blake?"

"Just a water, please."

"For me, as well," I tell her. "Extra ice, if you have it." Jonah looks at me. "To match my icy heart." I smile sweetly at him.

"That makes sense." He nods. He settles back into the white leather seats, his ankles casually crossed. He's got the vibe of a very successful, very confident man. "Why are you looking at me like that?"

"Like what?"

"Like I'm under a microscope. Are you a biologist, by chance?"

"No. I'm an editor. And I was just trying to read you. I'm an excellent judge of character."

He grins now, settling even farther into his seat. "Are you? Tell me. What's your read on me?"

I shake my head. "Oh, no. I'm not falling into that trap. I'm not going to offend a man and then sit next to him for six hours."

"You think I won't like what you see?"

"I don't know."

"Why don't you try me? I have very thick skin."

His eyes twinkle cockily, daring me.

"You're confident," I tell him. "Maybe too confident. Sometimes when that happens, it's because it's not real. I haven't decided yet if that's you or not."

He doesn't flinch.

"You're successful," I continue. "Obviously." I gesture around at the lavish appointments surrounding us. "You've definitely got the vibe of someone standing on top of the world. But I feel . . . almost like that's not enough for you. You want to be standing on top of the sun instead."

Jonah stares into my eyes for a long moment. "That sounds painful," he finally says. "I think I'd be burned alive."

I nod. "Yes. That happens when people get too greedy."

His eyes widen briefly. "I see what happened here. You googled me. You think I'm an ordinary run-of-the-mill wolf of Wall Street."

"No, I don't think you're ordinary," I answer. "But you definitely give off a wolf vibe. Like you almost prefer to be alone."

"Maybe I don't like to be disappointed," he offers.

"Has everyone always disappointed you?" I counter.

"Well, this got deep all of a sudden," he says, shifting in his seat and changing the tone. "I rarely discuss my motivations on a first date."

My heart does a funny little flip in spite of myself.

"You consider this a date?" I ask him.

"Well, we'll be spending six hours together. I'll be feeding you. We'll be exchanging stories and getting to know each other. I think it surely classifies as *some* kind of date."

"It won't be anything like the one you had last evening, I can assure you."

He flinches now.

"About that," he says. "That was a joke, sent to me by my ridiculous chief of operations. It was a thank-you and a joke."

"I'm sure." I nod. "It looked like you were both . . . laughing."

I picture the way she was hanging on him, and how he didn't seem to mind, and I get annoyed all over again. I pull out my earbuds.

"Now that Elliott is fast asleep and unlikely to do any more damage"—I gesture toward the mountainous heap by my feet—"I have audio samples to listen to. I'd been planning on getting it done on the flight. Do you mind?"

He shakes his head. "Not at all. I was planning on working, as well. First, though, you said last night that you have a question. What is it?"

My heart pounds as I remember the embarrassment of standing there last night.

"It doesn't matter now," I tell him limply, and I turn back to my phone. Before I start the audiobook, I check my email, out of habit. The thought of an overflowing inbox gives me hives. I'm surprised to see Padraig's name. I click on it.

From: <Padraig.Sinclair@sleighmail.com>
To: <n.turner@parkerhamiltonpublishing.com>
Subject: Character Building Question

Dear Ms. Turner,

May I call you Noel? I hope that isn't too presumptuous of me, nor this email itself. I was pondering one of our two main characters this evening: Jack. I need to give him a couple discerning character details that the other main character, Nora, will be drawn to. As a woman, do you have any insight you could share?

I do hope I'm not a bother,
Padraig

Normally, I wouldn't go back and forth with a writer who hadn't yet submitted a full manuscript. I'd wait for the chapters, and if I didn't like them, I'd pass. Very seldom, I might request a revise and resubmit. But very rarely—as in I can't remember a time when I've done it—would I help a fledgling writer write the actual chapters.

However, there's a first time for everything, and rules are made to be broken. Across from me, Jonah uncrosses his legs, then recrosses them. As he moves, his cologne wafts over to me. The man smells like a snowy day in an enchanted forest.

"You smell familiar," I tell him. "Like a professor I used to have. What cologne do you wear?"

"Tom Ford."

"That's what I thought. Thanks!"

I press reply to Padraig's email.

From: <n.turner@parkerhamiltonpublishing.com>
To: <Padraig.Sinclair@sleighmail.com>
Subject: Re: Character Building Question

Dear Padraig,

Here's an idea: have Jack wear Tom Ford cologne.

Best,
Noel

Jonah is sexy enough of his own accord, without adding in the fact that he smells like heaven.

"Why are you frowning?" Jonah asks.

I take out an earbud. "Pardon me?"

"You were frowning. Is your audio not good?"

"It will be excellent," I assure him. "This narrator is phenomenal. I was just answering emails. I have resting witch face, I guess."

"That's not it," he says. "But I'll let you off the hook. You don't have to tell me. Our dinner will be ready shortly. Daphne's bringing us toasted ham and cheese sammies."

"I'm surprised there's any ham left to make them," I mutter, staring down at the snoring animal at my feet.

"I've never heard a being, human or animal, snore that loud."

"Me either, to be honest. It's cartoonlike."

Elliott's lips are formed in a perfect O, like he's going to blow smoke rings, and his cheeks puff out with each exhale. We both chuckle, which wakes him.

Daphne brings our dinner, and Jonah turns to me.

"You have to explain how you wound up with him. Because it doesn't track with your image."

"What do you mean?" I demand, in mock anger. "Just who do you think I am?"

"I think you're elegant, refined, and you're wearing a cream-colored cashmere coat. You wouldn't wear things like that if you had planned on owning this beast. Also, is your purse Gucci?"

"Yes."

"He's chewing on the strap."

"Oh my gosh, Elliott! You were asleep two seconds ago," I exclaim, yanking it away from him and examining the damage. "Well, at least it's just a strap. I can replace that easily enough."

"You value your things, and you take care of them," he observes. "You like the classics and aren't swayed by trends."

"Is that a polite way of saying I look frumpy?" I ask.

"No, you look timeless," he answers. "It's a compliment, Miss Priss. Take it."

"Miss Priss is a compliment?" I chuckle now. "I'm not a schoolmarm."

"Is that still a word?" he asks, deadpan.

"Thank you again for letting us hitch a ride," I say, changing the subject. "I don't know what we would've done."

"Well, I do love playing the role of white knight. What's in Wyoming for you, anyway?"

"My parents. I'm headed home for the holidays. You?"

"Same. My dad needs my help."

"Well, we're both good kids, then," I decide.

"Do they know you're bringing . . . that?" He points at Elliott.

I shake my head. "Nope. I didn't want to ruin a good surprise."

"Oh, I'm sure they'll love it," he drawls, and I laugh again.

Every time he moves, the scent of a forest wafts over me and every time, I fight to ignore it.

Daphne returns to take our dishes. "The rest of the flight should be calm and easy," she tells us. "Can I get you anything else?"

"Not right now, thank you," I tell her. "Dinner was amazing."

She blushes and looks at Jonah. "Mr. Blake?"

She's got a crush on him, and I wonder if he knows.

"Nothing for me, Daph. Thank you. You're tops, as usual."

She blushes even deeper and bends to pat Elliott's big head before she leaves.

When she's gone, I look at him. "I actually should let my folks know about Elliott. They'll need to come pick me up in something big enough to hold him."

"They should borrow a flatbed semi," he advises.

"And you're prone to exaggeration," I say, adding to his list of personality traits.

"You do realize that I'm not a character in one of your books, right?" he asks me. "There's no need to identify all my parts."

"I do this with everyone," I assure him. "It's a character flaw."

"It's not a flaw," he says. "I just wonder how often *you're* disappointed. How often does reality not measure up to what you built in your head?"

"It happens," I admit. "But that's okay. That's life. It's part of the challenge."

"Is that what it is?" he asks, amused. "I generally call them detours."

"Oh, no. It's all part of the journey," I tell him.

"Do you have a sign in your living room that says 'Live, Laugh, Love'?" he asks.

I laugh. "No, I have a framed TV hanging over the fireplace that displays pictures of classic art."

"See? You're timeless."

I can't argue. He actually did peg that part of me right. I invest in quality things and take care of them forever.

"I've had this purse for ten years," I admit. He crows in delight.

"I knew it."

I smile but adjust my earbuds and begin the audiobook. Eloise St. James pulls me into a pre-WWII-era Irish romance, and I close my eyes and listen for the next five hours. I'm so absorbed in the story that I'm startled when Daphne emerges to prepare us for landing.

"It's time for seat belts, guys," Daphne says. We oblige and sit back in our seats, folding up our papers and closing out our apps.

"Where in Cheyenne do your parents live?" Jonah asks conversationally.

"Outside Cheyenne, actually. About thirty minutes. A little town called Winter Falls."

Jonah stares at me.

"You're joking," he finally says. "Your last name. Turner. You're . . . Susan and Rich's daughter."

"Yes," I answer slowly, staring him in the eye.

"My dad is Judd Blake. The mayor. Your dad has plans to overthrow him and turn Winter Falls into a tourist trap."

My breath catches in my throat. My heart beats a bit harder.

"It appears that you're my archnemesis," I say awkwardly.

"It certainly seems so."

We fall silent as we touch down and taxi in.

"My parents are good people," I tell him. "They're not trying to target your dad. They just . . ."

"They need something that he won't give them," Jonah says simply.

"Essentially."

We fall into silence until we stand up and coax Elliott down the steps with the last piece of ham.

When we're on the tarmac, I turn to him. "Thank you again. Truly."

"The pleasure was mine," Jonah answers. "Are you sure you don't need a ride into town?"

I shake my head. "My parents will be here."

He nods. "Then this is goodbye for now." He turns to leave, then pauses.

"Oh, and Noel?"

"Yes?"

"All is fair in love and war."

He strides away.

CHAPTER SEVEN

Jonah

As I drive into Winter Falls in the rental SUV, I can't stop thinking about the ridiculous situation I'm now in. When I call Jace to complain, he does nothing but laugh.

"You're telling me you met a beautiful woman who is smart and classy, but you're both involved in some small-town feud like the Hatfields and McCoys?"

"I hope there are no shotguns involved, but yes."

"Only you, Jonesy. Only you."

We hang up, and I can't find a station that isn't playing Christmas music, so I just turn off the radio and listen to the sound the tires make in the snow on the road.

It sounds like cornstarch.

The occasional house has Christmas lights up as I drive into town, and the old Park 'n' Shop's faded sign out front says "Merry Christmas."

There are no city decorations or lights.

There is no Christmas tree in the town square as some other cities have.

My dad has certainly seen to that.

I'm torn between finding it sadly dark during a time that should be festive and bright and being relieved that I don't have to pretend to enjoy a holiday that I've hated since I was four years old.

Heading down Main Street, I see that the Busy Bean has lights in the window, with silver tinsel and coffee-cup-shaped gift cards on display.

Both of the stoplights in town are red when I reach them.

As I wait at the main intersection, I see Nolan Greene, the police chief, sitting in the window of Nell's Café, having coffee with someone I can't make out. He glances up and catches my eye, then touches the tip of his cowboy hat in greeting.

I lift two fingers from the wheel to return the gesture.

I can't help but wonder what everyone thinks when they see me. I haven't been home in a long time. Do they fault me, or do they understand?

It's not like they don't know my family's story.

The light turns green, and I continue through town to my father's small ranch right outside the city limits.

I drive through the gates and park next to my father's old, battered pickup.

The house is dark. The porch lights aren't even on.

I find my father out in the shop behind the house, tinkering at his woodworking bench.

"Oh, hey, son!" he greets me when he turns around, a block of wood in his hands. He's got wood shavings in his hair, and I give him a hug.

"How're you doing, Pop?" I ask.

"Well, I'm a mite cold, if you want the truth. The heater out here can't seem to keep up with the winter."

"Nothing can," I say ruefully. "Let's go inside and get you warmed up."

We enter through the back porch, and the house feels colder than the shed.

"Why didn't you start a fire?" I ask, turning to him. "It's freezing in here."

"There's no reason to go to all the trouble when it's just me here." He shrugs.

"Staying warm isn't too much trouble," I chastise him. "I'll start one."

I get to work in the living room, laying the firewood and then tending it until it roars.

"There," I say with satisfaction. "That's better."

"Thanks, kiddo," he says, leaning against the door. "And thank you for coming. I really can use your help."

"I know. I met the Turners' daughter."

"Met? You went to school with her."

"I don't remember her," I tell him with a frown.

"Well, that's because you chased everything in a skirt, and she was too smart for that."

"Maybe," I say. *But you'd think I'd remember eyes like hers.*

"I don't know what Rich thinks is going to happen here," my

dad grumbles. "The town council is never going to boot me without a cause."

"Are you standing in the way of progress?" I ask bluntly.

He shakes his head adamantly. "A Christmas tourist trap? You really think that will work? It won't."

"You need to figure out a plan, then. Something to replace theirs. This town needs help, Dad. It's dying. Anyone can see that."

"Ever since Ridgemont went out of business, folks have been struggling," he admits. "We need a source of revenue. That's partly why I asked you here, to put that expensive business degree I paid for to use."

"Are you ever going to let me forget that you paid for my college?" I ask.

"Not as long as mentioning it gets you to do things." My dad winks.

"You know I'm almost forty years old, right?"

"I do," Dad answers cheerfully. "I'm hoping to get a few more good years out of it. I wasn't kidding—if you think of a good idea for revenue, let me know."

I glance at my watch. "It's almost midnight, Pop. We can discuss this more tomorrow. Did you happen to change the bedding on the guest bed?"

"No one has used it since the last time you were here," my dad says indignantly.

"That was over two years ago."

My dad's face clearly shows that he doesn't see a problem.

"Not an issue. I'll sleep out here in front of the fire tonight, and I'll deal with the bedroom tomorrow."

"That's up to you." My dad shrugs. "This couch is just as comfortable, anyway."

He slaps the back of the leather couch that he's had since I was a boy.

"Good night, son. And welcome home."

I don't say that this isn't my home anymore. I don't say it, because it would be hurtful.

"Night, Dad" is what I say instead.

When he disappears down the hall, I make my way to the guest bedroom, the room that used to be mine. It still has the dump truck wallpaper that my mother had picked out for my nursery. Even through high school, my father had never allowed me to change it.

I drop my duffel bag and dig out my overnight case before heading into the bathroom to brush my teeth. Afterward, I retrieve some extra blankets from the closet, grab a pillow, and head back to the living room to get settled on the couch.

The wind howls outside, and the snow flurries against the glass. As the fire crackles, I stare into it, remembering, just barely, what this room would've looked like during this time of year if my mother were still alive.

The tree was on the right side of the fireplace and had colored lights. It was topped with a gold star, which I remember clearly because I used to want to climb the tree and grab it. I'd only been four. My memories are hazy, but still there.

She and I had popped popcorn and strung it into garlands for the tree. We'd both eaten a piece and then strung a piece, over and over, until she said I'd never eat my dinner, and she was right. I didn't eat dinner that night.

I fall asleep staring through the windows at the night sky because as much as I love NYC, you just can't see the stars there like you can here.

I wake to the sun in my face, and the smell of bacon and coffee.

The fire is barely embers, so I step out into the cold to add more wood and poke at it.

"How many eggs do you want?" my father calls. "Two or three?"

"Two," I answer. "Please."

My father is spooning four onto my plate when I join him in the kitchen, joining a heap of bacon and a big cup of steaming black coffee.

"Thanks, Dad."

"I didn't know you were going to sleep in so late," he tells me. "I ate hours ago."

I glance at the clock, a bit bleary-eyed. "It's seven A.M."

"Yes," he says. "I know. I need to head out. If you need anything, you know my number."

"Wait. What do you want me to do today? To help?"

"You can go on up to Nell's for lunch and take the pulse of the folks there. See how they're feeling. Maybe swing by the Busy Bean to do the same. Then come join me at the office. Nance and I are working on budgets today. It ain't gonna be pretty."

He slaps me on the back as he passes by. "Wash up before you leave." The door slams behind him.

"Welcome home to me," I mutter.

I eat half of what's on my plate before I wash the breakfast dishes up. As I'm throwing my paper towel away, I find a stack of *Wall Street Journals* next to the recycle.

That gives me pause. My father, someone who makes fun of everything Wall Street, everything related to banking, and everything related to New York in general, subscribes to the *WSJ*?

Maybe he's not so oblivious to my life after all.

I can't help pondering that as I do a few rounds of push-ups and sit-ups, then shower. It doesn't make much sense, because my father hates to hear anything about my life. If I try to talk about something from my world, he shuts it down.

After I'm dressed, I check my messages. I only have one from Millie: The confirmation for your dad's thermal hip waders is in your email.

Nothing from Noel. I don't think I expected anything, since I didn't give her my info, but it's still a bit of a letdown. This is a small town and she knows my name. She could've looked my info up if she'd really wanted to. Her wit is quick, and sparring with her would be entertaining.

As I step out onto the front porch, I pause with my hand on the railing, remembering a time when I was so much smaller, my hands clinging to the rail as the red and blue lights had flashed against the snow. A female officer had held me while I cried as I watched my father get into the car.

I blink away the memory.

Memories like that are what keep me from coming back here. It's easier to not think about it at all.

I find that my father has taken my rental car and its heated seats, leaving me with his old truck, the keys in the ignition.

"Because nobody would want to steal you," I tell it as I turn the key.

The truck sputters to life, and I rub my hands together, trying to warm them. While the truck warms up, I jog back into the house to dig my leather gloves out of my bag.

The truck is ready to drive when I return, and it doesn't take long for me to remember what driving an old truck on the snow is like. The bed skids if I'm not careful.

I keep my foot off the accelerator for most of the short drive to Nell's, letting the downshifts do the braking. When I arrive at the little town café, it's already bustling with nearby farmers and other townspeople on their way to work.

I'm waiting for Nell to see me and show me to a table when I overhear a couple voices from a nearby booth.

"Saw Jonah Blake in town last night, Mandy. Want me to arrange a meetup?"

I recognize the voice. *Heather Reid.* I'd dated her in high school, and she always wanted more than I wanted to give.

"Nah, that's okay, Heather. I'll leave him for you."

"Jonah Blake!" Nell's old voice calls out from across the room. The conversation near me immediately stops, and Nell comes to hug me, her cotton-white hair barely reaching my chest. "It's about time you came back to town, boy."

"It's good to see you, Nell," I tell her honestly. "You're a sight for sore eyes."

She grins, her wrinkles parting. "I've got the perfect seat for you. Follow me."

She leads me to the two-seat table in the window. "This was always your favorite," she remembers proudly. "And you're in luck. We've got fresh peach pie today. I baked it myself last night."

"I thought I smelled something delicious when I drove past here," I tell her.

She slaps at me. "Oh, you. You were always a flatterer."

"Because it always works." I wink at her.

She pours a cup of coffee for me. "Do you want anything to eat?"

"No, my dad made me a big breakfast. But I'd sure take a piece of that pie to go."

"You got it, sugar."

She leaves to get it, and I inconspicuously try to glance at Heather's table.

She hasn't aged well. There's nothing wrong with her looks, per se. Her blond hair is still meticulously highlighted, and her makeup is still flawless. But there's a hardness around her eyes and mouth now that were never there before.

Nell sets a take-out box in front of me and sits down.

"Don't even look in that one's direction," she advises. "She's bad news, honey."

"I wasn't looking at her for that," I tell the elderly woman.

"Well, make sure you don't. She just divorced Matt Langford. Remember him?"

I nod.

"They're kaput, and she's on the prowl."

"Maybe she just wants to be alone for a while," I suggest.

Nell shakes her head. "Consider yourself warned," she says. "Now, let's talk about this ugly business between your father and the Turners."

"Well, you don't beat around the bush, do you?"

She chuckles. "You can't when you're as old as I am. I don't want to run out of time!"

"I'm just here trying to help him sort it out, Nell. He wants to figure out a way to bring in some revenue. But he also doesn't want to turn the town into a tacky tourist trap."

"I think it's a bit more than that, don't you?" Nell asks softly, and she pats my hand. "He hasn't so much as lit a Christmas tree in the town square since she died, Jonah. We all know what it's really about."

"I promise you, he only wants what's best for Winter Falls," I insist.

She nods in agreement. "I never said he didn't, Jonah. We all know that, too."

"So, knowing that, do you think the majority will back him?"

She takes too long to think about it, and the truth is on her face.

"It's close?"

She nods. "It's close. The thing is, Susan and Rich want what's best, too. And what would be the harm in having a Christmas village here? Everyone likes Christmas, Jonah. Well, except for you and your father."

"Don't listen to her, Jo-Jo," Heather says, from right behind me. "I don't like it much, either."

"Jonah was just leaving," Nell tells Heather. "So you'll have to do your catching up another time."

"You were?" Heather asks me, disappointed.

"I . . . uh . . ."

Nell digs her fingers into my back.

"Yes. I was just leaving."

I try to hand Nell money, but she waves me off. "It's on the house, kiddo. Welcome home."

"Thanks," I mumble, taking the pie and edging past Heather. "See you another time, Heather."

"Yes, definitely. Soon."

I'm not sure if that's a good thing or a bad thing.

CHAPTER EIGHT

Noel

From: <Padraig.Sinclair@sleighmail.com>
To: <n.turner@parkerhamiltonpublishing.com>
Subject: Re: Re: Character Building Question

Dear Noel,

Thank you for the cologne name! I'll work that into the story.

    Emily said that you were in Wyoming for the holidays! I hope that you enjoy it. I bet Elliott is loving the wide-open space! Thank you again for caring for him. I know it's a lot to ask. I hope I repay you by writing the best story you've read in a while. In fact, maybe it will be life-changing! ;)

Pad

From: <n.turner@parkerhamiltonpublishing.com>
To: <Padraig.Sinclair@sleighmail.com>
Subject: Re: Re: Re: Character Building Question

Dear Pad,

My holiday is fine so far, thank you for asking. Yes, I'm home for the holidays to help my parents. Winter Falls feels exactly as I remember it.

I love the wide-open sky, and the way the stars shine so bright here. I love the feeling that everyone is almost family. There are people here that I've known since childhood. Sometimes that's good, and sometimes it isn't, but either way it contributes to a part of me I hadn't realized that I miss: my roots.

Yes, Elliott loves it so far!

I don't know if you've done this yet, but a great way to make a story authentic is to truly get to know your characters. Sit down and list everything about them. What do they like, what do they not? What angers them? What makes them happy?

If you need help, I'm technically on vacation right now, so I'm free. Just let me know.

Best,
Noel

"Do you miss the city yet?" my mom asks as we walk to the store.

"You know, I was just thinking about how much I like the quiet here. I love the city, no question. I love the bustle and the hustle and the grind. But, man, I'd forgotten how much I love it here, too."

"You're getting older," my mom says, sipping at her hot coffee as we walk, her breath turning into misty billows in the air.

"What does that have to do with anything?" I demand.

Mom chuckles. "Well, besides the fact that you'll need an eye cream soon, if you haven't started using one already, it means that you're going to be drawn to your family. You haven't built one of your own yet, so of course it makes you feel good to come back to the one you *do* have."

"That was a very creative way to nudge me about getting married and giving you grandkids," I commend her.

She grins impishly. "I had to try."

"Do I really need an eye cream?"

My mom peers at me. "Not yet, darling girl. You're perfect."

"You're partial. Is that Heather Reid?" I ask, shielding my eyes from the morning sun.

"Yes."

"I didn't know she'd stayed here. I thought she got married and moved away right after high school."

"She did. But she recently got divorced, and now she's back."

"That makes no sense. Why would she come back just because she's divorced?"

"Some people actually like their hometown," Mom points out. "She wants to be around familiar things. I can understand it. She's rediscovering herself, I think."

We've almost reached her now, and it's definitely too late to pretend we don't see her.

Heather stops and gushes over my coat. "I heard you were in town!" she says, her hands fluttering. "I love, love your coat! I've heard people say that winter white is so last year, but I don't believe it. It's gorge!"

"I agree," I tell her. "It's timeless. It'll never go out of style."

"Well, you look fantastic," she says. "I'm sure you've heard that Jonah is back in town, too. He and I are going to meet up soon. Should I give him your regards?"

Even though I'm getting annoyed with everyone for assuming I'd remember Jonah Blake, I still take a little satisfaction with my answer.

"No, he and I shared a jet here. But thank you anyway. See you."

I tug on my mom's elbow, and we aren't more than twenty feet away when my mom hisses at me.

"You left that part out, young lady."

Shoot.

"It was the only way I could get here," I tell her quickly. "The commercial airlines wouldn't let me fly with Elliott."

"Speaking of," my mom says, her gray eyebrow lifted into her hairline, "he chewed up my favorite slipper this morning."

"I'm sorry," I say limply.

"I still don't understand why you're dog-sitting for an author you've never even met. Who does that, Noel Marie?"

"A crazy person."

"That's right," my mom sniffs. "We'll have to see if they've got something to feed him at Park 'n' Shop."

"Or maybe Tractor Supply."

Mom glances at me. "That closed last year."

"Really? How in the world?"

"When Ridgemont went out of business, too many folks moved away. The shops that are still here are barely hanging on."

"And Judd knows this, but he's still refusing to grant you the permits you need to bring this city back to life?"

My mom nods. "Yes. Now you see why we're so upset. Winter Falls is dying, Noel. It truly is."

And it is. I can see it in the empty storefronts.

"This isn't right," I murmur.

"No, it's not," my mom agrees. "Look at what it could be! Look how charming it already is. Just think if we cleaned it up, replaced the lampposts with vintage poles and fixtures, and built more, of course, on the outskirts of town. The Christmas village could be something straight out of the Christmas villages people put up for Christmas decorations, personified into a living, breathing place."

I don't correct her word choice because she's got a point. It's definitely an interesting business hook.

"Like a charming old-fashioned town over the holidays," I muse, thinking. It's easy to envision the vintage feel and the magical atmosphere. "I really like it, Mom."

"The Etsy store I've been building has grown so much. I need a physical shop to keep up with production."

"It will look almost like a town in a snow globe," I say, thinking aloud. "Charming, magical, festive, nostalgic. This could work."

She smiles at my enthusiasm. "I know, honey."

We finish our coffee as we reach Park 'n' Shop, and we throw our cups away on the way inside. We stamp off the snow and hunt for dog food, the rubber soles of our boots squeaking on the tile floors.

We hadn't anticipated the size of the bags, however.

"Sam, did you take all of Tractor Supply's bulk stock?" my mom asks the owner as we eye the fifty-pound bags. "We can't carry this home."

"I can send Mikey with it in a few minutes, if you'd like," Sam tells us.

"Perfect. Thank you," I say. I pay for the food.

"Do you think I should've gotten two?" I ask Mom on the way out.

"Good God, how much does he eat?"

"I looked it up last night, and it said up to eleven cups a day."

"Good. *God*," my mom breathes. "He's going to eat you out of house and home, Noel."

"Technically, he's in your house right now," I say cheerfully.

Mom scowls. "Don't remind me."

I laugh, and finally she smiles, too. "Your dad did look sweet with him earlier," she says.

"He's always wanted to get another dog after Panda died so long ago," I remember. "Why hasn't he ever gotten one?"

Mom shakes her head. "I don't know. I guess he doesn't want to lose one again. It's a hard thing to deal with, Noel."

I nod. "I know."

"We don't deserve dogs. They have the purest of motives."

"How about when Elliott ate your slipper?"

"You're going to need to get him some training," Mom tells me.

"I won't have him that long," I assure her. "Just until I go back to the city. Surely my assistant will be able to find a dog boarder for the author after the holidays."

"He seems pretty attached to you, though," my mom says. "He was sleeping on your feet last night when I walked past."

"I know," I answer. "I dreamed I was being crushed to death by an elephant."

"You weren't far off."

We keep walking, our boots crunching in the snow.

Mom glances at me. "So how was Jonah's private jet?" she asks.

"It's his company's," I tell her. "Not his personally."

Mom waits.

"But it was nice, for sure. The seats lie flat into beds."

Mom looks at me quickly.

"We didn't do *that*!" I say quickly. "Obviously."

"Everyone always thought you two would end up together," Mom says.

I shake my head. "Mom, I *do not* remember him from high school. When you talk like that, it weirds me out."

"Do you have a head injury?" My mom peers at me. "You definitely knew him. In fact, we probably have old pictures back at the house."

"Noel! Suze!" We squint into the distance as my father comes into focus, plowing through the calf-high snow in someone's yard.

"Honey!" my mom shouts. "What in the world are you doing?"

"Elliott's gone," he shouts back. "He got away!"

"Oh, no," I breathe. We jog back with my dad, branching out to call for the dog. The icy wind slaps at my face as I search in every direction.

He's nowhere to be found. My dad apologizes a dozen times, and it wasn't his fault, but that doesn't make Elliott any less gone.

"What am I going to tell Padraig?" I wonder to myself as I trudge back to the house an hour later. I can't feel my fingers or toes, but that doesn't matter. All I can see is that goofy dog's face and the way his eyes were so trusting.

I'd lost him.

My mom was right.

We don't deserve dogs.

I warm up and head back outside, hunting for another couple hours but coming up empty-handed and frozen footed.

I take a long hot bath when I finally get back home and then climb into my twin-sized canopy bed with the pink bedding, and text Emily.

> I lost Padraig's dog.

Three bubbles.

Then, she answers:

> I'm not even going to ask how.

> I take that back. How??

I tell her the whole story and even include my purse strap.

I end with: I'll go out hunting for him again in the morning when it's light.

She ends with a picture from her cousin Michel's last photo shoot and: Your date for NYE. She includes a fire emoji for emphasis.

The man is attractive, I'll give him that. With black hair and green eyes that seem to stare into my soul, he is beautiful, for sure. He's young and perfect and has a foreign appeal.

But he's not who I think about as I fall asleep.

No. After checking the backyard for Elliott, I settle into bed, keeping an ear tuned for whines or scratching at the front door. It is not Michel's cocky grin I think about as I drift into dreamland.

It's Jonah's.

CHAPTER NINE

Jonah

It's not the creaking of the porch swing that wakes me, although that's certainly there.

It's the snoring.

Bleary-eyed, I look at the clock. The snoring continues, and I think I'd know it anywhere. I climb out of bed, pad to the front windows, and look outside.

Sure enough, Elliott is stretched out on his back on the porch swing, swaying in the wind, snoring as loudly as his lungs can possibly operate. His legs are splayed straight in the air, where he makes running motions. His mouth is an O again.

If it weren't two A.M., I'd laugh.

As it is, I open the front door and hiss at the dog.

"Elliott, get your butt in here."

Happily, the dog wakes up and meanders inside, nuzzling the side of my leg with his cold, wet snout.

"Thanks," I mutter. "Come on in here. I don't know what

you're doing out and about, but I'm pretty sure you're not supposed to be."

Elliott takes me up on the invitation and jumps immediately into the middle of the guest bed.

"You're going to have to scoot over," I tell him. "It's only a full-sized bed in the first place."

He lays his head on my pillow and opens one eye to look at me.

I sigh and share half the pillow.

"I'm not spooning you," I tell him.

And I don't. I wake up at seven A.M. with him spooning *me*.

The back of my neck is wet from his drool, and his right paws are thrown over my side.

"This is out of hand," I mutter. But it's cold, and the dog is warm, and we fall back asleep, cuddled together under the covers. It's not until my father comes in at eight and starts howling about a dog being in the house that we wake back up.

"What in the heck is going on here?" my father demands. "Why is there a Shetland pony in bed with you?"

I explain, and Elliott sits politely on the bed.

"You're telling me that the Turners let this . . . *animal* off leash?" my father demands. "That's against ordinance and not acceptable. Its paws are as big as my hand. It could've attacked someone."

Elliott lays his head down, his large eyes staring soulfully into my father's.

"I'll take care of it," I tell him. "Right after breakfast. He's not aggressive, Dad."

"I'll be talking to Nolan about this," my father grumbles as he disappears back into the hall. "They should get ticketed. This is not acceptable."

"Well, now you've done it," I tell the dog. He perks his ears at me and lays his big paw on my hand. "You didn't do anything, though, did you? You were just sleeping here, minding your own business."

He looks at me as if to agree.

"I'll see what I can do," I tell him. "But you've got to start behaving. Noel isn't strong enough to control you, and you know it, don't you?"

He blinks angelically.

"Yeah, you know."

He blinks again.

I toss the covers back and brave the cold air, fussing at my father while I pull my ice-cold jeans on.

"Dad, it's too cold in here," I call to him. "Turn the heater up."

"Put some clothes on," he calls back to me. "I'm not made of money."

"You can afford the electric bill," I tell him as I join him in the kitchen, with Elliott on my heels. "And if you can't, I'll pay it for you."

"That's not the point," he grumbles. "Paying for heat is like burning dollar bills. You don't get anything in return."

"You get to be warm," I point out. "And *I* get to be warm." I cross to the thermostat on the wall and see that it's set at fifty-five. I shake my head and turn it up.

"I'll compromise and set it at sixty-eight, and I'll light a fire. But you're going to get pneumonia or something. Keep this heater on."

I leave Elliott in the kitchen while I start a fire, and when I return, Elliott is sitting at attention near my father. My father flicks a piece of sausage into the dog's waiting mouth.

My eyes widen just as my father notices me.

"You didn't see that," he snaps.

"But I *did* see it," I tell him.

He scowls. "I dropped that piece on the floor, anyway. It was dirty."

"Er, okay," I answer, unconvinced.

He puts a heaping plate of eggs and toast on the table, and I pretend not to notice that he puts another one on the floor for Elliott. He pushes the plate behind the chair with his foot, hoping I don't see.

After I eat, I clean up the dishes, and Dad puts on his hat to go check on the barn.

Elliott trots after him, and I watch through the window as the dog follows my father as he goes outside to feed the horses.

Elliott stays at my father's elbow, overseeing everything Dad does, right up to pouring grain into the feed troughs. Elliott watches the horses lap up the grain, and I laugh as he curiously lowers his own tongue and tries it.

He spits it out, and my father laughs, patting the massive dog's head.

Elliott is still on my father's heels when he comes back into the house.

"This dog is something else." My father chuckles.

"He is," I agree. "And you had him outside off leash, Mr. Mayor."

Dad glares. "I don't have his leash because he's a stray that turned up on our doorstep. I guess I could've used a lead rope from the horses. What is he, anyway? Half moose?"

"He's not a stray, and I believe he's an English mastiff."

"So, part moose seems about right."

"Yeah. Close enough."

"You're going to take him back today, I assume?" my father asks.

"Yes, just like I promised."

"Well, I'm going to be in the study for a while working. There's no rush. As long as he doesn't destroy the house."

My mouth twitches. "Okay, Dad. Thanks for understanding. I'm just going to take a quick shower, and then he'll be out of your hair."

"Good," Dad says gruffly, and heads to his study with Elliott right behind him.

When I emerge, the dog is sleeping on my father's feet.

"He's a good foot warmer," my father says when he glances up and sees me standing in the doorway. "But that's all a dog this large is good for. He'll eat them out of house and home. Takes up too much space. Doesn't have a real purpose. He could kill a small child with one bite."

Elliott yawns, his mouth huge. He flops his head back on my dad's foot.

"You were saying," I prod my dad.

"There's no good reason to have a dog this big."

"They must like him."

"I hope they like their five-hundred-dollar-a-month feed bill for him, too."

"You've gotten crotchety in your old age. You know that?"

My dad glares at me. "It's just common sense."

"Do you yell at neighborhood children to stay off your lawn, too?"

"There's no neighborhood children out here."

"Good. Because if there were, you'd yell at them."

"I would not. Not with the current state of things. I need to be out there kissing all the babies."

"Dad." I turn to him and sigh. "That's not the kind of elected official you are. You aren't fake. You don't say things to get elected. You care about this town, and that's all you need to do."

"That's not the way elected life works, Jonah."

"Sincerity has always worked for you in the past, Dad. I wouldn't give up on it now. Come on, Elliott. Let's get you home."

Elliott doesn't move.

"Looks like you've got a new friend." I chuckle.

Elliott follows me with one eye but doesn't move another muscle.

"Elliott, let's go." I pat my thighs to encourage him, and finally, he lumbers to his feet. He sniffs at my dad's pockets.

"Have you been feeding him something?"

"Of course not," my dad protests, even as Elliott snuffles more in depth in his pocket. I lift an eyebrow.

"Come on, dog," I tell him. "Let's let the old man have his secrets."

Elliott reluctantly follows me, but he looks soulfully over his shoulder at my dad, solidifying my belief that he was being fed something delicious.

I pause. "Does Avery Linton still do dog training on the side?"

"Yes."

"Perfect, thanks. I'll see you later this morning."

Elliott jumps right up onto the bench seat of my dad's truck and lies down so that his head doesn't hit the ceiling, leaving me about eight inches to fold myself into.

"Don't stress yourself," I tell him. "I'll fit."

He can lift his head and look out the window without even sitting up, so that's how he rides into town, with his big head filling up the window, his hot breath steaming up the glass. By the time we get to Susan and Rich's, there are about twenty nose prints on the passenger-side glass.

He sits politely next to me on the porch while I ring the doorbell.

When Noel comes to the door, her face instantly lights up when she sees Elliott, and she drops to her knees, wrapping her arms around his neck and burying her face in his fur.

"Oh my gosh, Elliott," she exclaims. "What happened to you? I thought you were gone."

To my surprise, her eyes are wet and her cheeks are flushed.

"He's okay," I rush to tell her. "He spent the night hogging my bed, actually. He's fine, Noel. I didn't know you were this attached to him."

"I didn't know, either," she admits, lifting her wet gaze to mine. "I thought something bad had happened to him because of me. At my age, most women are mothers. I can't even keep track of a simple dog."

"He's completely fine," I tell her again, helping her to her feet. "My father even made him eggs for breakfast. And I don't know if you've noticed, but Elliott isn't a 'simple' dog. He outweighs you, and he desperately needs training. Speaking of, Dr. Linton does dog training on the side. Some lessons might come in handy."

She glances at me and then nods. "It couldn't hurt. I don't have a pen—let's go inside and write that name down really quick, if you don't mind."

"Of course."

She opens the door, and the scent of baking washes over me.

"Mom's making Christmas cookies," Noel tells me.

The smell triggers a mountain of memories erupting from deep within, swirling around me in fragments and clips.

My mom is standing in the kitchen, doing the very same thing . . . lining up snowmen on the cookie tray, after my fingers cut them out and handed them to her. The smell of that day comes back to me . . . strong enough that it almost brings me to my knees.

I grab the door, my chest tight, and Noel and Susan look at me in alarm.

"Jonah, are you all right?" Noel asks.

I nod, my jaw clenched.

But I'm not, because my body remembers what happened after that, after the cookies, after the popcorn strings, and my stomach clenches hard.

Even still, I try to act normal.

"Susan, can you write down Avery Linton's name for Noel?" I manage to say.

"She does dog training," Noel tells her mother.

"Of course," Susan says, coming around the kitchen island, wiping her floury hands on her apron, her eyes scanning my face. "Jonah, maybe you should sit down for a second. You're white as a sheet."

"I'm sorry. I should've eaten breakfast," I tell her. "I'll just be going now. Thanks."

"Here, sit—" Susan says, but I can't get out of the room, out of the house, fast enough.

When I look back in the rearview mirror, I see Noel's face, framed in the living room curtains, watching me drive away. There's confusion in her eyes, and if I'm not mistaken, authentic concern.

I blink hard. I hate that look. I got a lot of those after my mother died, from people who didn't know what to say, or what to do, but tried anyway. It always resulted in awkward, uncomfortable conversations.

This is a big reason why I don't come back here. Too many people look at me the same way, even now.

Too many things here trigger memories . . . memories I'd stopped focusing on long ago. I'd hidden them away, and when I'm here, in Winter Falls, the hiding place crumples.

As if on cue, and almost of its own accord, the nose of my truck turns down the road that leads to Winter Falls Cemetery.

A moment later, I step out onto the snow.

"Hey, Mom," I say softly. "Long time no see."

CHAPTER TEN

Noel

I join my mother in the kitchen.

"That was the weirdest thing ever," I say. "I'm not just imagining that Jonah Blake almost passed out in our kitchen, right?"

Mom shakes her head. "Not at all. He looked like he'd seen a ghost." She glances at the kitchen table, where mountains of individual cellophane cookie bags are piled up, printed with my dad's name and the slogan *Vote Rich for Regrowth! Together, we'll grow back Winter Falls!*

"Maybe he thinks we're not fighting fair," Mom says.

"I don't think that's it," I answer. "You're making cookies, not offering bribes."

I don't know why I care, but the look on his face was one of sheer pain.

"Maybe he has a kidney stone," my mom suggests. "Nolan had one last spring, he thought he threw his back out!"

"Maybe," I say doubtfully.

She chuckles. "Can you deliver the first batch of cookies to-day? Hand them out to everyone you see, go door-to-door if you want, just get your dad's name out there."

"Everyone knows Dad," I remind her. "But yes. I'll go schmooze for you."

"Thanks, sweetie." Mom stacks layers of wrapped cookies in a pretty basket and hands it to me. "Here you go. Come back when you run out, and more will be ready."

"Aye, aye, Captain." I look for Elliott but find him napping with my dad.

"Can I leave him with you?" I ask my father. "I'm hitting the campaign trail for you." I hold up the basket.

He nods. "Sure. We don't want him terrifying the constituents."

"He's already had breakfast, so don't believe it if he says otherwise," I say.

Dad chuckles. "Will do."

I pull my mom's ankle-length parka on and draw the hood up.

"You look like Little Red Riding Hood in that thing." My dad laughs as I tug fleece-lined boots on.

"It's not a fashion show," I tell him. "I just want to schmooze for you. I don't intend to lose toes for you."

"Well, I'm glad to see where your loyalty ends," Dad answers.

"Frostbite," I say immediately. "It always ends at frostbite."

"Good to know."

I take the basket and head out the back door, making my way over the snow-covered sidewalk and down the street.

I talk to Sam Jones and Elijah Harris. I talk to Josephine

Clark for at least fifteen minutes and assure her that my father will never outlaw ostriches, which is a strange bone of contention, since Josephine doesn't actually own any.

It's when I'm headed toward the edge of town to knock on doors that I see Judd's beat-up old truck parked out in the cemetery, all alone amid the swirling snow flurries. The gravestones are topped with snow, and the flowers covering some of the graves are faded and buried in snow, as well, with just their tips emerging. The truck's red paint sticks out like a sore thumb against the snowy background, and something about how hauntingly lonesome it looks stops me in my tracks.

I don't know why, and I don't even know *when* . . . but I find myself walking down the long drive leading up to the cemetery gates. I head toward that battered red truck, and I don't stop until I'm standing right behind Jonah Blake as he sits in front of his mother's grave.

"Are you campaigning?" he asks quietly, having heard my footsteps in the snow.

"Yes."

"You won't get many votes here," he answers.

"I wasn't counting on it," I tell him. "I just saw you sitting here, and it's freezing. I came to make sure you were all right."

"I'm all right," he says immediately.

I stare at him. "I don't want to argue with you, but you're sitting in two feet of snow."

"I *did* notice that, yes."

I gather my long red coat around me tightly and then sit next to Jonah, wiggling into the snow to get settled.

"It's not that uncomfortable," I say in surprise. "I don't even feel the cold, really."

"You're wearing a sleeping bag," Jonah points out, glancing at me. I notice that his eyes are red, and I look away tactfully.

"I am," I agree. "It's really warm, too." I glance at his hands, which are also red. "You're not even wearing gloves."

"I wasn't planning on being out that long. I really just came to drop Elliott off with you."

"Thank you again for that," I tell him quickly. "You have no idea how worried I was."

"You do seem to be getting attached," he answers.

"My mom said the same thing."

He doesn't answer, and we don't talk.

We sit in silence, listening to the wind howl. At the same time, I feel like I shouldn't be intruding and also that I shouldn't leave this man alone. Sadness hangs in the air, and the things he's not saying are loud.

He's troubled.

That much is clear.

"You must have so many memories of your mother," he finally says.

"I do," I agree. "Some are great, some are not, from my turbulent teen years."

He smiles a bit. "I envy that."

"The turbulent teens? Don't. Trust me." I smile, then sigh. "I'm not great at situations like this, Jonah. I'm sorry. I know something is bothering you, but I don't know how to help."

"It's okay. I just don't like being here. In town. I left for college, and I've barely looked back."

"Same. Although I do come home for Christmas. My parents love it so much, especially my mom. She named me Noel, for Pete's sake."

"Now's not really the right moment to petition for them," he says stiffly, and I startle. "I know they love Christmas."

"That's not what I'm doing, I swear," I say. "I was just making small talk. No offense, but you seem like you need it." I almost stand up and leave him stewing in his own mood, but something about his tense form gives me pause.

I take a look at his tightened jaw and clenched hands, white at the knuckle.

Panic attack.

"I have a confession to make," I tell him, trying to think of something to talk about that will distract him. "I know we went to school together, but I don't remember you. I don't remember what happened with your family, even though I know it was something. So I'm not as unfeeling as I must appear. I just have a very bad memory, apparently."

Jonah looks over at me, his eyes gold in the winter sun. "You know what's weird? I'm the same way. I don't remember *you*, Noel."

"Awww, I bet you say that to all the girls."

"I remember everyone else very clearly, even though I tried to leave all these memories behind. But you . . . I don't remember at all."

"I'll try not to be offended."

"How can you be? You don't remember me, either."

We both chuckle, then fall into silence as we stare at the headstone in front of us.

SARA BLAKE
BELOVED WIFE AND MOTHER

"Oh goodness. She died on December 24? You were so young. That must've been so hard."

"It was," he agrees. "For me, and for my dad. He had no idea how to raise a kid alone."

"Well, it seems he did a pretty good job."

"Thanks."

"What happened back at my house?" I ask him. "What brought you out here? Am I being too pushy?"

He's quiet. "One of the last memories I have of my mom is baking cookies together. I cut them out, she laid them on the sheet. Your house smelled just like ours did that day."

My stomach tightens at the look on his face.

"I'm so sorry, Jonah."

"It just triggered so many memories that I've tried hard to forget, that's all."

"That's completely normal," I assure him, rubbing at his cold hands with my mittened ones.

"I've never talked about this with anyone before," he answers. "It feels odd."

"You've never talked about your mom? I bet a nice warm therapist's office would be better than sharing a snowbank with a stranger."

"You're not a stranger anymore," he reminds me. "We shared a jet."

"Yes, we did."

"I wonder sometimes what she would be like now," he

continues. "I remember her being young and blond. Would she be going gray now, like your mom? Would she be healthy? One of my friends . . . his mother took me under her wing in college. She has dementia now. One of these days, she won't remember me."

"It's such a cruel disease."

"It is," he agrees. "Eventually, she won't remember Jace."

I shake my head and press my hand to my heart.

"We're not being very good mortal enemies right now," he says.

"No, we're not." I sigh.

"I'm going to come up with an idea to help my dad," Jonah tells me. "He needs this job, Noel. It's all he has. He's been mayor for so long, he doesn't know anything else. If he lost this, I don't know what he would do."

The thought of Judd Blake, all alone since his wife died, raising a son who moved away . . . it tugs at my heartstrings, particularly when I think about my dad, and how close he and my mom are. Rich Turner is the world's farthest thing from lonely.

"Can't you talk to your dad?" I urge him. "All my folks really want to do is change this town for the better. They want to build their Christmas business and bring jobs back. If your dad would just approve it, I'm sure mine will back away from the mayorship. I doubt he really wants the headache of that. He just wants my mom to have her dream."

"When I came here," Jonah says, turning to me, "I wasn't sure what to expect. Dad needed me, so I came. I wasn't expecting to find him so . . . alone." His forehead furrows. "It was easy for me to put memories behind me since I wasn't here, but the second I came back, they surrounded me again. It's hard to imagine what my dad must go through, living here every day."

"It must be very difficult," I answer.

"I call him, you know. Every week or so. And I told myself that I was being a good son, but I don't think I was."

"I'm confused, Jonah," I tell him, touching his arm. "Are you upset for your dad, or are you upset because of your mom?"

"I don't know," he says honestly. "Maybe both." He climbs to his feet and holds a hand out to me. "I've been boring you long enough," he decides. "Let me give you a lift."

"Thank you," I answer, taking the hint. He's done talking about his feelings.

I set the basket on the seat of the truck and climb in.

Jonah glances at the cookies.

"You hungry?" I ask, offering him one.

"Yes, but not for those. We'll stop for some real breakfast."

"We will?"

He nods and doesn't wait for agreement as he turns toward Nell's.

"I like your confidence," I announce.

"Did you just decide?" he asks with a grin.

"Yes. I wasn't sure before if it was impressive or annoying."

"Well, I'm glad you landed on impressive."

He parks and comes around the side of the truck. I struggle with the door, trying to open it, before he finally opens it for me.

"It sticks," he says with a grin. "But I wanted to see if you've grown any muscles from wrestling with Elliott."

"Funny," I tell him as I step past him, trip on his foot, and then slip on the ice.

Like lightning, his arm shoots out to catch me, and he holds me upright.

My face is mere inches from his, and his woodsy smell envelops me.

"You smell good," I tell him before I step back.

"Thank you." He holds out an elbow. "Shall we?"

I take his arm and step onto the curb, then release his arm to walk into the café.

"Chicken," he says, his eyes twinkling.

"You know they'll be gossiping already," I answer.

"That's the fun part."

"Speak for yourself."

We step inside, and Nell greets us immediately, but she's clearly curious as to why we're together. I hold out the cookies.

"Can I leave a few cookies here for your customers?" I ask her.

"Oooh, strategic," Jonah commends me as Nell comes to hug me.

Nell reaches up to pinch my cheek. "You look pale," she tells me.

"I'm okay. I've been out in the cold. As soon as I warm up, I'll be right as rain."

"I've got the perfect table for you, then. It's under a vent."

She leads us to the back corner.

"Will this work?"

I look around. Everyone else is up front, and now it looks like Jonah and I want privacy.

"It's great," Jonah tells her. "Thanks, Nell."

I take a seat.

"Don't enjoy this so much," I advise him. He glances at a table full of ladies who keep peeking in our direction.

"The word will spread by dinnertime," he predicts. "We'll be well on our way to being married."

"Great. Our parents will kill us both."

"I'm more of a lover than a fighter, anyway," Jonah tells me. "I can't help it. On an unrelated note, this is our second date. You know what happens on the third, correct?"

My head snaps up, and he bursts out laughing.

"Just seeing if you were paying attention."

Nell returns with coffee and leaves the pot with us. "I can bring you a stack of pancakes that are so good, your *mama's* mouth will water," she tells me. "How does that sound?"

"Perfect," I tell her, and she turns to Jonah.

"And for you, I'll bring you some fresh biscuits and home-made sausage gravy."

She doesn't wait to see if that's fine with him, she just turns and walks away, sticking her order pad in her pocket, since she doesn't need it, anyway.

"Biscuits and gravy will be great, Nell, thanks," Jonah quips.

"I wonder if anyone has ever told her no?"

"No one is that brave," Jonah decides.

I pour sugar and cream in my coffee, then stir it up. As I blow on the surface, I look at Jonah.

"So, tell me more about you," I suggest. "Do you like your job?"

Jonah takes his coffee black, and draws in a long drink.

"Yes and no," he finally answers. "I like the control. I like the black and white of numbers—they're either right or they're not. There's no in-between or gray spaces."

"That's what I love about being an editor," I answer. "The gray spaces. It's the gray space where the most interesting things happen."

"Is that so?"

I nod. "Have you never heard of *Fifty Shades of Grey*?"

Jonah's eyes widen and it's my turn to burst out laughing at the look on his face.

"Touché." He chuckles. "Well played. The next thing I know, you'll be telling me you edited it."

"No, I didn't," I admit. "Although it would've perked up the workweek, for sure."

Jonah is still laughing at the thought when Nell brings our food. She sets a little dish of peanut butter next to my pancakes.

"You remembered!" I exclaim with a smile.

"Of course," she says. "Besides, I taught you that trick when you were an infant. Peanut butter plus syrup equals perfection."

After Nell leaves, Jonah returns his attention to me, his gaze trained on my face in a way that makes me feel he's *really* listening. It feels as though I'm the only person in the room right now to him.

"What's your favorite thing about being an editor?" he asks me, then takes a bite of his food.

"Hmm." I chew and swallow. "The possibility."

Jonah lifts an eyebrow. "How so?"

"Well, I never know what I'm about to discover. Right now, I have an interesting new author who I think is going to surprise me. I love being surprised. I've been in the field so long now that it seems like no one can surprise me anymore. But he might. And that's exciting."

"This new author wouldn't have anything to do with you having Elliott, would he?"

"He has *everything* to do with that." I laugh. "He's that author, yes."

"So that's the reason you agreed to keep his dog—because you think he can wake you up."

"From my literary coma?"

Jonah nods.

"Yes, I guess so. I wouldn't normally go to this trouble, I can assure you."

"You're jaded," Jonah announces, slapping the table as though he's figured something out. I jump a little.

"How so?" I turn his words around on him.

"You think you've seen everything. You don't think there's much to know that you don't already. Or new things to understand. You think you already get it. As in, *everything.*"

"I'm not a know-it-all," I protest, and he laughs.

"Miss Priss, if we were in Hogwarts right now, you'd be Hermione Granger."

I stare at him, at the way his eyes crinkle when he laughs.

"I can't decide if you using a Harry Potter reference is cute or weird."

"Oh, it's weird," Jonah tells me. "Especially when you remember that I don't have any kids."

"I think I knew that," I say. "From when I googled you. I'm kinda surprised you don't."

"Why? Because I'm almost forty? You don't have them, either."

"Please don't refer to thirty-seven as almost forty. And I do want them someday," I tell him with a shrug. "I'm up for editor in chief right now."

"Congratulations."

"Thanks. But it hasn't happened yet."

"Give it time." Jonah nods. "It will."

"Thanks for the vote of confidence."

"Confidence is a skill," Jonah says. "You simply choose to believe something. That's all there is to it."

The bells over the door to the café tinkle as it's opened, and I hear my father's voice.

"Hey there, Nell. I'm here to pick up those doughnuts that I ordered yesterday."

I freeze, and before I can ponder my next move, I find myself dropping to the floor on my hands and knees to hide from my father.

"Sure thing, Rich," Nell tells him. "Give me just one sec."

Please don't tell him I'm here, I try to relay to her telepathically.

Jonah bends toward me.

"Should I invite him over?" His eyes twinkle impishly, and I want to slap him. He lifts the edge of the tablecloth. "You could crawl under here, if you want. But if your dad saw you under there, I don't know how to explain what you were doing other than . . ."

I snarl.

He laughs.

"Thanks, Nell," I hear my dad say. "Everyone at city hall thanks you, too."

The bells tinkle again, and I exhale.

Nell comes round the corner and eyes me. "I was just coming to tell you that your father is gone," she says simply. And to her credit, she doesn't say a single word about me being on the floor.

CHAPTER ELEVEN

Jonah

I literally cannot control my laughter at the sight of the elegant woman in front of me sprawled on the ground hiding from her father.

"It's too much," I gasp after laughing for two straight minutes. "I think you have a french fry in your hair."

She reaches to see, which of course makes me laugh all the more. Finally, she smiles sheepishly at me.

"Fine, it's funny." She gets to her feet, then sits down.

"I know what you're feeling, though," I tell her. "I feel it, too. Being back here . . . it almost puts me in a younger state of mind, like I was the last time I lived at home. The dynamics feel almost the same."

"It makes perfect sense," she agrees immediately. "I almost let my mom cut my meat for me last night."

I laugh again. A quick wit is my Achilles' heel, and hers is lightning fast.

"I feel like we have roles that we play," I tell her. "Here, we resort back to being our parents' children. At work, I'm the guy everyone needs to fear. Maybe we start becoming our roles. Maybe that's all we are . . . a sum of the roles we play."

"Who are you really, though?" Noel asks me, her voice softer than I've heard it before. "If you weren't playing a role at all, who would you be? Do you know?"

I stare at her for a long time, because no, I do not know. "For as long as I can remember, I've been playing the role of *boy who lost his mother but never dealt with it and never thinks on it.*"

Noel stares into my eyes so intently, it makes me squirm.

"You're not that boy anymore," she tells me quietly. "Give yourself permission to process whatever happened and put it behind you."

I pause for a beat, then two. Her eyes are so sincere, and I didn't know that blue could ever feel so warm.

"I . . . I'm fine, truly," I tell her. "I'm sorry that I was acting oddly earlier. But I'm fine."

Noel doesn't buy that, but she doesn't push it, either. Instead, she sits back.

"Perfect. Well, then, I'll feel okay with leaving you on your own now while I finish lobbying for my father."

She stands up and puts some bills on the table to cover breakfast.

"I like to go Dutch," she says when I protest.

I acquiesce immediately. "And I like to give a woman what she wants."

"Sometimes, I don't know if you're trying to sound naughty on purpose, or . . ."

"I never do anything on accident," I assure her with a wink.

"Do you want a ride, or are you planning on practicing your door-to-door sales skills a bit more?"

"Oh, the latter, for sure," she answers. "I've almost achieved the level of vacuum salesman. Fingers crossed." She holds her fingers up, and smiles.

I blink. The way she moves seems so familiar.

"You okay?" she asks.

"Déjà vu, I guess. For a second, it felt like I'd known you forever."

"I have that kind of face," she answers.

I laugh again, glancing at her unique deep red hair and her stormy blue eyes. "No, you really don't," I tell her.

"No, I really don't," she agrees.

"I'll . . . see you later."

I turn around and get out of the place as fast as I can.

What in the world is it about that woman that makes me feel like an awkward teenager?

For God's sake, every time I'm around her, my chest flutters like I've got a schoolyard crush.

"Get it together, Blake," I mutter as I walk three doors down to city hall to find my dad. He and the city clerk are huddled at his desk, examining a dozen spreadsheets.

"Hey, Jonah," Nancy greets me, standing to hug me. "Would you like some coffee?"

"No, I'm fine, thank you." I skirt the desk to stand behind my dad. "You come up with any ideas yet?"

"Not yet," he mutters. "But I will."

"I actually might have something," I say. "Izzy Mulvaney's

dementia is getting much worse. Jace came to see me . . . he wants to raise capital for a business idea he has."

My father waits for me to get to the point.

"He wants to build a dementia village, of sorts. A place that looks like a retro town, a place where no cars are allowed, and everyone, from the ice cream man to the grocer, is trained medical staff. The patients can wander to their hearts' content, because everyone is keeping an eye on them and they're safe."

"That's an amazing idea," my dad says. Nancy is nodding, too.

"It could be complicated," I warn them. "Regulations and stuff."

"But think of the good it could do," Nancy says. "My father had dementia. He always tried to escape at night and wander. It killed us to put him in a home, but we didn't have any choice. We were too exhausted to watch him twenty-four/seven."

"I like this idea," my father says, clearly thinking through options. "We could become known as the world's preeminent memory treatment village."

"I like your confidence," I tell him, realizing in this moment where I get it. "There's apparently already a village like this in Norway. Jace wants to do something similar here in the States. He wants it outfitted as a retro town, because so many dementia patients remember long-ago memories. If they're surrounded by that atmosphere, they'll feel more at home. Less afraid."

"Like drive-in movies, hamburger stands, and malt shops," my dad says, scribbling onto a notepad. "Can you call Jace and have him come talk with us? I'd love for him to consider Winter Falls as the home of his venture."

"It's not a venture yet," I remind my father. "We'd still need to raise capital."

"Pish," Dad says. "You can do that in your sleep."

"Only if it's a sound investment," I tell him. "And we haven't done our due diligence yet."

"Then do it," my father suggests. "Meanwhile, ask Jace to come visit. The sooner, the better."

"I'll call him." I sigh. "But you're going to have to be patient. Big projects like this don't happen overnight. Research must be done, business plans designed . . ."

"I'm old, not stupid," my father replies without looking up.

"Right. Okay."

I make a call to Millie and let her know to watch for a business proposal from Jace.

"Send it straight to legal when it comes in, okay? Let them know to start due diligence immediately."

"Everyone else in the company shuts down for the week after Christmas," Millie reminds me. "Are you saying that you want the legal team to work over the holiday?"

"No. I'm saying I want them to get this done before the shutdown."

"Christmas is only a week away," she says slowly.

"I know. That's why I want them to start immediately."

"Understood." She hangs up, and I call Jace next.

"Get your business plan over to Millie. She's going to have our legal team start due diligence. My dad had an interesting idea, and I think you might like it. Care to come to Winter Falls?"

"Right now? Over the holidays?" He pauses, but then says, "What the heck—we'll come now. Mom doesn't remember anyone anyway."

That stings, even though he doesn't mean for it to.

We hang up, and I turn to my father.

"Jace and his mom will be here. I'll need to clean up the guest room for Izzy."

Dad crows in delight. "Just when they thought they had us, Nance!"

"I still wouldn't mind a Christmas tree in the town center, though," Nancy tells him. "Remember the giant one we used to have every year?"

He sobers immediately. "No. No, we're not doing that. It's a safety hazard." He scoops up papers and ends the conversation by going to file them.

"Oops," Nancy murmurs. "I didn't mean to upset him."

"He'll be okay," I assure her. "You know how he gets."

Of course she knows. She sees him far more than I do.

"You know," my father calls from the other room, "it wouldn't hurt you to get a haircut."

"For what?" I call back. "I don't have a hot date."

"That's not what I heard," Nancy says to me. "I heard that you were with No—"

"Shh." I hold my finger to my lips.

She smiles. "I won't tell if you don't."

Dad continues, "I need you on the campaign trail. Noel Turner was out and about all morning, handing out homemade cookies. You need to step up your game, son."

Nancy snorts into her coffee cup.

"I just figured out a business idea for you," I call back. "Cut me some slack."

"Get your hair cut," he says, coming back into the room. "You look like a hippie."

"People pay a lot of money for this look," I tell him.

"Are those people blind?"

I sigh. "I see you've committed yourself to the role of crusty old man."

"Get off my lawn," my dad answers, sitting down at his desk.

"I'll see you at home later." I look at Nancy. "Good luck with him."

She chuckles.

"Do you know of a good barber?"

"There's a hair salon in the back of the Busy Bean," she tells me. "It's the only one in town."

"Perfect." I wink and leave.

The cold is biting, and I pull the collar of my coat up to help shield my face.

I grab a coffee from the Busy Bean before I venture down the hallway to the back. I duck inside a small room, where Heather Reid is cutting someone's hair.

I'm a deer in the headlights as both Heather and her client notice me.

"Hey, sugar," Heather greets me. "Go ahead and have a seat. I'll be with you in just a few minutes."

I sit down and pull out my phone. As I do, Noel's business card falls out of my pocket.

I pick it up, and on a whim, I text the cell phone listed on the card.

> Miss Priss, I need help.

There are three immediate bubbles.

> Are you ok?

I answer quickly. My father sent me to get a haircut. No one told me who the hairstylist is.

> Well, do tell. Who is it?

> Heather Reid.

She sends back three crying-laughing emojis and a bit of helpful advice: Run.

> I can't. She already saw me.

Sucks to be you! she answers.

> You really ARE my mortal enemy, aren't you?

She sends another laughing emoji.

"Whatcha laughing at, sugar?" Heather asks, sweeping around her chair as her client gets up. "I'm ready for you."

I get settled in the chair as she rings the lady out.

She comes back and puts a smock over my head, snapping it at my neck. "Just cleaning you up a bit?"

"Yes, please. My father thinks I look like a hippie."

"I definitely wouldn't go that far." She laughs, running her fingers through the lengths of my hair. "I'll get you trimmed up."

She snips at the top and sides.

"I wouldn't have pegged you as someone who cares what your dad thinks," she says casually, checking the lengths of two strands.

"Why do you think that?"

"You haven't been home in years."

"That doesn't mean anything."

"Doesn't it?"

"No. My dad is a gruffy old goat, but I love him."

"Of course you do," Heather murmurs. "How's life been treating you, anyway?"

"It's great," I answer. "I work a lot, but I wouldn't have it any other way."

"Really? But work can't keep you warm at night."

"No, but I have an operational thermostat, and I'm not afraid to use it."

She smiles. "How's city life? If I lived in New York City, I'd probably never come home, either."

"It's got its pros and cons."

"What are three pros?"

"Hot dog stands. Pizza. The bluntness."

"The bluntness?"

"Yes. New Yorkers don't sugarcoat anything. They opt for brevity over manners. It's refreshing."

"Some might call it rude," Heather points out as she buzzes my neckline into a razor-sharp line.

"Some might. But a New Yorker wouldn't. They'd call it efficient."

"So what are three cons?"

"The crowds. The humidity. The cold."

"Those last two are cop-outs," Heather says as she brushes off my neck and holds up a mirror. "What do you think?"

"That is one handsome lad," I tell her. "Thank you."

"My pleasure. Hey, Jonah—a bunch of us get together on Friday nights at the Bear's Den for drinks. You're always welcome!"

I hand her my credit card. "Definitely. Maybe! Thank you for thinking of me."

"I'm not sure if you've just accepted or turned me down," Heather says as she runs my card.

I smile. "I just tentatively accepted. Depending on what my dad might have already planned for me. He's campaigning, and I'm apparently now his campaign manager."

"Then you'd best stop consorting with the enemy, shouldn't you?" Heather says with a wink. She laughs at my expression. "Oh, honey, you know nuthin's a secret for long in this town. Everyone knows you and Noel Turner have been getting cozy."

"We got breakfast," I say slowly. "I don't think that's classified as cozy."

"That's not what my sources say," Heather says lightly. "They say you're smitten, kitten."

"I hope you don't pay your sources much," I tell her. "Because they kinda suck."

"Uh-huh. You were smiling at your phone a little bit ago, in a way that only smitten men do. Who were you texting, Jonah?" She widens her eyes innocently, and blinks. "Who was the lucky girl?"

I don't answer.

Because of course, *the answer is Noel Turner.*

CHAPTER TWELVE

Noel

I smile and look at my phone one more time before I lay it down. Miss Priss, I need help.

I can't help but wonder what's happening now while Jonah is at Heather's mercy.

My amusement dies as I envision her fingers flitting along his neck, grazing his jaw.

The thought actually makes my stomach clench.

I force the thought away by focusing on my emails.

From: <n.turner@parkerhamiltonpublishing.com>
To: <Padraig.Sinclair@sleighmail.com>
Subject: Elliott is a lunatic

Dear Padraig,

Through no fault of my own, Elliott ran away last night and spent the night gallivanting around. He's sleeping peacefully now, but I have to wonder at your sanity for trusting me with your dog. I can't even keep a houseplant alive.

I'm sleeping in my childhood bed here, and it's only twin size. Needless to say, there's not enough room for Elliott AND me, so I'm ordering an air mattress. I'm also going to get him a couple dog training lessons so that I can handle him better while I still have him. Speaking of, do you have any new chapters for me to read?

All my best,
Noel

From: <Padraig.Sinclair@sleighmail.com>
To: <n.turner@parkerhamiltonpublishing.com>
Subject: Re: Elliott is a lunatic

Dear Noel,

Your note made me laugh out loud, and I thank you for telling me. He does get into hijinks sometimes, you'll need to watch him.

As far as trusting you with him . . . dear lady, I'm sure he's enjoying his time with you immensely! He likes you, and that scamp has good instincts. I've always listened to him myself.

I'm happy to report that I'll have new chapters for you tomorrow! Nora is coming along quite nicely. She's drawn to Jack, but doesn't want to admit it, or even believe it. He's feeling the same about her. They keep bumping into each other in serendipitous ways, and neither of them suspects a thing yet!

I really need to start ramping things up though—shake them up a bit so they realize how much they mean to each other. Then of course, I'll need to figure out . . . DO they belong together in the end? I'd love to take you up on your offer to brainstorm their characters. Do you have any time available?

Talk to you soon,
Pad

From: <n.turner@parkerhamiltonpublishing.com>
To: <Padraig.Sinclair@sleighmail.com>
Subject: Re: Re: Elliott is a lunatic

Dear Pad,

I actually have some free time right now. I'm sending you a Zoom link—if you have a chance, jump on and we'll brainstorm in real time.

Best,
Noel

I set up the Zoom call and send it to Pad before I join it myself. While I wait to see if he joins, I check my phone. Nothing more from Jonah.

Elliott is sprawled on his back on my bed, taking one of his six naps a day.

"You have two speeds," I tell him over the top of my laptop. His ear twitches, but he doesn't move. "Sloth and tornado."

While I wait for Pad to join, I browse Amazon for a few minutes, choosing the largest, thickest air mattress I can find. *Add to cart.*

I eye the pink ruffled canopy and comforter that I've slept on in this room for as long as I can remember. And then I browse for a red-and-black-buffalo-plaid flannel comforter. *Add to cart.*

Elliott turns over on the bed, and almost falls off. He looks startled, but promptly settles back into sleep by flopping onto his back, his ears falling straight down onto the bed.

I browse XXL dog shirts, find one that says *Size Matters*, and I snicker. *Add to cart.*

I choose my parents' address, since I'll be here another week. *Check out.*

I choose my card, and bam, I'm done.

Retail therapy: complete.

As if on cue, Pad emerges onto my laptop screen, looking befuddled as he peers at the screen. He's got wild white hair and a beard and instantly brings to mind Santa Claus but with merrier eyes.

He's even wearing spectacles.

"Noel?" he asks. "Can you see me?"

"I can." I nod, hiding a smile as he taps at the screen.

"Is this your first Zoom call?" I ask.

He nods. "It is. It's nice to meet you in person!"

"It's nice to meet you, too. You look as kind as you sound! I'm excited to do this brainstorming exercise with you. Once you flesh your characters out and get a feel for what they like, you'll be surprised at how the story unfolds."

Pad rubs his hands together. "I can't wait to try. This is such a treat. Let me get a pen and paper."

He turns around and rummages in what looks to be a trunk behind him. When he bends down, I see a bunch of old furniture and things on shelves. It seems to be a shop of some kind.

"Pad, you can just take notes on your laptop while we chat," I tell him. "It's easier."

He emerges triumphantly with a pen and notebook. The notebook isn't a normal composition notebook. It's leather bound, and is wrapped many times with a leather cord.

"I can't work that way," he replies. "I have to feel the pen in my hand as I write."

He twirls the pen around his fingers, then chews on the end.

"Do you think Nora is stubborn?" he asks thoughtfully, running his thumb around the pen. "I picture her as independent, and passionate, but rarely stubborn. Unless she really believes in something."

"I'd agree," I tell him, stroking Elliott's silky ear. "It seems to me that she only fights when she knows she can win. If she can't win straight out of the gate, she likes to fight smarter, not harder."

"Smart," Pad said. "Just like Nora."

I nod. "She comes across the pages as clear as day to me. She's got integrity, and she's mature, worldly. But she's also got this slight vulnerability to her, almost an ethereal quality. People gravitate to her. She glows a little. On the inside."

"I'm so glad it plays out on the page like I intended," Pad says in delight. "I worked hard to get her right."

I nod. "And you did. Get her right. She's likable, relatable, sarcastic, but in a funny way."

"I'm glad you think so," he says, and he's scribbling notes. "I wonder what her favorite flower is?"

"Hmm. The first thing that comes to mind when I think of her is a Himalayan blue poppy," I answer. "It's not a run-of-the-mill flower. It's a flower for those who research, and who appreciate the different. Nora doesn't blend into the crowd. She stands out."

"How right you are! I like that choice," Pad approves, and he takes note.

"Her favorite color is also ice blue," I continue. "Or that's what it seems like to me."

"She loves completely, too," Pad says, scribbling notes. "She likes to come across snarky at times, but she's got a very soft heart that she hides." He pauses. "Which is good, because Jack needs a soft heart in his life. He just doesn't realize it yet. He grew up in an environment where he wasn't overly nurtured. He's still trying to figure out what that looks like."

"Hmm," I answer. "You might want to tighten that message. I didn't completely get that on the page. It feels as though he's got an edge, for sure. And it feels as though he's scared, but I'm not sure that I've felt why yet. Why exactly is he scared? Is he scared of losing people?"

Pad nods. "That's definitely part of it. He lost someone dear to him at a very young age, so he's scarred from that, but he's also scared to look at that scar. He's afraid to know the extent of the true damage, and he's afraid that he'll spread that damage to those close to him."

"Whoa," I answer. "All that definitely hasn't come across the page yet, but I like where you're going with it. That would show a vulnerable side to him that I think we should see. Making your readers understand your characters' *why* is critical. If they are on board with the *why*, they'll follow you anywhere."

I think of Jonah in the cemetery, and *his* unexpected vulnerability.

"Excellent advice," Pad tells me without looking up from his notes. His fingers scribble quickly across the page, writing with flourishes and swirls. His writing has as much character as he does, and he should consider turning it into a font.

I tell him that, and he laughs.

"You know, where I come from, there was only one font. That one." He points over his shoulder. I peer at the shelf.

It's a typewriter.

"About that," I say. "If we sign your book, you'll have to deliver it to us in a Word document so we can edit it. The way you've been scanning your pages works for now, but it won't once the editing process begins."

"Understood." He nods. "I have no problem with that. I'll hire someone to type it for you."

"Wouldn't it be easier to just write it on a computer to begin with?" I ask, confused.

"Computers lack soul," he says simply. "Would a rock 'n' roll purist prefer digital sound or the crackles of a record?"

"They would probably say a record," I answer. "Which is something I don't really understand. The sound is perfect on digital. Why would you want the static of vinyl?"

"It's the imperfections that give it character," Pad answers. "We're the same, you know. People. Our flaws make us interesting. Perfection is an illusion, Noel. If that is what someone is chasing, they'll always be running."

"You're talking to an editor." I laugh. "My core DNA tells me that everything can always be made better."

"There's nothing a red pen can't fix," Pad chimes in.

I nod. "Yes."

"But there's the rub. Sometimes, things aren't actually broken. They're just rusty. All they need is some TLC, and then they're as shiny as new."

"You're making a lot of sense," I concede with a smile.

He shrugs. "You learn a lot when you're as old as I am.

"Now about Jack," Pad changes the subject. "What is the most important thing in the world to him?"

"Straight to the heart of the matter, I see. Let's definitely not do the easy stuff first."

He smiles. "Okay. We can work up to it. For these, just answer straight from your gut. First instinct."

I nod.

"What's his favorite color?"

"Gray. Like a stormy sky. That's why he likes Nora's blue eyes. Because when she's mad, they look like a storm."

"I like that." He notes it. "Favorite meal?"

"Skillet-seared duck breast with beets and watercress."

Pad stares at me. "That was a very specific gut reaction."

I laugh. "It's one of the most pretentious meals I know of, and so Jack would be drawn to it. He's trying to escape his past, it seems like. So he crafts himself into the person that he wants to be. He's meticulous about it. He'll wear designer shoes, and have ridiculously refined interests. Because he's afraid to let himself be otherwise."

Pad pauses his pen. "Wait right there. That's insightful. Can you elaborate?"

"He's afraid to allow himself to be anything other than the opposite of where he came from. He's afraid he'll find himself back there, and he'll be the same broken child he was when he began."

Pad nods. "That's impressive. You're good, Noel."

I smile, and his praise feels good. "I've been doing this a while."

"No, it's a knack, something that can't be learned. You have an innate gift. Why does he hate where he came from so much? Does he hate the people?"

I shake my head. "No. He hates it because of the memories. He can't unsee things, and when he goes back to where everything happened, he is immersed in them, and he feels helpless."

"What happened to him there?" Pad asks, his pen hovering over the page.

"I don't know. You tell me—you're the author." He smiles, and I scowl. "And you'd better have a doozy, because you've got me hanging on your every word at this point."

He smiles again. "That's the best compliment anyone could ever give me," he says, and he's flushed. "I thank you for it."

"It's the truth. You're a skilled storyteller, Pad. There's no way this is your debut novel."

"When I said it was my debut, I simply meant it's the only one I'm seeking publishing for. It's certainly not, by far, the first story I've written."

"You have others?"

He nods. "Many, many others, written across many generations, my girl."

"Would you ever consider letting me read them?" I ask, trying to hide my excitement.

"I suppose, but I'd need to check with my subject matter. I take inspiration for my stories from real ones. They're by far the most entertaining."

"You're a wonder, Pad," I tell him.

He grins. "Flattery, my girl, will get you everywhere." He scans his notes. "Let's get back to our unanswered question. What is the most important thing in the world to him?"

"His family." My answer is immediate. "He doesn't even realize that it's his Achilles' heel. He thinks he resents his family—his father. But in reality, he resents how vulnerable his family makes him. He never wants to feel that way again. So he holds his family at arm's length."

"He can't grow as a character until he realizes that," Pad says.

I nod. "You're right."

Pad notes that down, then closes the journal. "You've been an immense help today. Thank you."

"I can't wait to see what you do with it," I tell him. "Truly. Hurry up and write it. I'm impatient."

He chuckles, his palm pressed to his belly. "In due course." He nods. "The pacing has to be just right. You know that."

"Pacing is everything," I agree.

There's a knock on the door, and my father sticks his head in.

"Hey, punkin. I got Elliott a big soup bone at the store." He carries in a giant hunk of bone.

"I'm afraid I need to run, Pad. I look forward to reading your next chapters."

I close my laptop and eye the bone. It's got ribbons of fat surrounding it.

"Does that thing still have meat in the middle?" I ask, grimacing.

"Yes. Dogs love it."

He puts it down on the floor, and Elliott immediately investigates, nudging it with his nose, rolling it along the floor. He finally decides it will work for his purposes and gently nips it with his teeth before leaping back onto the bed with it.

I sigh. "I'm glad I just ordered an air mattress."

Dad chuckles. "That bed definitely seemed bigger when you were five. Do you remember when I used to sit on the edge of it and read to you every night?"

"Of course I do. No one could voice the Heffalump as good as you."

A light shines in my dad's eyes, and he turns to me with his Heffalump face.

"Oh, no," I murmur, squinting, for what I know is about to happen.

"And then," my dad says solemnly, creeping toward me bit by bit. "Suddenly . . ."

He holds his hands up like a monster with claws.

"Pooh's house shook like thunder!" he booms, like the line from my favorite Winnie the Pooh book when I was small. He tackles me and begins to tickle. I shriek, and the dog starts howling.

Dad digs his fingertips into my ribs, tickling and tickling. I shriek and shriek, and Elliott continues to wail. I desperately try to suck in air as I fight off my father.

It's then that Elliott decides to protect me.

He leaps against my father's back, his front paws on his back and his head hanging over my father's shoulder, examining me with his giant face and round concerned eyes.

"I'm fine, Elliott," I gasp. "Dad, stop. Seriously. I'm gonna pee my pants."

My dad rocks back on his heels, satisfied with himself.

"It's nice to see that some things never change," he says. "Also, it looks like you have a guardian."

He pats Elliott on the top of his head, and Elliott slides to the floor to sniff at me. I hold my hand out.

"I'm okay, boy," I tell him gently. He sniffs to make sure, then once he's satisfied, he sits next to me.

If I'm honest, it feels nice that something so strong is watching out for me.

I rub his muzzle, and he nuzzles into my hand. I ignore the slobber he leaves on my fingers. My dad looks so content, it makes my heart feel warm.

"Hey, Dad, if you win the election, what will you do?"

"What do you mean? I'll allow your mom to have her Christmas village."

"But what will *you* do? With the mayorship?"

He pauses, his forehead wrinkled. "I'll bring in revenue, honey. That's what this town needs."

"Are you going to sit with Nancy in city hall and pore over budgets and discuss zoning issues and sound ordinances?"

He blinks.

"As little as possible," he decides.

"I worry that you won't like it," I tell him. "It's not you. You want to be with Mom all day working in the Christmas village. You don't want to be stuck in city hall."

"Where's this coming from?" he asks curiously.

"I just want you to be happy. I was talking to Jonah—"

"Ohhhh, now I see. They're trying to play you." My dad nods, as though he understands everything. "They're using my own daughter against me. I knew politics could get nasty, but I didn't know it would happen so soon."

I fight the urge to roll my eyes.

"Dad, that is not what this is." He appears unconvinced. "I just want to make sure that outside of this Christmas village issue, you want to be mayor."

"There isn't anything outside of that issue," he answers. "That's the dream."

"That's *Mom's* dream. What's yours?"

He looks at me seriously and sits on the corner of the bed, staying far from Elliott's messy bone.

"Punkin, my dream is to make your mom happy. That's all I've ever wanted."

His sincerity causes my heart to swell because I know he's telling the truth.

"Dad, all these years, you worked for us. You worked for my college, you worked for this house . . . Don't you want *something* for yourself?"

He chuckles. "Sweetheart, I've *got* something. I've got you and your mother, and that's all a guy could want." He gets up and squeezes my shoulder. "We're happy you're here."

"Me too, Dad," I answer. "Dad?"

"Yes, sweetie?"

"What happened to Judd Blake's wife? I know I'm supposed to know this, but I don't."

"It was a long time ago," Dad says gruffly. "Sara Blake was hit by a car."

"Right before Christmas."

"Yes, right before Christmas. It was very tragic. Jonah was so little, and Judd didn't know what to do without Sara."

"What was she like?" I sit back on my heels, and my father stares pensively out my bedroom window.

"She was a free spirit," he finally says. "She was young and liked to laugh. She and Judd were really happy." He looks at me now. "Are you trying to make me feel bad for Judd? This was a long time ago, Noel."

"Not at all," I tell him. "I was just wondering about her."

"Well, she was a lovely person," my dad admits. "I think that Judd would be someone else entirely today if she hadn't died."

"Jonah, too, probably," I reply.

Dad nods. "Most certainly. Judd did the best he could, but he didn't know how to raise a little kid. He was too hard on Jonah by half. He refused to let the poor kid talk about Sara. I have no idea how such a tiny kid heals from something like that without talking about it."

"They don't," I say softly.

"But like I said, Judd did the best he could."

"Careful, Dad. It almost sounds like you like him."

"I do," he declares. "You know that. This is just a little conflict of interest right now."

"I hope things go back to normal for you guys after this election," I tell him. "It's not worth it to let something like this tear a friendship apart."

"We're adults, Noel. We know how to behave."

"Good. Because in fourth grade, when I was running for class president against Julia Witt, you told me we couldn't buy sparkly erasers for everyone because Julia's parents couldn't afford to do the same, and that it would make the election too unfair."

"And your point is?"

"We already handed out homemade Christmas cookies with your name on them. You need to think about what you're willing to do for this election, and what the consequences might be."

My dad stares at me, and I can't tell if he's annoyed or offended, or both.

But then he smiles.

"You can remember that, but you don't remember Jonah?"

"It was a great lesson, Dad," I insist. "You taught me that, and I haven't forgotten. And you have to abide by the same life rules that fourth-grade me had to live by."

"I'm offended that you'd think otherwise." His tone is light, but his expression is not.

"I don't, Daddy," I tell him sweetly. "You're the best person I know. On an unrelated note, how would you like to take the Clydesdale for his walk?"

"Sure, I'll—yes. If you don't have time, I can do it." He pauses. "I came in here to see if you want to go to Wyatt Jones's hog roast tonight? There'll be a bonfire, and it will be good for us to mingle with everyone."

I sigh. "Okay. I'll go with you."

"Perfect." He smiles, then looks at Elliott. "Walk?"

Elliott leaps from the bed and to the bedroom door in a single bound, like an oversized flying squirrel. My dad jumps out of the way, and I hear things getting knocked over down the hall as Elliott lumbers toward the front door.

"We need a dog trainer," my dad calls. *"Yesterday."*

I get up and hunt for the paper that I'd written the name on earlier. I find it in the kitchen, dusty with flour.

Avery Linton. I google her, then dial her number.

CHAPTER THIRTEEN

Jonah

I have no desire to go to a hog roast," I tell my father. He looks at me like I have two heads.

"Of course you do. Why wouldn't you? Great food, free beer, friendly folks."

"If I remember correctly, a hog roast entails the roasting of a whole pig."

"And?" My father lifts an eyebrow. "It's delicious."

"What do you do while it roasts? Form a circle around it and watch?"

"Now you're being ridiculous." He sighs. "A good pig will take at least ten hours. It's been roasting all day already."

I empty my water glass into the sink, rinse it out, and set it in the dish drainer on the counter. My phone buzzes. I pull it out to find a text from Noel.

Prepare yourself—there's a hog roast tonight.

Too late, I answer. It's been mentioned.

Dad sits at the table reading the newspaper, although he can't seem to wipe the indignant look off his face.

"You're acting like I insulted your best friend," I tell him.

He sniffs. "You're insulting good food," he answers. "That's almost worse. I think you've gotten too big for your britches out there in the city."

Now I can't help but roll my eyes. "I'm not too big for my britches," I reply. "At all."

"Prove it," he challenges me. "Come eat a nice big plate at Wyatt's. I need you there, son. I don't want you acting like a snob, either."

"I'm not a snob," I tell him.

"Prove it," he challenges me again.

"Whatever."

I leave him to his paper and head to the barn to feed the horses.

The air is cold, and my nose instantly freezes, while my boots crunch in the snow.

I call the horses in and watch them canter easily through the pasture to me. One dapple, one gray, one buckskin.

I rub their heads, inhaling their horsey smell, then check their water. One of their troughs is frozen over, so I fiddle with the tank heater, fixing the cord that had come loose. I break the ice, careful not to splash it on me, then top it off with fresh water.

My phone buzzes, and my gut tells me it's Noel again. It is.

> Oops, sorry I didn't give you a heads-up quicker. Have you been drawn and quartered into going, too?

> Almost. Have you given in yet?

> Oh, yes. Why is it that we're grown adults, and our parents can still talk us into anything?

> Well, in my father's case, he can talk me into going tonight because of one simple reason.

> And that is?

> You'll be there. ;)

I feel almost giddy as I slide my phone back into my pocket, trying to imagine the look on Noel's face right now. Is she smiling?

"I'll make a farmhand of you yet," my dad says from the door of the barn. He leans on it easily and, wearing his cowboy hat, looks like something out of an old Marlboro commercial.

"I was your farmhand my entire life," I remind him. "Well, it was more of an unpaid internship."

"I paid for college. I think we're square."

"If I write you a check today for my tuition, can you stop bringing that up?" I ask, only half kidding.

"Heck no. I don't accept checks. Cash or money orders only. But your money's no good here, anyway. I did what I did."

"Then stop rubbing my nose in it, please," I request politely.

"Heck no. That's all the fun. I've got to remind you that I contributed."

"I know you did," I tell him. "I'm not going to forget."

"Nope, because I won't let you," he answers cheerfully.

I sigh. It's never going to end. I resign myself to the fact.

"What time is your shindig tonight?" I ask instead.

"Six."

"I have some work to do this afternoon," I tell him as we walk back to the warmth of the house. "But I'll go with you after."

I close myself in the office and keep an eye on my dad through the window as I scan through the emails on my laptop.

He fiddles around outdoors, checking tire pressures and snowblowing the drive.

I text Millie about a few work-related things, which she answers. Then she asks:

How's your dad?

I take a photo of him snowblowing and send it to her.

She answers immediately.

Jonah! Go outside and help him!

Can't, I answer. It's a matter of pride for him. I already fed the horses. He needs things to do around this place, or he gets restless.

I'm watching him though, I add. If he starts getting tired, I'll go out there. He's stubborn.

Must be a family trait, my secretary answers.

I sniff and choose not to answer.

Instead, I scroll through the two hundred unread emails in my inbox. The rate at which they accumulate astounds me.

I've sorted through at least twenty when one takes an unusual turn. It's from Bertie Hofflinger, a direct (and fierce) competitor, and also friend, who I've known for fifteen years.

Jonah,

I'm not going to beat around the bush. After the way you handled the Massaqua portfolio, we want you to run the London office of BIK Enterprises. We need someone with a deft hand, smooth tongue, and killer instincts to really break into the European market.

Think about it over the holidays, and get back to me with your list of demands.

Merry Christmas—
Hoff

I stare at the words without moving.

He's hinted before. Last year when I led his friend into the seven-figure club, Hoff raised a glass but didn't make a formal offer. So it's not like this is a total surprise.

But it's still a total surprise.

I sit back in my seat, watching my dad.

Would I want to move to England?

To drive on the left-hand side of the road . . . eat chips, not fries . . . have blood pudding and Scotch eggs and even stranger things like head cheese?

And . . . be an ocean away from a father who complains about me being too far away already.

"Dang it, Hoff," I mutter. Leave it to him to get my attention with *your list of demands*.

I type a brief response.

I'll think on it. My list will be long, however.

Not five minutes later, a text with a photo comes through on my phone.

It's a photo of the London cityscape at night, from a hotel balcony.

This would be your view.

I answer quickly.

Not pictured: rain and abject dreariness.

He answers just as quickly.

Also not pictured: a 7-figure salary, fully furnished penthouse, and a car service.

Slow down, champ. Don't you want me to work for it?

The answer is immediate.

> No. I trust you and trust is priceless.

> I'll think on it.

I put my phone back in my pocket and read a couple business plans before I put everything away to shower.

It's when the hot water is streaming over my body that it occurs to me.

I could always talk Pop into coming with me.

He could have a new start in a place where there aren't bad memories, or headaches like the Turners.

As I rinse my face, I remember the photo of the cityscape.

London is not my father's idea of home. But perhaps there are suburbs he could live in, somewhere near, but rural.

It's worth a thought.

After I'm out of the shower and have pulled jeans and a black turtleneck sweater on, I text Millie.

> Can you do some research on quiet rural towns within driving distance of London?

The likelihood of my father agreeing is slim, but you just never know.

I throw a bit of product in my hair, spritz cologne on my neck, and then find my father in the kitchen, a thick pair of wool socks in my hand.

"My, you look fancy," my father drawls as I pull on my socks. I glance at him.

"I'm sorry, I was fresh out of plaid flannel."

Dad cocks an eyebrow, while wearing his red plaid shirt, and doesn't answer.

I pull on my Hermès boots, and then we head for the car. We're a few minutes down the road when my dad speaks up.

"I have to admit, I do like the seat warmers."

I glance at him and smile. "You know, you can get seat warmers in a new truck, too."

"I'm not buying a new truck. I don't need one."

"There's no shame in comfort, Dad, that's all I'm saying."

We bump down the gravel road a few more miles until we reach Wyatt's place, a sprawling farm with a huge, heated barn.

A giant bonfire is already roaring, and townspeople mill about, chatting with drinks in hand and plates piled high.

I see Heather Reid with Connie Crespin, and Wyatt stands at the hog pit, serving the meat. To his left, there's a buffet of side dishes, brought by the guests. Merrill Landry and Nolan man the beer kegs. I don't see Noel. There are dozens of people that I don't remember, and my father is clearly intent on talking with them all. He's waving and calling out names before we are even out of the truck.

"This is going to be a long night," I mutter.

My dad winks, closes the truck door, and walks away.

Winter dusk comes quickly and soon darkness envelops us, while the orange flames from the bonfire light the sky for miles. I wait my turn for a plate of meat, and when I'm at the front of the line, Wyatt breaks out in a grin.

"Jonesy! I can't believe you're finally home!"

He sets down the plate in his hand and clasps me in a bear hug, lifting me off the ground.

"Lightweight," he sniffs.

I roll my eyes. "I'm the same as when we were seniors," I tell him. I eye his slight beer gut, and he scowls.

"Don't even say it."

I laugh, and he hands me a plate of shredded pork. "You saw the sides, and the beer, I'm assuming?"

"Heck yeah," my father pipes up from behind me. "This is a feast fit for a king!"

"Or a mayor," Wyatt says with a smile.

"Does that mean I can count on your support?" my dad asks, never willing to miss an opportunity.

Wyatt glances away. "Rich Turner is here tonight, too, Judd. I don't want to make anyone uncomfortable. You're both good men."

"Of course we are," Rich's voice booms. "And your vote is your own, Wyatt. Don't you feel pressured to do anything."

I turn to find him, his wife, and his daughter in line behind us.

"I would never pressure anyone," my dad sputters.

"Of course you wouldn't," Noel says quickly. "You didn't really think that, did you, Dad?"

She looks radiant in the glow of the bonfire, with her white coat and creamy skin. Her hair is a richer red than even the flames, and for a second, I'm mesmerized.

Rich looks at her now, clearly not wanting to answer.

"Dad?" she prompts.

"Of course I didn't," Rich finally says. "Not at all."

"If you believe that, I've got a three-headed goat to sell ya," my dad says. His words are joking, his tone is not.

"And now you're saying I'm *lying*?" Rich booms.

"Dad." Noel grabs his arm, and her gaze meets mine. *Help*, her eyes say.

"Dad," I interject. "It's fine. This is just a misunderstanding. Right, Rich?"

I've taken a step to stand in between the two men, and I meet Rich's gaze.

"Yes," he answers. "It's a misunderstanding."

His words are stiff, and so is his hand as he offers it to my father. Dad hesitates for a scant second before shaking it.

Susan breaks the awkward silence a few moments later. "There's Becky Johnson," she tells Rich. "Come on, we need to talk to her."

"If you're talking about the petition, I need to be there, as well," my father says, following them.

"Be nice!" Noel calls after them. When she turns back to me, her cheeks are flushed.

"Are we having fun yet?" she asks with a wry grimace.

Wyatt grins and hands her a full plate. "What's a little bickering to keep us on our toes?" he asks. "We're all friends here. It's good to see you, Noel."

"You too, Wy. How's Lizzie doing with the twins? When I was home last, they'd learned to walk! What are they up to now?"

"Mainly keeping Daddy awake." Wyatt laughs. "They don't sleep a lick past six A.M. on their *best* days."

I shudder, and Noel notices.

"Thank you for having us all tonight, Wy. If you see Lizzie, send her my way."

We take our plates and step out of the line, and Noel turns to me.

"You looked a bit terrified there for a second." She laughs. "Does the idea of kids scare you?"

"I'm never having kids," I tell her quickly.

"Never?" She raises an eyebrow.

I nod, quite sure of myself. "Never."

"Wow," she says softly. "That's a pretty definite answer."

I can't tell how she feels about it, and I don't even know why that matters. I find myself studying her face, but instead of finding answers, I get distracted by how lovely she is. Her red hair flows in loose curls down her back, and her eyes are as blue as the cerulean sea.

"You look beautiful this evening," I tell her.

Red stain immediately spreads across her cheekbones.

"Um, thank you," she answers. "I wasn't sure what to wear to a hog roast. I know, I know. I grew up here. I should know. But times change, and I haven't been to one since I was in high school—it was for Molly Atkins's wedding."

I wrinkle my forehead. "I was at that one, too. I remember because my father and I got into an argument about it. I didn't want to go. I wanted to go to—"

"Abigail Wood's party," she finishes for me. "Right?"

I nod. "Yeah. I don't remember you being there."

"Same."

It's undeniably weird.

"Hey, I see spiked apple cider," Noel says suddenly. "I think we've earned some. How about you?"

"Definitely."

We skirt around the bonfire and weave through the throngs of people. We reach the long table filled with stacks of cups, napkins, and a massive stainless steel dispenser filled with the mulled cider.

I fill two cups and sniff at mine before handing Noel hers.

"Don't light a match near that," I warn.

She grins and takes a big gulp without fear or hesitation.

I admire that. So I do the same.

I cough and sputter, while Noel looks at me innocently. "Too much for you?"

"Never," I tell her. I take another drink as if to prove the point.

I cough again. "What's in this? Turpentine?" I gasp.

She laughs.

"Don't show weakness," she advises. "You're wearing two-thousand-dollar shoes and a ten-thousand-dollar watch. You already stand out. Don't give them more reason to think you're different."

"I *am* different," I tell her bluntly. "And so are you."

She shrugs. "Are we, though? Deep down, where it matters?"

"Maybe not," I decide.

She nods. "Exactly."

I don't know precisely what we just agreed upon, but it seems to make her happy, so I don't ask.

"Your dad is in his element," she says, nodding toward him.

I turn to look, and he truly is. He mingles, he laughs, he winks. He talks to children, he drinks beer with the men, he chats with the women.

This is his home.

My stomach sinks a bit.

I'll never convince him to move away.

As if to prove the point, my father bursts out laughing and slaps someone on the back.

There's no way he'll leave here.

Not now, not ever.

CHAPTER FOURTEEN

Noel

Jonah looks past me, his eyes fixed on something and his expression pained. I glance over my shoulder and find that he's watching his dad.

His dad looks completely happy: laughing and friendly. I don't see anything that would warrant the pained look on Jonah's face.

"You okay?" I ask, my hand on his elbow.

He breaks his gaze and looks at me.

"I'm fine," he answers with a slight sigh. "Something just became apparent to me."

I wait for him to elaborate, but he doesn't.

"Care to share?" I prompt.

"My dad will never leave this town," he answers simply without offering context. Without context, I lack an appropriate response.

I take another drink of the spiked cider while I mull over a reply, forcing myself not to flinch at its bite. Someone must've dumped three bottles of vodka into this batch.

"I think my breath is flammable now," I tell Jonah. He laughs, throwing his head back, because out of anything I could've said in reply, I chose *that.* Something about it makes my belly tighten.

He was upset about something, but I made him laugh instead. It's a heady feeling.

"You're very funny. Do you realize that?" he asks me with a small smile still on his full lips.

"I'm pretty *awkward,*" I correct him. "My assistant could tell you stories of me getting myself into trouble."

"They certainly know our secrets and skeletons," he answers. "Mine does, anyway. She could write a book on my missteps and exploits."

She.

It's crazy, but I feel a twinge of jealousy. If he and his assistant are like Emily and me, they spend a *lot* of time together. I have no claim on this man whatsoever, and I have no right to feel jealous, yet I do.

I don't like how that makes me feel.

"Good assistants are hard to find," I say. "I'd be lost without Emily. And she knows it."

We chuckle, and he nods.

"Millie is old-school, and she treats me like the prodigal son she never had. She even arranges my dinners at night."

My jealousy twinges again.

"I'd better go find my folks," I tell him. "Thank you for keeping me company."

"Anytime," he answers. His dark hazel eyes seem to smolder, and I really need to get out of here. Smoldering eyes are my Achilles' heel. He also has a cleft in his chin, something I didn't notice until just now.

It's at this exact moment that I hear my parents' raised voices.

My head snaps around to find my father arguing with Judd again. Jonah and I rush to get to our fathers. When we reach them, the vein is popped on my father's temple—a telltale sign that everything is getting ready to go south.

"Rich, stop," my mother implores him. A small crowd has gathered. My father shakes his head.

"Suze, he doesn't get the right to ruin this opportunity for everyone. I'm sorry, but he doesn't."

"I'm not trying to ruin anything," Judd demands, his face a deep red. "The risk is too great. It's not going to work. I have an idea that will, though. No risk."

"Everything has risk, you dummy," Rich thunders.

"Rich," my mom warns. My father glances at her.

"Everything has risk," he repeats, a bit calmer. "Including whatever plan you're cooking up. There is always risk."

"My plan has *less* risk," Judd says. "You can ask my son. He's a finance genius."

All eyes turn to Jonah, who stands at Judd's elbow.

"Yes, Jonah. What plan are you two cooking up?" I find coming out of my mouth. It annoys me that he hasn't mentioned a *plan* before now.

Jonah glances at me, his brow wrinkled.

"I can't compare the two ideas, since I haven't seen the Turners' business plan. But I can tell you that in order for my father's idea to come to fruition, my business teams will be doing due diligence on the viability. If we think it's lucrative, we'll finance it. When we finance something, the risk involved is always worth it for us."

The crowd murmurs. I can't ignore the fact that he just made a sound case.

It's annoying.

"That's good to know," I tell him. "But as you said, you can't compare the ideas, since you haven't seen my father's business plan."

"Does your father have a business plan?" Jonah asks, his eyebrow raised a bit.

"Of course he does," I answer. "My father is a serious contender for mayor. He obviously has a business case for the plans he's basing his campaign on."

"If you trust me enough to do it, I'd be happy to do a side-by-side comparison of the two business cases and report back to you, and to the rest of the town, regarding the viability of both."

Everyone around nods and murmurs.

"That's generous of you, son," Judd tells him. He looks at the rest of us. "My son's time is very expensive," he tells us. "Because he's the best at what he does. We should take advantage of his offer. We'd never be able to afford him otherwise."

My father starts to protest, but I interrupt. "We'll consider it on one condition: you keep me informed every step of the way, and we reserve the right to get an alternate assessment."

I ignore my dad's protests and lock eyes with Jonah.

Jonah's mouth twitches.

"That's two conditions."

There are chuckles around us.

"Do you accept?" I ask.

He nods. "We accept."

"Does anyone want to ask Judd or me for our agreement?" Dad asks.

Jonah and I reply at the same time: "No."

Everyone laughs, except Dad and Judd, and the contentious energy dissipates.

Crisis averted.

Jonah guides his father away, and the people around us restart their conversations.

As my parents and I walk away, I turn to my dad.

"Send me your business plan, and I'll talk with Jonah about it."

He looks away and doesn't answer.

"It's the easiest path forward," I tell him. "I'm sure your plan is sound, so there's no harm done to let him do a risk assessment. I don't know him well, but he seems professional. If the results seem skewed, we'll hire someone individually. Just email me the plan, and I'll handle it."

Dad still doesn't answer. It's my mom who eventually pipes up.

"There isn't one, Noel."

I look at her. "There isn't . . . a plan?"

She shakes her head.

"Do you have a value proposition?"

She shakes her head again.

"Do you have a project plan, at least?"

"We don't have any of that," my dad snaps. "But it's an excellent idea, and I know it's viable."

I sigh, not quite believing my father's childish attitude.

"Dad, it's impossible to know if something is financially viable unless a business case is done—outlining all the risks, all the costs, all the potential. It's a lot of research. That's the only way a good decision can be made."

"Are you Warren Buffett now?" Dad asks, annoyed. "The last I knew, you edited books for a living."

"Every book I acquire is a business choice, Dad. I have to do a risk assessment on all of them. You don't get to my position by making bad business decisions. And, if you remember correctly, in college you had me minor in business. As a backup plan."

My dad looks away mulishly.

"Trust me, you don't want to win the mayorship and then execute a bad business plan. It'll wreck your reputation and ruin any chance of reelection."

"*This* is why we brought you home," Mom announces proudly, and she's beaming. "She's right, Rich."

"He knows I'm right," I tell her. "Even if he won't admit it."

"I'm ready to go home," my mom says. "How about you two?"

"Now you're speaking my love language," I agree. "Let's go home, and I'll take a long hot bath and have a nice cup of cocoa."

I glance around to find Jonah—but he's standing with his back to me.

Nice seeing you tonight, I text as we walk toward the car. I appreciate your unbiased help with everything.

I don't know if he'll interpret that as snarky or as hopeful. I'm not even sure how I meant it myself.

It's when we're in the car and on the way home that my father meets my gaze in the rearview mirror.

"I'll gather everything I have, and you can look at it tomorrow. You can see what else we need to put together a plan. Does that work?"

I nod. "Perfect. Thanks, Dad."

"Thank *you*. You were right. Just don't rub it in."

"I would never."

I do, of course. Every chance I get for the rest of the night.

"I mean, it's not like this happens often," I tell Dad as I make hot cocoa a few hours later. "I can't remember the last time you admitted I was right. In fact, I don't think you *ever have*. So this is momentous. Unprecedented."

Elliott leans longingly against my legs, hoping against hope that something delicious will fall into his waiting mouth.

"You can't have this, boy," I say. "Chocolate is poison for you."

"He doesn't believe you," Dad points out. "Look at that face."

Elliott actually does have an indignant look about him.

"Don't you start," I tell him. "I wouldn't lie to you."

He literally sits in the corner and turns his back to me.

Two seconds later, he peeks over his shoulder to make sure I notice that he's upset.

"He's pouting." My dad laughs. "I've never in my life seen something like this."

Elliott pouts for a good twenty minutes, checking over his shoulder with soulful eyes every few minutes to make sure we're still paying attention.

"You're ridiculous," I tell him. "I'll take you outside to make up for it."

At the word *outside*, Elliott perks up and gallops toward the back door. When he gets there, he surprises both my dad and me by using his nose to push up the handle, and with ease, he opens the door and strolls outside like he owns the place.

My mouth falls open. "Did he . . . just figure out how to open the door by himself?"

"Well, we'll need to keep that locked," my dad says with a sigh, handing me a steaming cup.

I hurry after the dog, careful to not spill my hot cocoa.

CHAPTER FIFTEEN

Jonah

That was a heckuva party," my dad says happily, a couple hours later. "Rich and Suze have no idea what they're up against." He reaches for the coffee. "They have no idea what they're in for. Thank you for volunteering your time, kiddo. It means the world to me."

"Of course," I tell him, a bit taken aback. I can't remember the last time my father thanked me for something.

"Shoot," he says, shaking the coffee can. "We're out."

"I'll go back into town for more." I stand up. "I can't face the day tomorrow without coffee."

"Me either," he admits.

I grab my coat, and before I talk myself out of going back into the snow, I march out into the cold.

"Millie would not have let me run out of coffee," I mutter, realizing once again how much easier she makes my life.

The SUV is still warm, and as I nose it out of the drive, I

make a mental note to get Millie something extra for Christmas, something she doesn't have to buy herself.

At the first red light, I text Noel. What should I get Millie for Christmas?

The light turns green, and I drive into town. The snow gleams in the moonlight, like stars have been scattered across the surface. It's quiet, and I'm sure that most are still out at Wyatt's.

Houses are lit up for the holidays, with green, red, blue, and white lights. I see Christmas trees through windows, but the streetlight poles are bare. The city hasn't decorated at all, something that doesn't bother me, but even I have to admit the town doesn't look festive at all.

There are no other cars at Park 'n' Shop, which should've been my first clue that it's closed. But no, I get out into the cold and get my feet wet in a puddle of slush on my way to the door, which of course is locked.

Because it's nine thirty P.M. and I'm in a one-horse town. I check my phone for an answer from Noel, then head to the convenience store out on the highway instead.

Before I head inside, I check my phone again. Still nothing.

I put my phone away and go inside, determined to stop fixating. I pore over the shelves, hunting for any brand of coffee, but there isn't a one.

"Can I buy some coffee?" I ask the clerk. She looks at me.

"Of course—there are several to choose from." She gestures toward the coffee bar.

"No. My dad ran out of grounds, and if I don't find some to brew in the morning, he and I will kill each other," I confide.

She laughs and tucks her hair behind her ear. "It can't be all that bad." She chuckles. "We have energy drinks, if that helps."

"My father would rather chew off his own arm than skip his morning coffee." I glance at the coffeemakers. "Can I buy a pack of whatever you used to brew that? I'll pay any amount. Whatever you think is fair."

The woman digs out a single-use bag from beneath the coffee bar. "Colombian okay?"

"I'll take anything you have."

She won't let me pay for it, even though I try to insist. She shakes her head. "It's not a problem," she assures me. "It's annoying that the Park 'n' Shop closes so early."

"I live in New York City now," I tell her. "There's never a time of day when I can't find something I want. I forget sometimes that the rest of the country isn't awake around the clock."

"I would give anything to live in NYC for a while," she answers, a dreamy look in her eye.

"Winter Falls is quaint," I reply. "It has potential."

"I hope so. Merry Christmas, Jonah," she answers. Her tone is a bit familiar now.

I hesitate, and she smiles again. "Nicole Ruffalo. We took trig together our senior year."

"Oh! Of course!" I say, although I still have no clue who she is. "Of course. It's so good seeing you!"

"We also shared a bus seat back from the Fairfield game our senior year. You strained your wrist, and I helped you hold the ice pack on it."

Ohhhhh. Now *that* I do remember.

"I remember," I tell her. "Thank you again for your help that day."

"You gave your all in that game. It was the least I could do." She smiles sweetly.

"Well, I can gauge the weather with this thing now, so it all worked out." I hold up the wrist in question and chuckle.

"Heck, who needs a meteorologist? You just need an old football injury."

We laugh, and I try to think of something to say that will get me home to a quiet house where I can recharge my social battery in front of the fireplace.

I'm saved by the bell, though. The landline behind the counter rings, and she has to walk away to answer it. I wave and duck out while I can.

It's when I'm backing out that my phone rings, and I see from a glance that it's Noel.

I pull back into the parking spot to answer.

"Hey," I say, surprised that she's calling me instead of answering my text.

"I need your help," she says, and she sounds out of breath. "I don't suppose you have a few minutes?"

"Of course, what's wrong?"

"It's hard to explain. Can you come to the playground at the elementary school? There's a wooden Timber Town out back."

"The playground?"

"Long story."

"I'll be right there."

It takes less than five minutes to drive to the elementary

school and park out front. It's dark, of course, and the street-lights don't light up the school grounds. I circle the building in the dark, wondering what the heck I'm walking into.

It's shadowy, it's quiet.

"Noel?" I call out.

She steps out of the shadows near the Timber Town, by a bridge and a tire swing. She waves, then ducks back behind the play center.

I eye the scene suspiciously as I approach. "Are you trying to frame me for a drug deal so that I can't help my father win the election?"

I can't see her yet, but she laughs.

"No, we need your help. Over here!"

I follow the sound of her voice and find her up a few ladders, in a secluded portion of the play area. She's with Elliott.

He thumps his tail when he sees me.

"What's wrong?" I ask. "You and Fluffy out here for a night-time playdate?"

Now that I'm with her, I can see that her white coat is splashed with what looks like coffee and mud, and her hair is plastered to her forehead with sweat.

"What the heck happened?" I add.

"Elliott, of course." She sighs. "He was excited about going outside, and he took off and I chased him through town."

"And you need my help . . . how?"

"I can't get him down, and my parents aren't answering their phones. I almost called the fire department but remembered that it's a volunteer department. I don't want to interrupt their fun at Wyatt's."

The fact that she'd called *me* for help makes me feel a certain way that I can't define.

The dog outweighs Noel by a hundred pounds, so watching her try to move him now is pretty amusing, and I can't help but chuckle as she pushes at his haunches. Which, of course, makes him dig in even deeper, refusing to budge.

"I'm not exactly sure what to do here," I say, watching Noel practically on her hands and knees.

She glances down at me, her hair disheveled and in her face. "Well, whatever it is, you can't do it from down there."

She's frustrated, tired, and even though I won't tell her this, utterly adorable.

"Hold on." I climb up the ladders to reach her. "How did he even get up here?"

"He's a devil dog, that's how."

The devil dog is absolutely thrilled to see me and noses my pockets.

"I don't have anything for you, boy," I tell him.

He eyes me doubtfully, his eyes large, brown, and woeful.

"You have trust issues," I tell him. I glance at my watch, and Noel catches me.

"I'm so sorry for bothering you tonight. I just got frustrated. I've been here forever, it seems like."

"You're not a bother. I was checking the time to see if the gas station is going to close soon. We could get some food to lure him with. It worked last time."

"The gas station closes at eleven," she tells me.

"I'm not going to leave you here in the dark. Can you take my car and get some beef jerky or something? Maybe a Slim

Jim or two?" I ask her, pulling out the key fob and offering it to her. "I'll wait here with the Moose."

"Are you my guardian angel?" She wastes no time in grabbing the key and shinnying down the ladder . . . making her escape.

"You have to come back, though!" I call after her rapidly retreating back. She waves over her shoulder in response. I look at the dog, who has his slobbery face pressed against my leg.

"If I didn't know better," I tell him, "I'd think you purposely cause trouble."

He blinks innocently and holds up his paw for me to shake.

I flatten my palm out against it, measuring.

"Are you sure you're not part bear?" I ask him. "Your paw is almost as big as my hand."

He swipes at me with it, trying to get me to shake it again. He's so big, so strong, that it actually hurts if I'm not paying attention.

"You really do need training," I say. "You know, some dogs, when they're given a command, they obey it. Let's practice.

"Down," I order.

He looks at me.

"Down," I repeat.

He blinks.

"Sit," I try again.

He sits, then immediately stands.

"That was a good try," I tell him. "Sit," I say again.

Instead, his head snaps up, he looks into the darkness, and he takes off, chasing something I can't see.

"I did not say *run!*" I yell as I follow him.

He bounds from the top level onto the wooden bridge hanging from chains. It clatters and ripples as he lumbers across it, and then he leaps to the ground.

He looks over his shoulder at me, and I could swear he laughs.

"Come back here," I yell. "Right now."

He doesn't even miss a step. He races toward a tree line on the edge of the property. I think I see a tiny flash of movement, and I hope against hope that he's not chasing a skunk or a raccoon.

I pursue him, slipping in patches of snow and ice and mud.

Elliott's brindle coat disappears into the night, and when I reach the copse of trees, I slow to a jog. There's no sign of the dog, but I can hear twigs snapping and then a spitting sound.

I reach Elliott in time to see him nosing a kitten over and over on the ground, rolling it to and fro with his big nose.

"Elliott, no," I tell him sternly. The small wad of hair looks to be only a couple months old and is quite small. It's got long hair, which is wet now and standing up in angry spikes as the cat hisses at Elliott in tiny, terrified bursts.

"It's okay," I assure it as I draw closer. "Elliott won't hurt you." I'm telling Elliott as much as I'm telling the cat.

The dog breathes in the cat in huffs and snorts as he examines it.

"Have you never seen a cat before?" I ask him. "He's your friend."

The kitten hisses.

I reach to pick him up, but Elliott picks him up instead, more gently than I would've imagined, and trots away, toward the school.

"Elliott, stop," I call, rushing to try to grab his collar. I slide on a patch of ice instead and fall into a pool of slush.

It's freezing, it's muddy, and I'm covered in it as I climb to my feet just in time to see that Noel had witnessed the entire thing. She claps a hand over her mouth, whether in horror or to hide her laughter, I don't know.

Her eyes widen as she takes in Elliott with the kitten's scruff in his mouth.

She lunges for his collar and rescues the kitten before I can reach them.

"Remind me not to hire you as a babysitter," she says. She eyes my clothing. "Are you okay? I'm so sorry about your clothes."

"That's something you seem to tell me often," I remark. "Also, you have a new kitten."

She shakes her head, with the furry kitten cradled to her chest.

"Oh, no I don't. I left you here with a dog. Any addition of an animal is on you."

The kitten looks like an indignant baby owl as he watches us with round eyes. His long gray fur is even wetter now from slobber, but instead of being scared, he seems outraged as he stares down his wet nose at Elliott.

Elliott, for his part, seems quite concerned about the cat and doesn't attempt to eat him, as I'd feared.

"He's taken a liking to the kitten," I say needlessly. "On the bright side, he's no longer stuck on the playground. I solved your problem!"

"Gee, thanks," she says, and she seems a bit shell-shocked.

"Let me give you a lift home," I offer. "I've got to get these wet clothes off."

"I'll trust that you can do that alone," she says with a grin. "And I'd love a ride, thank you."

It's a whole other debacle getting Elliott into the SUV, one that involves Elliott's back paw in my mouth. The Slim Jim that Noel brought back ultimately helped.

He lies across the entire back seat now with his giant head pressed up between our seats.

Noel holds the wet kitten under her stained coat, and I sit in my wet jeans.

Noel and I both reach to turn the heater up at the same time, our fingers touching.

She blushes. "I'm sorry. It's your car. You were just shivering."

"It's a rental," I tell her. "Thank goodness. It will probably never be the same now."

As if to agree, Elliott licks his chops, and a drop of saliva flies onto the ceiling.

Noel sighs and cuddles the kitten.

"I'm surprised he didn't eat this little guy," she says as I turn out onto the road.

"Me too," I tell her. "He took off like a bolt of lightning. I was afraid he was chasing a skunk."

She shudders at the thought.

The kitten mews, and Elliott snaps to attention, worriedly snuffling at Noel's arm to check on the cat.

"I take Elliott tomorrow for an obedience lesson with Avery Linton. I'll see if she knows if someone lost a kitten, and if not, if she can help me find a home for it."

"Is it a girl or a boy?" I ask, not taking my eyes off the road.

She holds it up and looks.

"Girl," she confirms.

If I'm not mistaken, she cuddles the kitten a bit closer.

"What will you name her?" I ask with a smile.

"I'm not keeping her," she insists.

"You might not, but Elliott plans to."

With his worried face wedged in between us, it's hard to argue that.

"Elliott doesn't call the shots," Noel decides.

"Okay," I agree.

I turn onto her parents' street, and I can see their house from here.

It's lit up like the Christmas tree in Rockefeller Center. It is covered in white lights, and it manages to look classy even though it's overdone.

They have several animated deer in the yard, and giant lit wreaths on the door.

"Welcome to the North Pole," I say as I pull into the drive. "Apparently."

Noel chuckles.

"My parents do have Christmas spirit in abundance." She turns to me. "Jonah, thank you for coming to my rescue tonight. It was very, very kind of you. I'm so sorry that Elliott ruined your clothes. Again."

"It's fine," I assure her. "If I hadn't been rescuing a damsel in distress, I would've just been sitting in front of the warm, cozy fireplace, perfectly comfortable and dry, sipping a hot toddy with my father."

She looks at me, unfazed.

"Being warm and dry is overrated," she says. "I'd much rather be in the mud with a handsome man than at home putting a puzzle together with my mom any day. But that's just me."

"Miss Turner, are you calling me handsome?" I ask, lifting my brow.

She rolls her eyes. "You're quite aware of your good qualities."

"I'd rather hear them from your perspective, though," I answer. "To see if we agree."

She laughs now, her eyes twinkling. "Can you hold the kitten while I get the Moose?"

I nod and reach out my hands.

The kitten doesn't necessarily want to leave the safety of Noel's sweater. After glaring at me for disturbing her, she burrows deeper into Noel's chest.

"Because I'm a gentleman," I say, "I'm not going to reach in after her. I'll get the dog instead."

Noel chuckles. "Your gallantry is noted."

With a firm hold on Elliott's collar, I walk him to the door. I wait for Noel on the porch, and if I'm not mistaken, the drapes part a bit, and someone peeks out.

I wave, but the curtains quickly close.

"They don't want to talk to me," I say quietly to Noel. "In fact, I think you might be grounded when you go in for consorting with the enemy again."

She snorts. "You joke, but . . ."

I chuckle, and tell her good night.

"It's always an adventure," I add, glancing down and noticing the way her hair falls against her neck.

"That's my goal in life," she answers. She meets my gaze and holds it. "Drive safely going home, Jonah."

"This isn't home," I remind her.

But as I drive back down the snowy street, I'll be darned if that statement doesn't feel less true than it used to.

CHAPTER SIXTEEN

Noel

I wake up in the morning to find the dog curled up with the kitten. More specifically, Elliott is curled *around* the kitten. As in, the kitten is the center of Elliott's cinnamon roll. She purrs happily, safe and warm. I've never seen anything like it.

I take a picture and email it to Padraig.

You'll get a kick out of this, I tell him.

I also ask him a question: Do Jack and Nora have a happy ending?

I pad out to the kitchen in search of coffee. I smell it, so I know someone is awake.

My mom is in her red fuzzy Christmas robe, her feet in reindeer slippers.

"Good morning," she tells me, pouring me a cup without asking. She hands it to me. "How'd you sleep?"

"Well, Elliott shoved me out of bed on accident, so I'm happy the air mattress arrives today."

"You *think* it was an accident," she says knowingly. I laugh and take a sip of coffee.

"So, about last night," I start to say. She raises an eyebrow and waits. I sigh. "I know you were up last night, but you ran to your room when I came in."

"I did not," she denies.

"You did. I saw you. I know you saw Jonah Blake bringing me home."

My mom sighs. "I don't want to know any of it. If your dad finds out, he'll be beside himself, and I don't want to have to lie."

"Nothing happened that would upset Dad." I pause. "But seriously, about last night, there *is* something I need to tell you . . ."

It's at this moment that Elliott comes trotting in, the kitten dangling from his mouth.

My mom screeches and lunges for the kitten, trying to save her little life.

"Mom, it's fine," I tell her, holding her elbow. *"This is what I needed to tell you."*

We watch as Elliott gently sets the kitten down and nuzzles her with his big nose. The tiny kitten arches her back and rubs against his ear.

"I think she thinks he's her mom," I say. "I don't know how else to explain it. They slept together all night, and she has no fear of him now. At all."

As if to prove the point, the kitten quickly scales his leg like she's climbing a rock wall, jumps onto his back, and lies back down. Then Elliott somehow manages to sink to the ground and lie down without disturbing the kitten.

My mom's eyes widen.

"Where did you get it? Was Jonah with you?"

"So you did see me coming in," I say.

She scowls. "I already admitted it."

I smile. "You did. Grudgingly. But yes, Jonah was with me. After I chased the dog all over kingdom come, I couldn't get ahold of you or Dad, and . . . You know what, never mind. The story is long. Let's just say, you guys didn't answer your phone and I needed help with Elliott."

"So you called Jonah?" my mom asks. "That's an interesting choice."

"I don't know why," I tell her. "He's here, he knows me, and he's already got experience with Elliott. Plus, he's way stronger than me, and I thought that might come in handy."

"You're probably not wrong about that," she says.

"Anyway, the dog found the kitten. I'll check with Avery today to see if she knows of anyone who lost her."

The kitten is bathing Elliott now, her tiny tongue working her way up and down his big, floppy ear. When she's done, she curls up under it like a blanket.

"I guess she likes clean bedding," my mother says wryly.

We sit in the breakfast nook and sip our coffee, with me in my bare feet and my mom in her slippers with felt antlers.

The winter sun shines through the window, momentarily breaking through the white sky.

"It's nice having you here, Noel," Mom says. "I wish you could stay longer."

"I'll be here for almost two weeks when all is said and done," I point out. "I don't have to be back until New Year's Eve."

"Well, I'll just have to soak you up until then."

"You can come visit me, too, you know," I tell her. "You haven't in forever."

"You know how your father hates the city," she answers.

"You can come alone. We can have a girls' weekend. We'll get massages and facials and go shopping."

"Tell me more," she says with her hands under her chin.

I laugh, and as I do, my father comes in wearing his robe and with his salt-and-pepper hair mussed.

"Good morning, ladies," he greets us.

"I'm going to New York for a girls' weekend sometime soon," Mom announces. Dad's eyes widen.

"You feel comfortable traveling to the city alone?"

"Mom is a strong, independent woman," I tell him. "She'll be fine."

"Plus, Noel will be there," Mom says to him.

He winks at me.

"Noel can protect you," he decides. "She's scary. We're lucky to have you on our side, punkin. Ol' Judd won't know what hit him."

"Dad," I warn. "We're going to be civil, we're going to flesh out the business plan, and then the voters will decide. We're not fighting dirty."

"We're not?"

"Of course not. That's not who we are."

"You better believe Judd will," Dad tells me.

I shrug. "That's his prerogative. Voters will see through it."

Both of my parents stare at me now.

"How long have you lived in this country?" Dad asks, dumb-founded.

I shake my head. "It'll be fine. The best man for the job will win, and isn't that what we should want?"

My mom shakes her head in turn. "I want my Christmas village."

I sigh. "Do you have a name for it, or will it just be Christmas Village?"

"I mean, it's good marketing," Dad pipes up. "It says right in the name what it is."

I can't argue with that.

"How about Winter Falls Christmas Village?" I suggest. "That way, it's marketing for Winter Falls, too."

"You're a genius," Dad decides.

"I am," I agree. "But now this genius has to get dressed for Elliott's obedience lesson."

I take my coffee and return to my room.

While there, I check my email as the shower water gets hot.

From: <Padraig.Sinclair@sleighmail.com>
To: <n.turner@parkerhamiltonpublishing.com>
Subject: Re: Snuggle Buddies

Dear Noel,

I loved this picture! Thank you so much for sending it. I have to ask . . . how did this interesting friendship come about? Please tell me—I need to include some fun Elliott stories in this book, and with him gone, it's hard to think of them.

As far as Nora and Jack . . . well, now. Surely you don't want me to spoil the ending, do you?

Only 7 days 'til Christmas!

—Dad

Of course he wouldn't answer.

I do, however, write him back and tell him about alllll of Elliott's escapades lately.

I fear I will owe a friend of mine thousands in dry-cleaning bills by the time this is over, I type.

I glance out the window after noticing movement in my periphery, and find my father taking Elliott outside. Unlike normal, when Elliott plows through everything in his path to get outside, he's walking slowly and carefully, because the kitten is standing on top of his back, riding him like an ancient charioteer.

"Oh my word," I breathe. I snap another picture and attach it to the email before I hit send. I stare out the window at them for a few minutes more, marveling that when the kitten sits between Elliott's shoulder blades, she doesn't lose her balance at all. She doesn't even wobble.

"Very queenlike," I murmur. *Maybe Cleocatra would be a good name.*

The shower feels incredibly good today, and I allow the hot water to flow over me for longer than I really should. There are water shortages somewhere in the world, and I try not to waste just because I can.

Today, though, I let the hot water work out the kinks in my shoulders while I ponder a decent name for the kitten.

Poppy?

Holly?

Daisy?

Smudge?

I get dressed in jeans and a sweater, pull on my warm boots, and blow-dry my hair. I'm listening to music when I think of the name Halsey.

It could be cute, but shouldn't a name mean something?

When I emerge from my bedroom, there's no one to be found, and I set out to see where everyone is.

I find my father in his heated shop out back, with Elliott and the kitten playing rambunctiously. No matter how vigorous the kitten gets, Elliott shows restraint, as if he knows that she is so much more fragile than he is. He moves suddenly, and it startles the kitten, and she paws at him with a brief hiss.

"Man, that kitten has moxie," my dad says, shaking his head. "The Moose could eat her in half a bite, yet she's not afraid."

"He won't, and she knows it," I tell him. "But *thank you, Dad.* Moxie is a *perfect* name!"

"I think if you name a kitten, you pretty much have to keep it," he says. "I think that's the law."

"Is it? You might want to brush up on your penal codes before you take office, Mayor."

He chuckles.

"I've got to take Elliott for his lesson," I remind him. "I don't want to wrestle with a cat and a dog. Will you keep the kitten here? I'm going to talk to Avery about her."

"Sure," he says, sanding a long table leg. "She's fine in here with me."

"You're the best." I bend and kiss his cheek.

"We should put that on voter buttons!" he calls after me as I take Elliott and leave.

We're driving through town with his nose pressed against the passenger window a few minutes later.

"That's going to be impossible to clean, you know that?" I ask him, glancing at all the giant nose prints.

He is unconcerned and continues staring diligently out the window.

We come to a stop at the stoplight, and a tiny elderly woman and a much younger man, probably in his forties, cross in front of my car. She holds on to his elbow, and he has no problem at all supporting her slight weight.

He's big, muscular, and I feel like I've seen him before but I know I haven't.

He stares at me, though, like he either knows me or is *interested* in knowing me.

Blond and blue-eyed isn't my usual type, but there's something almost ornery around his eyes that piques my curiosity. *Who is this guy?*

The light turns green, and I go. In my rearview mirror, I watch as he continues with her down the street, and I idly wonder where they are headed.

I stop wondering, though, when I pull up in front of Avery's vet practice. I can see her out back in tall muddy boots, walking from her barn.

She waves in greeting, and once I open Elliott's door, he bounds out and runs straight to her, as though he's greeting a long-lost friend.

He wags his tail, she pats his head.

"Sit," she tells him, her hand held up above his nose.

He sniffs her hand, then sits, his butt on the ground.

She gives him a treat. "Good boy."

"You're a wizard, Harry." I breathe the Harry Potter reference in disbelief. My disbelief continues when she does it two more times.

"Now you're just showing off," I announce.

She laughs, and holds out her now-empty and now-slightly-slimy hand.

"You must be Noel. We've not had the pleasure of meeting. I only just moved here last year."

I shake her hand and then wipe mine off on my jeans. She chuckles.

"Mastiffs are amazing, but their slobber game is strong," she says.

"It's almost atomic," I agree. "It doesn't want to come out of my sweaters."

She laughs. "I've heard that, yes. Come on in out of the cold. I can't wait to get to know this magnificent creature."

We go inside, and she does a quick checkup and weighs him. She lures him onto her scale and has him sit again.

She peers at the number. "Two hundred one point five."

"Good Lord." I gulp. "No wonder he yanks me around like I'm nothing."

"We'll fix that," she tells me, "but it will take some work on your end. I'll teach the skills, but you'll need to practice with him."

"I will," I vow.

"He could stand to lose a few pounds, honestly," she says. "He looks fit, but he's carrying just a little extra weight, and that will weigh on his joints. So I recommend a diet."

"Oh my word. I have no idea how I'll go about that," I tell her. "I think I'll just relay that information to his owner."

"He's not yours?" she asks.

"No, I'm dog-sitting for a while."

"Not many would take on a mastiff," she says, and I think I've gone up in her eyes. "But honestly, most mastiffs are just big teddy bears. They call them gentle giants for a reason."

I tell her about the kitten, which she finds delightful.

"I'm glad to hear he doesn't have a high prey drive," she answers. "Some do, some don't." She pats his head, and we get to our first lesson.

For the next thirty minutes, I learn how to give the sit command, the down command, and the stay command.

She also gives me some tips for teaching him to heel.

"This will take practice," she tells me again, at the end of the lesson. "But all great things do."

"I'll do it as long as he's with me," I promise. "And then I'll teach his owner how to continue."

"He looks so attached to you," she remarks, watching the

way he leans casually into my side. "Have you known him long?"

"Nope," I answer. "Just a matter of days, really."

"Wow," she says. "I would never have guessed that. He's very comfortable with you."

"This dog doesn't know a stranger," I reply. "He thinks everyone is the new best friend he just hasn't met yet."

"Well, I think you're taking amazing care of him," she tells me. "I'm impressed at your commitment. Do you want to come back for another lesson in a couple days?"

I nod. "That would be absolutely perfect."

She gives me a small bag of healthy dog treats to use for training, and Elliott eyes them as I put them into my purse.

"Don't even think about it," I tell him. When Avery looks at me, I shrug. "He's already chewed up the strap, see?"

I hold it up and she nods. "You'll want to keep everything picked up that you don't want him chewing. He's past the puppy chew stage, but any dog, if they are bored, will chew. So keep your shoes picked up, too."

"Good advice. Thank you."

"Anytime. I'm always here to help."

I try to pay her, but she won't take it.

"I'm just happy to meet you," she says. "Your parents have told me so much about you. They're very proud."

"It's very good to meet you, too."

Elliott and I make our way back out to the car, and he jumps in without hesitation. He also slams his head against the top of the car door frame, because he's just that clumsy. I rub it for him and close the door.

His head perks up, and he watches to make sure that I'm getting in, too.

"I'm not trying to trick you," I tell him. But he sniffs at my purse, and I realize that he's just concerned about the treats. "And yes, I have the treats. But those are for later."

If a dog can purse his lips, he does so now, staring at me with complete sorrow.

"You'll live," I say. He doesn't look convinced.

As I drive back through town and am stopped at a red light yet again, I glance through the window of Nell's and see Jonah sitting at a table. Across from him, the blond man and elderly woman I'd seen earlier are sitting. The man appears to be helping the woman cut her food.

Jonah looks up and catches my gaze, and his eyes burn into my own. I don't know what expression I see there, whether he's happy to see me or annoyed that I'm watching his companions.

The light turns green, and I drive away.

CHAPTER SEVENTEEN

Jonah

I watch Noel's car drive away before I turn back to Jace.

"I'm so happy you guys are here," I say. "I had no idea you'd be able to get here so quickly."

"I told you, we didn't have Christmas plans. It'll be nice to be with a friend for the holidays."

"Errrr, I don't know if you remember, but my house isn't the most festive."

He shakes his head. "Yes, I do remember. How's your dad, anyway?"

"Still at it! You know how he is."

"I do," Jace answers.

"Jerry, can I have some more water?" Izzy asks, her blue eyes cloudy as she looks at her son.

"She thinks I'm my father," Jace explains as he hands her his untouched glass. "Sometimes. Actually, *most* of the time, lately."

My heart clenches a bit as I watch the tiny woman across from me. Her hair is wild, which is unlike her. She used to wear it pulled neatly into a chignon every day. Her hands are gnarled from arthritis. Her eyes don't comprehend like they used to. The difference in her from just a few months ago is apparent.

"Well, there are worse people to be," I answer lightly. "Your father was a great man."

Jace nods. "Yes, he was."

We finish our breakfast, and then Jace and Izzy follow me to my father's place.

In my rearview mirror, I notice that Izzy can barely see over the dash. All I can see is her puff of white hair.

When we arrive, my father is riding the buckskin mare, Sugar, to check the property. He sees us from the back pasture and heads in our direction.

As he approaches, Izzy turns to Jace. "Your father always did like to ride horses," she says. She starts walking to meet my father, and when she does, she calls him Jerry.

Jace sighs, then holds out his hand to my dad. "Good seeing you again, Judd," he says.

"You're a sight for sore eyes," Dad answers. "I hear you've got a solution to my problem."

"Maybe!" Jace says. "And you might have the solution for mine. We walked around the town square today. It has a lot of potential, and it's just the right size."

"Let me go rub this mare down, and then I'll be in to chat," Dad promises. "Jonah, you'll want to check the fire. I started it this morning, but I haven't been inside in a while."

"Will do, Dad."

I check the fire while Izzy and Jace put their things in the guest room.

"I washed the sheets myself," I tell him. "So feel privileged."

"You know how to use a washer?" he asks, his brow raised. "That doesn't track, partner."

I punch him lightly on the shoulder. "It's just like riding a bike."

"Did you use laundry detergent?" he asks doubtfully.

"Of course. I'm not stupid." I try to recall if I had, in fact, put in the soap. Sadly, I don't remember. "And I cleaned the guest room. Myself. So feel very special."

"Oh, I do," Jace assures me. "Do you happen to have an extra blanket? I'm going to get my mom settled for her nap, and then I'll bring some paperwork out here that we can go over with your dad."

"Clean blankets are in the hall closet. There are clean towels in there, too, although I think I put a couple in your room."

"You did. Thanks. Be right back."

While I wait, I text Noel.

> How's the kitten getting along?

Her name is Moxie

> 😆 You named it? I knew you'd keep her.

Elliott would be devastated if I found her another home

> Isn't Elliott only with you for a little while?

At the rate this author is writing,
it could be a LONG while

Well, that's good

I think he's good for you

What are you basing that upon?

I can tell you're an editor

Normal people don't use the word "upon"

She doesn't reply, so I continue.

And I'm basing it UPON what I've seen so far

He'll make you less uptight. Less stressed.

Her answer is immediate.

You think I'm stressed?

Aren't you?

Isn't everyone?

Probably so

> You just seem more tightly wound than most

You seem so, too. Do you think it's because our parents have started WWIII against each other, and they're drawing our entire hometown into the mix?

> Touché

> How long are you in town for?

Hmm. I have to be back in the city by NYE.

> Big date?

Something like that.

My stomach tightens, which is stupid. She doesn't belong to me.

> How did the obedience training go?

Very well. I'm now perfectly trained to give him treats on cue.

> I don't think that's how it's supposed to work

Can you explain that to Elliott?

My father comes in the back door and stomps the snow from his boots. Then he sweeps it up with a broom and dustpan.

"Some would do that on the porch so it didn't make a mess," I point out.

"Some don't have a son who has gotten really good at cleaning and laundry," he shoots back.

"Don't count on those skills," I tell him. "They're rusty."

"I thought they were like riding a bike?" Jace says, joining us with his laptop and satchel.

"You have terrible timing," I remark. He laughs, then grabs my father's hand, shaking it and pulling him in for a hug.

"Thank you for having me," Jace says. "I was telling Jonah earlier, it'll be nice to be with friends over the holidays."

"You're always welcome here, you know that," my dad answers, taking off his coat and hanging it up on the hook by the back door.

Jace spreads his things out on the kitchen table and opens his laptop. Over the next hour, we sit around the table and discuss Jace's vision, how it could transform Winter Falls, and how it could benefit the lives of memory patients all across the country.

"Alzheimer's ran in your mother's family," my father tells me randomly. I freeze and look at him. He's never, ever liked to discuss her.

"It did? Do you remember who?" Jace asks. "Because it can be hereditary."

I must look concerned, because he rushes to continue.

"But it's not the only factor."

My dad turns to me. "Her grandfather had it," he says. "And then, after your mother died, her father got it."

I vaguely remember my grandfather's decline.

"It's a dreadful disease," I say. "I'll keep an eye out for signs as I age."

"They're learning more about it all the time," Jace says. "Hopefully, we'll be able to find a cure in our lifetime."

My dad pulls a drawing toward him with one finger. He studies how Winter Falls would look once the face-lift is complete.

"I like how it seems like a town from the fifties," he says. "It's nostalgic."

"This generation of dementia patients will find the fifties comforting," Jace answers. "As the memory village is around longer and longer, it will adapt with its demographic."

"So if I get Alzheimer's, I might find the nineties comforting?" I ask. "Someone will have to tight-roll my jeans, and if I have any hair left, I'll wear a mullet."

Jace chuckles. "Everyone is different," he says. "But dementia patients tend to remember things from long ago, rather than recent memories. So when they are surrounded by modern things, it confuses them. Scares them, even. They don't remember how these things work; my mom has forgotten how to use a cell phone. In theory, surrounding them with an atmosphere that resembles their youth, the era that they remember, will comfort them."

"I'm not a doctor, but it makes sense to me," Dad says. "This is a good idea, all around."

Jace glances at me. "We'll have a business plan within a day or two. I'll work on it nonstop."

I nod. "I'll help."

"Hmmmm," my father says dramatically. "Won't that be interfering? Aren't you supposed to be an impartial observer, someone who will examine the business plans? I don't think it would be fair if you helped prepare one."

I stare at him, my mouth open.

"I thought you wanted to fight dirty," I say.

"Not *too* dirty," he answers. "I still have to look myself in the mirror every morning."

"That's the father I remember and love."

"I'm sorry my mom thought you were my dad," Jace tells my dad, changing the subject. "She thinks I'm him, too."

Dad's eyes soften. "Don't apologize, son," he says. "If me being Jerry for a while brings her comfort, I'm happy to do it."

My chest swells a bit. Beneath his hardened and crusty exterior, my dad is a really good man.

He glances at me. "I got some coffee today. How about you keep polishing your domestic skills and make us a pot?"

"There's the father I grew up with." I sigh.

He smiles, unabashed, and I make the coffee, as requested.

"If the banking thing doesn't work out, I see a bright future for you as a housekeeper." Jace grins at me. I flip him off behind my father's back. Jace winks.

My phone buzzes in my pocket. Then again. Then again one more time.

I pause.

Is it Noel?

I glance at my dad and Jace. They're chatting now, not paying attention to me.

Discreetly, I pull out my phone and see that it was Millie.

> Jonah, I'm sorry to bother you, but Bertie Hofflinger is pressuring me for your home address there in WY.

> He said he needs to overnight you something important.

> Should I give it to him? Please advise.

Interesting. I wonder what he's up to. There's only one way to find out.

Sure, I answer. Go ahead.

"Hey, kiddo," my dad says. I look up. "I took Sugar for a ride, but Diesel and Denim could still use exercise. Do you and Jace want to do it? It's not half bad outside today."

"We're seeing the sun for the first time since I've been here," I tell Jace. "You up for a ride?"

"I am if you are."

"Why not?" I decide. "Let's do it. It's been many, many years since these glutes have seen a saddle."

"Just what every rural father dreams of hearing," my father mutters.

"I'll meet you in the barn," Jace tells me. "I just want to check on Mom. If she gets up while I'm out—"

"Don't worry," my father interjects. "I'm here if she wakes up."

"Thanks," Jace answers.

He walks into the hall, and I bend next to my dad's ear.

"Thank you, Dad."

He looks up at me. "For what?"

"For being a good person."

His eyes widen.

"Don't worry," I assure him. "I won't tell anyone."

He laughs. "Tell *everyone*! Don't forget, I'm running a mayoral race!"

I shake my head and pull my coat on, then my boots.

On a whim, I pick up one of my dad's cowboy hats from a hook, and it actually fits. Well enough, anyway.

"Yes, you may borrow it," my dad says from the table. "Thanks for asking."

"Just so you know," I tell him, "becoming a curmudgeon is *not* a prerequisite of growing older."

He's still chuckling when I close the door behind me.

I slide the heavy barn door open, and the air inside is warm. By the time Jace arrives, I've almost got both horses saddled.

"I'm impressed," Jace says. "But also nervous. Did you pull the cinch tight enough? Will my saddle come off midride? I'm too pretty for a broken neck."

I laugh. "Feel free to check it yourself. I know my dad drilled this into your head during the summers you visited."

"I'll never forget it," Jace says. He does, in fact, check his cinch before he swings up onto Denim.

We nudge our horses out of the barn and over the snow. The pasture is a pristine bed of white, gleaming in the afternoon sun.

"Deer," Jace says, pointing at tracks to our right.

"Yep."

We ride a bit farther. "Are those dog tracks?" Jace asks, pointing again.

I look.

"No, that looks like a wolf."

"A *lot* of wolves," Jace corrects.

"A pack of wolves," I agree. "They were probably tracking the deer that passed through here."

We keep riding, the horses' hooves crunching in the snow. The sound is comforting somehow, a memory from my youth.

The air is achingly cold, but the sunlight distracts from it a bit.

My cheeks burn from the wind, but I block it out. I'm communing with nature now, I'm enjoying myself.

I can't feel my toes, and I should've worn two pairs of socks. *Why am I so stupid?*

Diesel flicks his ear, and his hot breath puffs big white clouds into the air.

"Should we ride down by the river?" Jace asks.

"Do you remember that time—I think we were sophomores—you got thrown while we were by the river, got the breath knocked out of you, and I had to figure out how to get you up and back on that horse?"

"Ahhh, good times," Jace says wryly. "I think my ribs still hurt."

"Let's not tempt fate," I decide. "Let's go through the woods instead."

"Your call. I'm fine either way."

The light dims slightly as we enter the forest. Pines surround us, and combined with the snowy air, they smell like something straight out of a candle. I make a mental note to ask Millie to find candles with that scent.

It'll be easier to enjoy it from the comfort of my living room than on a frigid horseback ride.

To block out the cold, I try to envision myself sitting in front of a fireplace. My hands are warm, I can feel my feet again. I'm wrapped in a fleece blanket. My toes are practically hot, in fact.

It takes me a few minutes to realize that the fireplace I'm envisioning isn't the modern fireplace in my NYC condo with its blue flames. No, the fireplace in my head is rustic, and real, with great flames unfurling and lapping at the stones in the flue.

I can't take the time to analyze that. I have to keep envisioning it, no matter which fire it is, or my hands will freeze and fall off.

I won't be the first to give up, I tell myself, glancing over at my friend.

Don't be a sissy.

Don't be a sissy.

"Hey, Jonesy? I'm freezing my . . . I'm freezing, dude. My thighs are stinging."

"Well, if you want to be a sissy, let's turn back."

I rein Diesel around and laugh at the look on Jace's face. "I'm completely messing with you. I thought my toes were going to turn to ice."

Jace laughs, and we head back. We're not too far away from the edge of the forest when I see something interesting.

"Is that a heart?" I ask, pointing at the big tree trunk ahead of us.

Jace peers at it. "Yeah, I think so."

As we draw nearer, the letters inside the heart come into focus.

JB

+

NT

The heart is faded and old, likely carved years ago.

JB and NT.

Jonah Blake and Noel Turner?

A few thoughts collide in my head at once.

The one that stands out the most is: *That poor girl. Was she in love with me all those years ago, and I don't even remember her?*

CHAPTER EIGHTEEN

Noel

Check your email.

Emily's text interrupts me while I'm making marinara for dinner. I keep stirring the sauce with one hand and click into my email with the other.

From: <Padraig.Sinclair@sleighmail.com>
To: <n.turner@parkerhamiltonpublishing.com>
Subject: Next 2 Chapters

Noel,

Attached are the next two chapters for your perusal. I hope you find that I'm fleshing out Nora and Jack. Their characters are so nuanced and multifaceted that I have to peel their layers back like an onion. Please let me know if I revealed anything too quickly, or too slowly, or if the dialogue between Nora and Jack is authentic. I'm open to your input—after all, you're the expert on that. A friend once told me that there's nothing a good red pen can't fix, so I'm counting on your red pen, my dear!

Another thing: Can you help me watch that they don't come across as unlikable? Remember: They have no idea that they've been thrust back in time to fulfill their Christmas wish. We have to be patient with them while they figure everything out. If they figure it out. That, of course, remains to be seen.

All best,
Pad

PS: Please give Elliott a hug for me, and tell him that he's really helping with this story.

I smile, because it's actually quite adorable that Pad is integrating Elliott's shenanigans into his book. I love that Elliott's mischief here in Winter Falls will be immortalized in print.

I spend the next twenty minutes reading both chapters. When Nora starts flirting with Jack's best friend, I suck in a breath.

Nooooooo, I text Emily.

I knowwwww, she answers, with a sobbing emoji. But keep reading.

So I do.

A few minutes later, I text her again.

> She's only flirting with Jett to annoy Jack. Also, there's a lot of J names in this. I'm not sold on these names, but that's the only complaint I have so far.

Emily sends back a quick response. I can't with you right now! Your "only complaint"? This man is a treasure. The way he portrays Jack's inner thoughts and emotions . . . he keeps him masculine, but still so expressive. It's the perfect balance, and I bow to his skill.

You know I'm right, she adds.

I know you're a drama queen, I correct.

> When is he sending the next chapters?

I don't know. When he finishes them, I answer.

> Well, tell him my health and well-being depend on them. That might hurry him along.

I don't even answer that one. The girl can be outrageous. I love her for it.

I put my phone down and add more basil to the sauce, then taste it again. I turn around to call my parents for dinner and see that my dad is already sitting at the table, with Moxie in his lap.

Moxie is wearing a fuzzy pink sweater.

I blink. "Dad, why is the cat wearing a sweater?"

Elliott lifts his head off my dad's foot and makes a weird noise, almost like he wants to know the same thing.

"She's tiny, Noel. It's freezing. I bumped into Avery earlier—she said she hasn't heard of anyone who lost a long-haired gray kitten."

"Good," I say before I realize it. My dad looks at me. "I mean, Elliott would be devastated," I add.

"Oh, yes," Dad agrees, smiling. It's an annoying *knowing* smile, though.

"Where did you even get a cat sweater?" I ask.

"Your mom knitted it last night. It didn't take her long at all. I think she's working on a Christmas sweater for her today."

"Of course she is," I agree, as though it were the most normal thing in the world.

He pets Moxie, and the kitten purrs, then jumps down onto Elliott's head. That's where she stays, like a bee on a flower.

Elliott tries to see what she's doing but ends up cross-eyed from his efforts.

He gives up and puts his head back on my dad's foot, and Moxie adjusts herself to sit on the side of his head instead. He sighs in resignation and closes his eyes.

"I didn't know that Mom was knitting again," I mention as I set the table. "I thought it hurt her hands too much now."

"It's her way of handling anxiety," Dad says. "It's rhythmic and keeps her focused on the moment rather than worrying about things that might not even come to pass. Plus, she's on a different med now for her arthritis, so it doesn't hurt as much as it used to."

I feel like I should've known that, and I feel badly that I didn't. It was a big deal for Mom when she couldn't knit anymore. If she can again, it's a huge win that should be celebrated.

"I need to call home more," I decide.

Dad looks at me. "We know you're busy, Noel."

"Still."

Mom joins us for dinner, and as we eat the pasta and bread, she shows me a few pictures of sweaters she wants to knit for the cat.

"Mom, those are super cute, but I'm not sure that cats like to wear sweaters."

"She doesn't seem to mind," Mom says, staring pointedly at the kitten, who is sound asleep on Elliott's head in her fuzzy pink sweater. "Look how nice the pink looks with her gray fur."

"Hey, did an Amazon box come for me today?" I ask. "I'm waiting on—"

"It came," Mom answers. "I put the air mattress in your room—you were smart to get one with a pump built in. Also, that shirt for the dog . . . you can't have him wear that around town, Noel. It's not seemly."

"It's just a joke," I answer with a grin. "He's enormous."

"What's the joke?" Dad asks. "I want to laugh."

I tell him, and he looks down his nose at me. "No sexual innuendos, young lady. I'm running for mayor."

"I know, Dad." I sigh.

"I'll knit him a Christmas sweater, instead," my mom says. "He and Moxie will have matching sweaters. That will be lovely for the Christmas Eve party."

"Whose party?" I ask.

"Ours," she answers. "We're going to hold a holiday celebration in the town square on Christmas Eve."

I stare at her hesitantly.

"I think you'll need permission from city hall for that."

"I know. I'm going to send you there for that today. You've been hanging out with Jonah Blake enough lately—that will surely come in handy."

My parents are both staring at me now, and I feel like this moment is some sort of loyalty test. They're waiting intently to see if I'll pass.

"Of course I'll try to help," I say slowly. "But don't count on my acquaintance with Jonah to hold any weight."

"Pish," my dad says. "I don't know if you've seen the way that man looks at you, but I have."

"What do you mean?"

My mom pats my hand. "Everyone was talking about it at Wyatt's," she says. "At first, your father and I were taken aback, but then we started thinking . . . it could benefit this whole thing."

"You mean, you decided that your political aspirations could benefit from using a relationship that I have? I'm disappointed in that, Mom. Seriously. I don't like the changes I'm seeing in you guys with this."

"Don't lecture us, young lady," my dad says gently. "We've been patient with Judd Blake for years, and he's shut down our every attempt to chase our business idea. We've been tolerant. But it's time to stand up for our rights."

"You don't have to *use* people to do that," I point out.

"Harnessing advantages is how people win," he answers. "All's fair in love, war, and business."

"That's not how that saying goes."

"I know." He winks. "But it should be."

"You're incorrigible, honey," Mom says, grinning proudly at her husband.

"Where are the parents who raised me?" I demand. "Because they aren't in this room."

Mom rolls her eyes. "You're so dramatic, sweetie. I truly don't know where you get it."

She takes her plate and pads over to the sink, wearing a different set of Christmas slippers. These feature flashing Christmas lights in blue, red, and green.

"Yeah, I have no idea where those genes came from," I mutter.

My father chuckles, but Mom gives him a look over her shoulder that silences him.

I glance at him smugly.

He gives me the "dad look." The last time I saw one of those was when I'd tried to sneak wine coolers to prom my senior year and he'd found them in my car beforehand.

It's still effective.

I wipe the smirk off my face.

He smirks now instead.

"So, will you be going to city hall tomorrow to get permission for the party?" Mom asks brightly as she washes the pots. "The sooner, the better, of course. I only have a few days to prepare as it is."

"You're killing me," I groan. "I'll think about it. Right now, I have a bit of work to do."

I get to my feet and motion for Elliott. He stands to join me, and somehow Moxie clings to his head as he does. Then she whips her little body onto his back, and that's where she rides, all the way to my bedroom, once again a tiny feline pharaoh on her chariot.

"The two of you look ridiculous," I tell them, which is a lie. They look adorable and only a little bit ridiculous. "I hope you know you're natural-born enemies."

They clearly do not.

Elliott is so gentle with her, which only amplifies the difference in their sizes. He has to be ever mindful not to squash her, and he actually is. He watches after her like a mother duck, and she's his duckling.

I find that my mother hasn't just set the air mattress in here, she's unboxed it, set it up, and made the bed. Because of course she has.

She always makes sure I'm taken care of.

If she knows I'm swamped at work, she has food delivered, since she's afraid I don't take care of myself. She sends care boxes filled with vitamins and home remedies and useful recipes that she knows I won't try, but she's ever hopeful.

"The least I can do is try to arrange their party." I sigh to Elliott.

He looks up at me without moving his head, since Moxie has once again lain upon it.

"I mean, how hard can it be to get permission for a Christmas party?" I ask. "It's not an unreasonable ask. We're not asking for funding, just the space for the party."

Elliott blinks, as though he agrees.

"Thanks, boy. We'll go tomorrow. Maybe you'll help my cause. Everyone likes you."

He blinks demurely now, accepting the compliment.

"You've got very expressive blinks," I tell him.

I pull out my laptop and sort through emails and, sadly, find nothing from Padraig. I do approve a few covers, a few expenses, and a few deadline extensions.

I accidentally click into a promo email from a spa, and although I mean to click right back out, the pictures of glass-domed bedrooms to watch the northern lights from and huge mineral hot springs in the middle of snow intrigue me.

Great Expectations Spa and Resort, Wander, Alaska.

I love the name, I love the premise, I even love the town name.

It's a great setting for a book, I absently think.

I bookmark their website. After this Christmas holiday, I might need a separate holiday to recover.

I yawn and realize that my eyes are slightly blurry. It feels like this day has gone on for a hundred years.

An air mattress has never looked so inviting. My mother made it up with the new Christmas bedding, and she even added a faux fur throw on top with a matching accent pillow.

I take a hot shower, pull on comfy flannel pajamas, and curl up on the air mattress with a few chapters from another author.

I comment in the margins and find myself engrossed.

I'm so engrossed that a few hours later, when an owl hoots outside the window, I barely register it.

Until it hoots again, and this time, Elliott snaps his head up, scrambles out of my twin bed, gallops to my air mattress, and dives on top of me so that I can save him.

I laugh and pet him.

"It's just an owl, Elliott. You're far larger, far stronger, and far braver than a little bird, aren't you?"

He looks at me, and I almost expect him to shake his head in argument.

"Go back over to the bed, boy. There's no room here."

He doesn't move, not one inch, and his expression is mulish.

But Moxie moves.

She scampers over to join us, and somehow, the three of us share one air mattress until morning.

CHAPTER NINETEEN

Jonah

After Jace and I do the morning chores for my father, we traipse back inside and find a full, steaming breakfast on the table.

Eggs, bacon, toast, orange juice, and stiff black coffee.

"You've outdone yourself," Jace tells my father as he pulls off his coat and boots. "I haven't had food like this since . . . I don't remember when."

I do.

Since before his mother forgot how to cook.

Whenever we'd spent school breaks at his house instead of mine, his mother had spoiled us rotten with home-cooked meals and treats. She certainly showed her love for us through food.

"My father isn't as good a cook as your mom," I tell him. "But he'll do."

"Hey," Dad growls. "I've never had any complaints."

Izzy comes in wearing red slacks, a yellow top, and mismatched socks.

"Mom, I laid out your clothes for you," Jace tells her. "Didn't you see them?"

She smiles at him. "I liked these better. Aren't the colors pretty?"

I melt. "You look lovely, Izzy. Are you ready for something to eat?"

She nods happily. "I hope there's chocolate milk."

My dad's eyes widen, and he shakes his head silently at me.

"I don't think there is right now," I tell her. "But after breakfast, I'll go get you some. Will that work?"

She pats my shoulder and leans her head against mine. "You spoil me, Jerry."

"You're easy to spoil," I answer, and she beams.

I guide her to a chair and help her get settled, while Jace makes her a plate.

"Would you boys stop by city hall and talk to Nance today?" Dad asks. "I'll keep Izzy company. I'd like for Nancy to be up to speed on the plan we discussed, and she can create packets for the city council."

"Sure," Jace answers. "We'd love to."

We eat, then Jace and I get showered and dressed while Izzy and my dad linger over breakfast. When we return to the kitchen, Izzy is rearranging the utensil drawer, her uneaten plate of food waiting for her on the table.

She holds up a tiny shrimp fork.

"Look at this, Jerry!" she says in delight. All three of us turn our heads to look, unsure which of us is currently her husband. "What in the world will they think of next?"

"It's for shrimp, Ma," Jace tells her.

She wrinkles her nose as she sits down at the table. "Do you know what shrimp *eat*?" she asks. "They're filthy little things."

My dad chuckles. "You're not wrong. They're still delicious, though."

She's unconvinced.

"It's okay, Ma," Jace assures her. "You don't have to eat any."

That pacifies her, and she eats her eggs happily now.

"Do you have any ketchup?" she asks sweetly.

"Of course," I tell her, and I retrieve it.

"She's never eaten ketchup on her eggs before," Jace says with interest.

"Of course I have," she answers. "Jenny and I do it all the time."

"Aunt Jenny has been dead for ten years," Jace murmurs to me, turning away so his mother can't hear his low voice.

"Not to her right now," I answer. "And that's okay." I watch over Jace's shoulder as Izzy gets back up and wanders to look out the window, trailing her finger along the glass.

"They used to do reality orientation as treatment," Jace says. "Where they'd try to convince dementia patients that their memories are incorrect and remind them of the current reality. But it's a futile thing that just upsets them. So I just go along with whatever she believes is true."

"Makes sense," I answer. "Why upset her?"

"Exactly." Jace crosses to the window where he puts his arm around his mother's slender shoulders.

"Ma, I'm going out for a bit with Jonah. You're going to stay here with Judd, okay?"

She nods, unconcerned.

"Don't forget my chocolate milk," she reminds me.

"I'd never," I promise.

We bundle back up, and head to town in Dad's truck. When we get to city hall, I text my father.

> Left the SUV for you, in case you and Izzy need to go anywhere.

When we get inside, Nancy has doughnuts and coffee waiting for us.

"I figured you boys would be hungry," she says with a giant grin on her face. She's clearly pleased with herself, and something about her reminds me a bit of Millie.

"We're always hungry," I assure her. She beams.

Jace and I each grab a couple of doughnuts and big cups of coffee.

When she walks away, Jace leans toward me.

"Fair warning: with all this caffeine and sugar, I'm going to hang from the ceiling fans today."

"Great."

We do our parts, though, and put away two frosted doughnuts apiece and enough coffee to bring Frankenstein's bride back to life.

Nancy answers calls from the desk across the room while Jace and I assemble the business plan for the Winter Falls Memory Village.

"Did you get the financial projections from your finance team?" I ask him.

He nods. "I've got them in my email. I'll forward them to

you. Keep in mind, these are preliminary. There hasn't been time for a deep dive."

"Initial numbers are fine," I tell him. "I can help flesh them out. In fact, I'll connect my finance team to you right now."

I send a quick email to Millie, asking her to arrange it.

When I turn back around to tell Jace, the front door of city hall opens, and Noel and Elliott stroll into the room.

She's holding a plate of frosted Christmas cookies. Elliott keeps glancing at it longingly.

Nancy rushes to hug her and takes the cookies.

"To what do we owe this pleasure," I ask lightly, trying not to show that I'm almost entranced with the way the sunlight in the window backlights her flaming-red hair. It's a sight that doesn't get old.

Jace doesn't try quite so hard. He outright stares.

"This is Jace Mulvaney, Noel," I tell her. "My best friend from college. Jace, this is Noel Turner. Her parents are running against my dad in the mayoral race."

"Otherwise known as Mack Daddy," Jace says, offering his hand.

She glances at him, only momentarily fazed. She refocuses quickly, however, after shaking his hand.

"You look so familiar," Jace continues. "Have we met?"

She looks at him, her head cocked. "You do seem familiar," she agrees. "But I think I'd remember meeting a real live mack daddy."

He grins, pleased.

I frown, *dis*pleased. Her playful tone with him grates on my nerves.

"He was called Mack Daddy in college for a reason," I warn her. "Don't be fooled."

"I wasn't planning on it," she assures us both. "I'm actually here to see how to go about getting an event permit."

"I can help you with that," Nancy tells her, pulling out a packet of forms from her desk.

I think about the carved heart in the woods, and I think about how beautiful this woman is. If she had a crush on me in high school, I really missed the boat on that one.

While Nancy gathers a few other forms, I join Noel and scratch Elliott behind the ears. He thumps his tail against my legs like a whip.

"Ow." I grimace. "Love doesn't hurt, boy."

Noel titters. "An owl scared him last night, and he took a flying leap on top of me on the bed. I think I have bruises on my ribs."

"Speaking of owls," I say, coming up with the world's worst segue, "Jace and I were out riding in the woods yesterday. Look what we came across."

I pull up the photo I'd snapped and show her.

Her eyes widen. "Did you have a crush on me in high school or something?" she asks, grinning. "Are you just pretending that you don't remember me?"

"I was going to ask you the same thing," I reply. "Have you been secretly in love with me for years now?"

She throws her head back and laughs.

"Hardly. I swear to you, I have no recollection of you at all."

"And I of you," I tell her, a bit coolly. The idea of being in love with me wasn't *that funny*.

"Well, there must've been another NT and JB who live here in Winter Falls and who carved that tree," Jace says soothingly.

"Yes, on my father's property," I say. "That makes perfect sense."

Jace gives me a look. "Dude, you don't own those initials. Plenty of people have the same ones."

"How many people live in Winter Falls, Nancy?" I call.

"Five thousand two hundred and eleven at the last census," she answers without looking up. "But, of course, a few moved away after the Ridgemont closed."

"I'm not sure if enough people still live here to have the same initials," I say. "But sure, we can stick with that story."

Noel's eyes widen, then narrow. "You are just a bit arrogant, do you realize that? I have absolutely not been pining for you all these years. *I literally did not know you existed.*"

I smirk. "Of course. We'll go with that."

"We're not *going with that*," she says slowly. "That's the truth."

"Okay," I agree.

She grits her teeth.

"I've got the forms," Nancy says. "If you're ready, Noel."

Noel heads to her desk, and I follow.

"What's the event?" I ask curiously.

"That was going to be my first question," Nancy says, her pen poised.

"A Christmas Eve party for the community in the town square," Noel answers. "My parents will fund the entire thing. They just think the community can use a little perking up this year."

"So you want to throw a party for the town, which will be directly followed by the mayoral vote. That feels akin to bribery," I tell her.

She turns to look at me. "Voting for my parents will not be a prerequisite for attending the party," she says.

"That doesn't matter," I answer. "They'll still associate the party with your folks, and they'll remember that in the voting box."

"I can't help if they have goodwill for my parents," she answers. "It's a holiday party, Jonah. Not a bribe."

"I don't know," I muse. "Nancy, who has final approval over potential community events?"

"Your dad," she says. "And if the applicant contests the decision, the town council."

"And they aren't meeting until Christmas Eve anyway," I answer. "So it might be a moot point, due to timing."

When Noel meets my gaze, her blue eyes are fiery.

"If you try to block this party, I will file an injunction so fast your head will spin," she warns, her voice laced with steel. This is her New York City side, her Wyoming side long gone.

"I didn't say I was planning to block it," I tell her. "I'm just examining the optics. It looks bad. Like a bribe."

"Well, you can let me worry about their image," she says. "Meanwhile, maybe you should consider the optics of you putting your head together with your college buddy. That seems a little biased to me." While I sputter, she turns away from me, ending the conversation. "Nancy, can I file the application with you?"

Nancy nods. "Of course."

Jace pipes up from across the room, where he's playing with Elliott. "Miss Noel, let me assure you, he's not doing a thing to help me right now because he's too busy checking his phone for texts from *you*. Also, please know that I don't share the beliefs of my friend here. I think a holiday party is a magnificent idea, and I hope you'll save me a dance, assuming there's music. If there isn't, we can make our own."

I flip him off.

"We'll see," Noel answers him, and her face relaxes, her cheeks growing a bit pink. "Let's get this permit approved first."

"Good luck," I tell her.

Her back stiffens, but she doesn't turn around.

CHAPTER TWENTY

Noel

"Can you believe the nerve of that man?" I demand to my parents when I get back home with Elliott in tow. "Who does he think he is?"

"This is what we're talking about," my father says patiently. "This whole time. They can't let their personal whims bleed over into the decisions for this town."

"I'm just astounded," I say, shaking my head. "If Judd is like this, it's completely unprofessional."

"Judd is worse," my mom replies. "Where do you think Jonah learned it?"

"I'm not going to tolerate it," I answer.

"There's our girl," Dad says approvingly.

"The nerve." I'm still fuming.

"Put it out of your head, Noel," my mom suggests.

But Dad interrupts. "No, don't. Keep it in your head as fuel. Things need to change. Starting now."

"That could be your campaign slogan," I tell him. *"Right here, right now.* Or something like that."

"Genius, honey," Dad approves, and he scribbles it down. "I'll get buttons and refrigerator magnets made."

"I'm making a list of townspeople who would directly benefit from a Christmas village," Mom tells me. "Merchants, shops, et cetera. We'll reach out to them directly."

"You know, I should put you in contact with our marketing department," I tell her. "One of the marketing directors owes me a favor."

"That would be *perfect*," she gasps. "Would you really?"

"Of course," I answer, already pulling out my phone to text Emily. "I'm arranging it right now. Expect a call or email from her today. Tell her your ideas, and see if she can polish it all up."

"You are our favorite child," she declares.

"I'm your *only* child," I answer.

Elliott is sprawled in front of the fireplace, recharging after our walk downtown.

I curl up on the sofa with my laptop, and Moxie folds into my side. Her purrs bring my blood pressure down, and after a few minutes, I'm feeling much calmer.

I'm emailing Padraig for an update when Avery texts.

> Hey girl. I have an opening this afternoon if you and Elliott want it? We can have coffee after.

YES, I answer. Name the time.

I'll see you at 2pm, she replies.

Time passes quickly until then, and I let Elliott nap until the last possible minute.

"I figure it's best if he's well rested," I tell my dad when I go to rouse him.

"Smart thinking," he agrees. "Kind of like a toddler."

"Exactly."

"Wait," my mom calls, rushing in. She's got a green-and-red sweater in her hands. "I finished his sweater last night."

"Already?" My jaw drops. "Are you powered by rocket fuel now?"

She laughs. "It's just nice to be able to knit again. I get carried away sometimes. I'm working on Moxie's today. Hers won't take long."

Elliott does surprisingly well as I put his new sweater on. He holds out his paws obediently, and once it's on, he prances around like a preening peacock.

"It fits perfectly," I tell my mom. "You did a fantastic job."

She preens along with Elliott.

Elliott gets into the car easily enough. It's almost like he's eager to show off his new threads. He has no idea that he looks like a giant Christmas decoration.

Or if he does, he doesn't care.

He prances jauntily out of the car when we arrive at Avery's, heading through the door like he's done it a thousand times before.

Avery greets us with a smile and a command for Elliott to sit.

He sits.

She rewards him.

We spend the next hour working on his new skills, with me

doing the commands and taking him through his paces. By the end I feel like *I'm* the one who was taken through my paces.

"This is stressful," I tell Avery when we sit in her kitchen afterward as she makes us two cups of coffee. "I worry that if I don't get him trained, he'll accidentally hurt someone. Namely, me."

Avery nods. "He doesn't know his own size and strength. He could *easily* knock a small child over just by getting excited."

"We don't want that," I agree. "He's not around any children right now while he's with me, but I have no idea who his owner takes him around. He needs to learn to control himself."

"So his owner . . . has he checked on him at all?" Avery asks, and I hear a little judgment in her voice.

I rush to defend Padraig. "He's elderly, and he's writing a book that he's hoping I'll publish. I think, maybe due to his age, that he just needs solitude while he writes. He definitely cares about Elliott, and we email back and forth about him all the time. In fact, I keep him abreast of Elliott's shenanigans every day. I have a bunch of content to work with, trust me."

I tell her all about the kitten, and how Elliott is so gentle.

She laughs. "I've heard stories of that happening sometimes," she says. "What a hoot!"

"I know," I agree. "He's like her giant mother, and she's his adopted duckling. If he's not carrying her on his back, then he's carrying her in his mouth, and she likes it. He's careful not to hurt her with his teeth. I've never seen such a thing."

"Just watch them carefully," Avery advises. "Animals can be unpredictable."

"I will," I promise.

Avery and I chat for a while, about our alma maters and our early careers.

"I always knew I wanted to be in New York," I tell her. "From the time I was in high school. I had this idea of myself dressed very stylishly, with my Gucci briefcase and designer shoes, hailing cabs and living in a high-rise penthouse suite."

"Did it work out like that?" Avery asks.

"Mostly," I concede. "I have the briefcase, and I have the designer shoes—and the toe calluses to prove it. I hail cabs, and it isn't nearly as glamorous as I thought *that* would be. In fact, they smell like hamster cages most of the time, so I tend to take Ubers instead."

Avery laughs.

"But it's made me independent. And strong. I have an edge that I wouldn't have had otherwise."

"That's commendable," Avery says. "I feel really strongly that women need to focus on becoming independent when they're young. Even when it's uncomfortable."

"*Especially* when it's uncomfortable," I answer. "I was terrified the first time I took the subway. But guess what? I do it now without blinking. I know that if I can navigate New York, I can navigate myself through any city in the world."

"That's true," Avery agrees. "I'm envious of that. I don't have that skill yet."

"Well, you've got an open invitation to come visit me, and I'll tutor you. Just like you're tutoring me with Elliott."

Her face lights up. "Really? I'd *love* that. Truly."

"I would, too," I tell her, and I'm being honest. She seems like great friend material.

"Have you ever noticed how hard it is to make new friends as an adult?" Avery asks, as though she's read my mind.

"I was just thinking about that," I reply. "I live in a city of over eight million, and I've not yet come across someone who was friend material, except my assistant. And she's also my cousin, so I'm not sure that counts. Therefore, I think you and I might be soul sisters."

She laughs. "Well, I dunno. How do you feel about pineapple on pizza?"

"Never."

"How about no-carb diets?"

"Of the devil."

"And pumpkin spice?"

"Overrated."

"You're right," she decides. "We're soul sisters. Shall we sign a binding contract in blood?"

"Now you're scaring me."

We laugh and each take a sip of coffee. I idly stroke Elliott's ears as he lays his big head against my side.

Avery glances at me. "I hear your parents might be throwing quite the shindig for Christmas Eve."

"My goodness, word travels quickly around here," I exclaim. "I literally was at city hall about it this morning."

Avery grins. "Welcome to Winter Falls."

I chuckle. "I forget sometimes."

"I'll be surprised if you get the permit," Avery says. "With the way things happened for them, I just don't see it happening."

"What do you mean?"

"The town square? On Christmas Eve? That hits too close to home for them. They'll die before they allow it."

"What happened in the town square on Christmas Eve?" I ask her, and I feel my forehead furrow.

"Frowning causes wrinkles," Avery says, trying to distract me. I give her my dad's look, or at least, my best rendition of it. She's unfazed.

"It's not my story to tell," she finally says with a sigh. "I'm sorry. I didn't realize that you didn't know."

"Come on. I won't tell anyone," I press.

"Would you disclose information that wasn't yours to tell?" she asks me.

I pause. Then sigh. "No."

"And that is why we're soul sisters. Neither would I."

My shoulders slump. *"Fine.* I'll just be the only person in town who doesn't know."

"That's the spirit!" she says enthusiastically. I glower.

She laughs. "I like you," she decides.

"And I like you, too," I tell her. "I love this for us!"

"I love *Schitt's Creek*," she breathes. "Marry me now, woman!"

We giggle and finish our coffee.

"Thank you again for today," I tell her as I leave. "You were just what the doctor ordered."

She's staring over my shoulder in amazement, and I turn to find the most exotic-looking car I've ever seen being hauled on a flatbed truck.

"What in the world is that?" I wonder.

"I don't know for sure, but to me, that looks like a Caterham Seven. A *very* rare car."

"It looks . . . like the Love Bug and the Model T had a love child," I say doubtfully.

She laughs. "Don't be deceived," she says, gazing in appreciation. "It's a car for performance. It's lightning fast, and all about focus, not comfort. This car is legendary. It's a statement. This is for someone who could literally have *anything* in the world . . . but they chose *this car*."

"Wow," I say. "You're quite the fangirl. How in the world do you know all this?"

"Brothers." She shrugs. "You'd be surprised what I could tell you about cars."

"I always wanted an older brother," I tell her. "You're lucky."

"They talked me into jumping out of a tree house when I was five," she says. "And eating a grasshopper when I was three."

"Maybe I'm okay being an only child," I decide. "I'll talk to you soon."

"Oh!" she says, bending to scratch Elliott's ears. "I forgot to tell you. You look very handsome in your sweater!"

He beams the entire way home.

CHAPTER TWENTY-ONE

Jonah

Y ou've got to be kidding me," I mutter, examining the document presented to me by the delivery driver standing in front of me.

"No, sir," he says. "This is a gift. For you. From Mr. Bertie Hofflinger. He sends his best regards and wants you to know there is more where this came from."

"Subtle," Jace says from my elbow, as he examines the masterpiece sitting in front of us. "Some might say understated."

The driver laughs. "This Caterham Seven is minted number seven out of only twenty cars like it ever made, built in 1977. You *could* say it's the most dramatic statement in the world."

"There are only twenty cars like this one?" Jace asks, his eyebrow raised. *"In the world?"*

"That's what I'm saying, yes," the driver answers.

Jace turns to me. "And this guy *overnighted* you this thing?"

"Essentially, yes."

He shakes his head in wonder. "You must be *really* good at what you do."

"I've been telling you that for years."

I sign the acceptance, because I'm not insane enough to send it back. The driver hands me the keys and the title and drives away, leaving the red work of art in my driveway.

"You have permission to help me with my business idea," Jace tells me. "I trust you."

"Just now?"

The sun glistens on the red fender.

"Where are we going to put it?" Jace asks. "Can we make space in the barn?"

I laugh at the idea of rolling this car into a barn. "My dad's workshop has a one-car stall on the backside. We'll put it in there."

"Will you drive it back to New York?"

"Are you nuts? I'll have it delivered. I'm not putting that many miles on her, or risking her out on the road. This baby will only be driven on a closed track."

"Wearing white gloves?" Jace guesses.

"Pretty much."

I dust my coat and jeans off before I open the door and sit down. Jace goes to the passenger door.

"Clean your feet off," I tell him, running my hands over the dash in reverence.

I turn the key.

The sound of the engine is an operatic symphony to my ear. It purrs and roars at the same time. It's enough to lure my father out to the porch, where he stands with a confused look on his face.

We drive around the workshop and carefully nose into the garage stall. To be on the safe side, I also pull a tarp over her.

We walk up to the house, where my dumbstruck father is still on the porch, waiting for an explanation.

"I need to borrow your extra garage stall for a few days, please. There's a Caterham Seven in there."

My father's mouth falls open, and I enjoy strolling casually past as though it's no big deal.

"You need to get insurance on that thing," he says. "Right away."

"I don't know yet if I'll be keeping it," I answer.

"Why in the world would you *not*?" he asks.

"Because it's attached to a job offer," I say simply. "Think of it as a bonus. If I were to accept the position."

"What's the position?" Dad asks.

"CEO of my biggest competitor's London office."

Jace's jaw drops, and my father is visibly stunned.

"London?" he asks. "England?"

"That's the one." I nod, waiting for a follow-up reaction. He doesn't give one. "Big Ben," I add. "Parliament. Buckingham Palace."

Still nothing. His face is expressionless as he says, "That's quite an offer."

"It is," I agree. "I have a lot to think about."

"You do," he agrees. "But what it should always boil down to is: do the best you can for *you*." He slaps me on the back and goes inside.

Jace turns to me. "Did he just give you permission to move to London?"

"I think so," I answer. "I think that's *exactly* what he just did."

"But maaaan, that's a tough choice. You're the only thing he has in the world, and he's getting older."

My gut clenches. "I know. Thank you for the reminder, though."

"Sorry, man. I don't think I could do it to my mom. It'd break her heart."

"You could take her with you, though. If it were you."

"I could," he says. "But she'd never want to go. Not if she was given a choice. It would turn everything she knows upside down."

He's right. And I know it's the same for my dad. If I were to accept that job, and if I were to ask him to accompany me, I'd be the most selfish man in the world.

"You're right," I tell him. "Of course you're right."

"Can we keep it for now, though?" he asks hopefully.

"You'd better believe it."

He fist-bumps me, and we join my dad and Izzy inside.

We're halfway through dinner when there's a firm knock on the front door.

I open it and am surprised to find Noel standing in front of me.

"I'm here to lodge a complaint," she announces.

My head snaps back. "A complaint? What in the world for?"

"You volunteered your services to determine the risks associated with both mayoral candidates' business plans, and you were to evaluate each impartially. I trusted you to be impartial." With that last line, her voice is thin, and I meet her gaze. "But after I was told that, the vehicle I saw delivered to you today might indicate that you are, in fact, not impartial."

It takes me a moment. Then it hits me.

"You think I'm being bribed by my father?" I ask, my voice louder than I intended. "You think my father could afford that car?" I turn to him. "No offense, Dad."

"None taken," he assures me.

"It could be Jace, not your father. I have no idea," she continues. "And if you're willing to do that, and if *they* are willing to do that, how can I possibly know that your father will be impartial about my parents' petition?" she asks. "So that's my complaint."

She takes a breath.

I eye her. "Are you done?"

She nods.

"You're here to lodge a complaint about something that hasn't happened. My father hasn't yet made a decision about the party, and in fact, I don't think he even knows about it."

"I do not know what you're talking about," my dad confirms.

"Your complaint is based upon an assumption," I tell her.

"The optics are bad on this, Jonah," Noel says. "Whether or not my assumption is correct, it's the same one that everyone else will make."

"I'm not being bribed by a political candidate on either side," I tell her stiffly. "I'm not being bribed at *all*. It's an *attempted* bribe. By someone who wants me to work for him. I, however, have integrity and don't want to be obligated to anyone for anything. The fact that I'd be willing to walk away from a bribe *like that*, well . . . that should tell you all you need to know about my integrity. Good day, Noel."

I walk to the door, then pause. "Oh, and to show you that I haven't been compromised, I'll make sure your parents' request gets approved. You can have your party, and the town council will meet that evening to deliberate your proposals and the request for an emergency election."

"Do you mean that?" she asks. "Their application will be approved?"

"I'll make sure of it. Your parents and my father can present their proposals that evening. It will be unbiased. You have my word."

I hold out my hand and raise my eyebrows.

She pauses, then places her hand in mine. We shake.

Oddly, I don't want to release her hand. I want to pull her closer, and . . .

"Jonah?" she asks, raising her own eyebrows. I realize that I'd been about to drift into a lovely daydream.

"Yes?"

"May the best man win?"

"Oh! Yes, absolutely. *May the best man win.*"

"Thank you, Jonah," she says softly. "This means a lot."

She turns and walks back to her car. I have the maddening impulse to chase after her and to open her car door for her, to make sure she's buckled in, and to kiss her goodbye.

I shake my head, trying to clear the errant thoughts away.

I turn, close the door, and come toe-to-toe with my father as he waits for me with thunder on his face.

"You didn't have the authority to do that," he says evenly, and I can tell he's trying to hold on to his temper.

"I didn't tell her I'd authorize it," I answer. "I said I'd make sure that *you* do. I wasn't usurping your authority."

"That isn't my concern," he says. "And you know it."

"Dad, it was a matter of principle," I tell him. "Of honor, actually. She thought I'd be open to bribery."

"Why do you *care* what she thinks?" he demands.

My mouth snaps closed. I have no idea why her opinion matters and didn't, until this very moment, realize that it did.

"I don't," I lie. "I don't like anyone believing something like that of me."

"So if you aren't interested in her," Jace says, "I can be, right?"

My gut clenches. "Of course. A hundred percent."

He grins.

I feel like punching him.

"Want a beer?" he asks, already past it.

"In a minute." I turn back to my dad. "You need to authorize this party, because it's a celebration. It's not a business that might be a risky venture. But if you don't authorize a fully-paid-for Christmas party for this town, the townspeople aren't going to appreciate that."

My father opens his mouth but then closes it, because he knows I'm right.

"Jace, I'll take that beer now."

We sit down in front of the fireplace and take gulps from longnecks. The fire crackles and pops in a way my gas fireplace in New York doesn't. My dad crosses his cowboy boots at the ankle and lays back his head.

"This isn't so bad, you know," Jace tells me. "I've always loved it here. I never quite understood why you wanted to get away from it."

"You can't understand?" I ask. "Really?"

"Obviously, I understand one reason. But I don't think that's the entire reason. I really don't."

I stare him down, not blinking. Neither does he.

Finally, I sigh. "I like the city because I disappear there. If I'd stayed here, everyone would've expected things from me. Traditional things. Things like having a white picket fence, two point five children, and a golden retriever. I never want those things," I say limply, and it honestly feels good to say the words aloud after keeping them silent for so long.

"You *never* want to settle down?" Jace asks dubiously. "I don't believe that. That's a midlife crisis talking."

"I grew up without a mother. I understand better than anyone that life can change in the blink of an eye, that a kid can be orphaned, that someone can die. I'm never putting a child through that risk of . . . emotional annihilation. Not when I know very, very well what it feels like."

Jace stares at me. "Dude, you're willing to never have a family because there's a slight risk that something could happen and your kids could be orphaned? Do you understand how illogical that is?"

He means well, but it's a knife that cuts clean and deep. I flinch.

"Do you know what it feels like to live it?" I ask. "If not, then do not debate this with me. It's not your business, anyway."

I rock back into the sofa.

"You're right," he agrees. "It's not my decision to make. But you're wrong—I do understand the fear. Because let's be honest here. You're coming from a place of fear. You're afraid to feel those very deep emotions again, and you want to protect others from it.

"But guess what? You can't. You will feel pain again—and so will I. I live in fear that today is the day my mom forgets me forever. I know that one of these days, it will be true. But instead of letting that fear control me, I focus on living each moment that I can with her right now, and on making every moment count for her."

I stare at Jace, and pins seem to prick the backs of my eyes. "I'm sure you do, man. I didn't mean otherwise."

He nods. "I know. You're just not the only one who understands pain."

"I know," I agree. "I'm not. I'm sorry. We good, man?"

"Of course," he says quickly, slapping me on the shoulder. "We'll always be good."

My father snores lightly, oblivious to our conversation.

"About Noel . . ." My voice trails off as I watch the orange flames.

"I knew it!" Jace crows. "You're into her, too."

"It's complicated," I grumble.

"The best things always are. May the best man win?"

I nod. "May the best man win."

"No hard feelings?"

I shake my head. "Never."

Then we shake on it.

It's as I'm getting ready for bed that my phone dings with a text. I look immediately, thinking it might be Noel.

It's not. It's Heather.

I need to talk to you in person ASAP.

Well, that's mysterious, I answer.

It has to do with the election.

You have my attention, I reply. I can meet you tomorrow.

CHAPTER TWENTY-TWO

Noel

*W*ater drips onto my face, and somehow, even in sleep, I feel a dark shadow.

I shriek and try to jump up. Elliott yelps and jumps away, running down the hallway. He'd been crouching over me, drooling on me. It wasn't an intruder in a rainstorm.

Moxie chases after Elliott, and I wipe my face off with my blanket and sigh, looking at the time.

7:30 A.M.

It is *much* too early for this.

My feet are freezing, so I get up and stuff them into fleece socks. Since I'm up, I head down to the kitchen to make coffee.

It's dark, and while I'm turning on lamps, I find Elliott crouched behind the chair in the living room.

I bend down. "Hey," I say softly. "I didn't mean to scare you."

He turns his big eyes up toward me.

"I promise," I say, kissing him on the forehead.

His tail thumps the floor, and I smile. I'm forgiven.

"Why were you hovering over me like that, anyway?" I ask him. "Were you checking on me, bud?"

He pants and soaks up the attention, unbothered.

After I make my coffee, I take a steaming cup with me back to my bedroom so I can work before my parents get up.

My eyes light up when I see Pad's name in my inbox.

From: <Padraig.Sinclair@sleighmail.com>
To: <n.turner@parkerhamiltonpublishing.com>
Subject: One More

Dear Noel,

I find myself in a bit of a creative flow. I'm hoping to get several more chapters done soon. In the meantime, here is one more chapter.

Thank you for your patience,
Pad

PS: I trust our resident House Horse is well? ;)

I eye the House Horse and watch how he's already asleep again, already snoring, his lips making a perfect O.

From: <n.turner@parkerhamiltonpublishing.com>
To: <Padraig.Sinclair@sleighmail.com>
Subject: Re: One More

Dear Pad,

House Horse is extremely well. In fact, if you ever need to go out of town in the future, I'd be happy to Horse-sit. We're growing rather attached to him.

I'm diving into your chapter now!

Best,
Noel

When he'd left this dog with me, I would never have imagined that I'd end up liking him so much. Or that I could sleep through such loud snoring.

Elliott's eyes open, and he stares at me as though he can sense that I'm thinking about him. There is such unconditional approval in his eyes that I shake my head.

"We don't deserve dogs," I tell him. "Although I'm still mad that you splashed hot chocolate on my coat."

He thumps his tail.

"You're forgiven." I sigh. "Like always."

He thumps his tail again.

"You're a good boy," I tell him.

"Noel," my mother calls. "We have a visitor!"

At eight A.M.?

I pull my robe on and walk to the kitchen with Elliott on my heels. Moxie is on his back, yawning.

I find Jace in the kitchen, having a cup of coffee and a piece of toast.

"I came with a delivery; I wasn't expecting to be fed," he says. "But I never turn down food."

My mom laughs. She loves feeding people.

"Good morning," I greet them. "Everyone is up so early."

"I'm sorry," Jace tells me, although his grin says that he is decidedly not. "I wanted to give your permit approval to you in person. Judd signed it this morning."

"He did?"

Jace nods and hands the signed document to my mom. "The ink is barely dry."

"Will wonders never cease," my mom says, shaking her head. "Rich, you'd better go buy a Powerball ticket before our luck runs out."

"No joke," my dad agrees, taking a swig of black coffee. I reach for the pot.

"Pardon me, but is that cat riding your dog?" Jace inquires politely.

"That's what they do now," I tell him. "It's not weird."

"Not at all," he agrees, eyeing them in amazement. "Anyway. I know you'll be rushing around to prepare for your party, so I wanted to offer my services. If you need help, I'm happy to give it."

"Well, that's so kind of you," my mother gushes, catching my eye over his head. Her expression plainly says, *This one is a keeper.*

I give my head one shake. A clear message: *Knock it off.*

She grins.

I glare.

Jace stares. "I'm sorry, did I do something?"

"Not you," I tell him sweetly. "Not you at all. Thank you for the offer. I'm sure we can use you in a hundred different ways. But won't the Blakes be annoyed?"

"Of course not," he answers. "I'll be helping them, too."

"Smart man," Dad says. "What idea did you bring to Judd, anyway? The one that's better than mine?"

Jace pauses, and I can see that he doesn't know how much to say.

"You don't have to say anything," I tell him. "At all."

"You'll know soon enough anyway," he decides. "It's not a secret. My mother has struggled with Alzheimer's for years. It's a cruel disease that strips people of their dignity. I read about a 'memory village' in Norway, where they turn a small town into an amazing care facility." He talks of the details for a few minutes, then ends with "It could change lives."

My mouth is open, so I close it.

"That's . . . very noble," I manage to say.

Jace smiles. "Not really. I just want to take care of my mom. She's given me everything over the years. It's time I give back."

My heart melts inside of my ribs.

"That's . . ."

"We'll need to see how your business plan shakes out," my father interrupts.

"Of course," Jace says, standing up. "Anyway. I didn't mean to hijack your morning. I just wanted to deliver the good news in person. Have a lovely day."

I show him to the door and close it after him.

"Just because he has a good idea, and a good reason, doesn't mean that his idea is better than ours," my mom says when I return.

"No, it doesn't," I agree. "But, man. He has a really noble 'why' factor."

"So?"

I shrug. "When you're trying to sell an idea to an audience, you need to sell them on the *why*. They don't always buy your product, but they buy why you're doing it. He wants to do this for a noble reason. What is *your* 'why' factor? How will you convince the people in this town that your idea is just as noble?"

"We need to talk to your marketing team today," my mom says quickly. My dad nods.

"You do that," I say. "Get your ducks in a row."

"What will you be doing?"

"I have a chapter to read," I say as I get a refill of coffee. "For my *real* job."

I return to my bedroom and close the door.

Pad's chapter pulls me in within seconds and weaves a tale that brings a threat in the form of another woman who chases after Jack before he and Nora can figure out that they're meant to be.

I pick up my phone and text Emily.

> Check your email.

She answers me twenty minutes later.

> If he has Jack misstep with her, I'll kill Pad.
> Seriously. Where have all the good guys gone?

I don't know that it's considered stepping out if he's not dating Nora, I answer.

He should want NO ONE other than Nora, she says. That's true love.

Sometimes it takes people awhile to understand what is meant for them, I answer.

A while, she corrects.

I send her a glaring face.

She sends me a crying-laughing face. And so the student becomes the master.

> Not quite yet, padawan.

I set my phone down and stretch.

I'm half afraid to emerge from the bedroom because I'm sure my mom's to-do list for me is ten miles long. On the other hand, the longer I put it off, the later I'll have to stay up tonight to do it all.

I get dressed, pull my hair into a bun, and go fresh-faced. I find my mom in the dining room, the entire table covered with refrigerator magnets.

Right here, right now.
Rich Turner: It's time for change.

"I'd like for you and Elliott to go hand these out in the town square today," she requests while counting the magnets. "Can you?"

"What else?"

"Pardon?" Mom looks up now.

"What else do you have on my list? I know that wasn't all."

She sniffs. "I don't know what on earth you're talking about."

"There's literally a list right there with my name on it," I point out, and I grab it. She lunges but doesn't get there in time.

Noel To-Do

Hand out magnets

Pick up lights from Lowe's in Cheyenne

Stop by post office with Christmas party mailers

"You want me to drive to Cheyenne today after I hand out the magnets? Do you intend on me being able to come home tonight, or should I just pitch a tent somewhere?"

"You're really so dramatic." My mom sighs. "Yes, if you could, that would be so helpful. We've got a lot of preparing to do in just a few days. The town square has never seen as many lights as we're going to hang in it." She hums as she stacks and stamps mailers.

"Oh, and I made this for when you hand out the magnets." She holds up a smocklike apron with a huge pocket. It's filled with mini candy canes.

"It's a fanny pack for Elliott," she says proudly. "So, he'll be 'handing out' candy canes. People will love it."

"You're beginning to scare me," I tell her. "I had no idea you were so calculating."

She cackles, taking it as a compliment. I'm still not sure if I meant it as one, but I do take the smock. That's when I notice the letters.

VOTE FOR RICH.

"Um," I say, holding it out and looking at it.

"Yes?" Mom says.

"Nothing." I decide to pick my battles. She already has Elliott dressed in his Christmas sweater. I'm almost surprised that she hasn't arranged an elf costume for me to wear.

When I mention as much, her eyes light up.

"NO," I say, holding up my hand. "That's where I put my foot down. I'm not dressing up as an elf to Elliott's Santa."

"But . . ."

"No."

My mom gives up, sensing a losing battle.

"I'm sorry, boy," I tell him as I suit him up in the smock. A pocketful of candy canes hangs on each of his sides.

"It's a nice design," I commend her. "It's like . . . a candy saddle. You're talented."

It takes Elliott a moment to get used to the crackling sound of the candy cane wrappers as he walks, but then it doesn't faze him.

"You're a natural, boy," I tell him when we're walking down the street.

Once we get to the town square, we start to gather some stares. I begin handing out the magnets, and children flock to Elliott. He eats up the attention, and the kids love getting candy from a dog.

"It's good to see you," Becky Tanler tells me as she takes a magnet.

"Your hair looks gorgeous," Sydney Welsh says to me later, and she bends to get a candy from Elliott.

Then I hear, "You give a new meaning to the phrase *giving*

candy to babies." And Jonah is standing in front of me in a tailored peacoat, one hand in a pocket and the other holding a coffee.

His eyes seem a bit gold in the sunlight.

"That's not how the saying goes," I answer, and I feel my cheeks flush.

"I know," he replies. "I have a habit of changing things to fit my needs."

"Do you?" I ask, amused now.

He pats Elliott's head.

"It's a bad habit," he admits.

"When is the last time you can remember not getting something you want?" I ask.

He thinks on that.

"Hmm. I can't remember a recent instance."

His tawny hair curls just below his ear, and I fight the urge to reach out and smooth down that curl.

"Noel?" he says politely, and I realize that I haven't been paying attention.

"Yes?"

"Would you be so kind as to call Elliott off my foot?" He smiles politely and gestures to the dog, who has literally collapsed onto his boot.

I sigh. "When he's done, he's done, and the timing is always inconvenient."

Jonah chuckles. "Well, if you can't get him to walk home, I promise that if you're still here when I'm done with my appointment, I'll give you both a ride."

"In your new car?" I ask, perking up.

He laughs. "No."

"Do you still have it?" I ask.

"For the time being."

I can't tell if that means he's giving it back. "I thought you weren't accepting it?"

"I'm taking my time returning it." He shrugs. "What can I say? You can't fault a man for liking to look at beautiful things."

The way he watches me now, as though *I'm* the beautiful thing, makes my belly flutter a bit.

"Is it a deal?" he asks. "If you're still here when I get back, I'll drive you home."

"It's a deal," I tell him.

I manage to pull Elliott just enough to slide him off Jonah's shoe, and he walks away, his collar up against the winter wind.

He looks utterly dashing. There is absolutely no denying it.

I coax, lure, and beg Elliott to move just enough to get off the sidewalk, and it's when we're standing on a patch of grass that I look up and see Heather Reid with Jonah.

He's leaning against the building, and she reaches up to touch his collar. It's an invasion of his personal space, and he looks perfectly fine with it. In fact, a minute later, he touches her wrist.

It makes my stomach clench, and I turn away.

CHAPTER TWENTY-THREE

Jonah

I blink against the cold wind as I watch Noel beg Elliott to get off the sidewalk. She bends, pats her knees, crouches, and then practically hangs around his neck to get the big animal to move.

I chuckle aloud, and Heather eyes me.

"Well?" she says. "What do you say?"

Shoot. I have no idea what she's asked. In fact, I had no idea that her hand was on the top button of my coat.

It makes me uncomfortable, and I pull away a bit.

She notices.

"So you aren't free tonight?"

I shake my head. "I'm sorry. I can't tonight. I promised my dad I'd help with something. I should be doing that now, but your text said it was urgent." I'm hinting for her to get to the point.

Noel won't wait forever, I'm sure.

"I'm sorry for the mysterious vibe—I just didn't want to text this," she says hesitantly. "My dad is on the town council. If you want, I can talk to him for you."

"Talk to him?"

"On your behalf," she says slowly, as though I'm a bit dense. "I can try to sway the vote."

"I hope that my father's business plan is enough to stand on its own," I say, because there's no way I'm taking a favor. Not from anyone. The unintended consequences never pan out well.

"Oh, I'm sure it will," she says quickly. "But just to be on the safe side, I'll talk to him. It's fine, Jonah. I've got you." She starts to walk away, so I grab her wrist. Lightly, but still.

I release it quickly.

"Don't talk to him," I tell her. "Please."

She looks up at me, her eyes wide. "But I can sway him to your side."

I shake my head. "I don't want it that way. It needs to be fair."

"Sure, Jonah. Whatever you want." She's clearly confused, maybe even offended.

I'm walking away when she speaks again. "It's not a crime to accept help from people, Jonah."

I turn. "The plan for Winter Falls needs to stand on its own merit—the people here deserve to choose."

"Okay," she says, giving in. "Okay."

I nod and walk away. By the time I get back across the town square, Noel is gone. I glance up and down the street, and she's nowhere to be found.

I climb in the SUV and motor down the street, keeping an eye out for Noel.

Shoppers come in and out of the town square shops, their

hands filled with gifts and wrapping paper. I think I spot Elliott but realize it's a small woman carrying an oversized stuffed bear.

As I putter past city hall, I instinctively glance through the window to see if my dad is at his desk. He's not, of course. He's at home, and I know that.

But I find myself thinking of all the other times he *wasn't*. All the days and nights and weekends that he'd been at that desk, every time I'd looked, every time I'd driven past with a friend's family or my grandmother or a babysitter.

He's spent a *lot* of time away from the house because he just couldn't bring himself to be there without my mom . . . and he'd never seemed to realize what an effect that had on me.

And then he has the nerve to guilt *me* because I don't like coming back here?

I turn into the drive, my knuckles white as I grip the wheel. I see my father peering through the kitchen window, a glower on his face.

"You said you'd go pick up the grain first thing this morning," he says as I come through the door, stomping snow off my boots. "But you weren't here, so I had to send Jace."

Crap. I'd forgotten.

"I had an errand that took longer than I planned," I say, not quite apologizing. "Why didn't you just go? Jace isn't used to driving a truck."

"I had a meeting I couldn't miss. Zoom meetings are something else, aren't they?"

"Everyone hates them," I agree.

"Can you hear me? You're on mute. Patty, you're still on mute. It was painful."

"When should Jace be back? I'd like to review his financials."

"It's hard to say. At least an hour, maybe an hour and a half. Izzy's here, in her room. I gave her your mom's old jar of buttons to look through. She seems to be having fun."

"Do you mind if I use your den for a while?" I ask Dad, my voice cool. He shakes his head.

"Sure—go ahead. Everything okay?"

"I just need to work for a bit. Thanks."

I feel him staring after me, but I don't look back. For some reason, pent-up resentment is boiling, and I don't know why here and why now, but I do know that if I don't get some space from him, I just might blow.

I set up shop at his desk. I answer emails, get back to Millie on a few things, and have two conference calls: one with my COO and one with my CFO.

I check in with my CMO, and then when I'm finished meeting with my senior staff, I close my laptop.

A picture frame pokes out from a pile of paperwork, and I pull it out.

It's an old photo of my mother and me.

I remember this one. My grandmother framed it and put it in my room after Mom died, hoping to keep her memory alive. One day, after the housekeeper had cleaned my room, I noticed it was gone. No one could find it.

And here it is, years later, on my father's desk.

I take it to him. "Where did you find this?" I ask, my fingers wrapped around the frame.

He looks away. "I had it in my den," he finally answers.

I pause, meeting his gaze. "This whole time?"

He nods, once, and I feel my blood pulsing in my forehead.

"Son, I didn't want you to dwell on things that couldn't be changed. Your mom was gone, and you needed to wrap your mind around that. When your gran gave you that picture, all you wanted to do was sit and look at it."

"So *you took it*?" I ask in disbelief. "You took a child's photo of his dead mother? Dad, that's messed up. I looked at that picture because *I didn't want to forget her face*."

"Don't villainize me," he says, and there is real pain in his voice. "You weren't the one who had to explain to his four-year-old son that his mother was never coming home."

"No, but I was the four-year-old son who had to hear that message," I say. "It was no picnic, either. And when you didn't let me even talk about her . . . what do you think that does to a kid, Dad? And then you stopped coming home, too. First Mom, and then you. I was all alone. *What do you think that does to a kid?*"

My father is a deer in the headlights, but I can't stop.

"I was a child who needed a therapist. I needed to process that loss, I needed for you to be present so that I wasn't afraid of losing you. But you weren't."

"I couldn't be in this house," my dad says, his voice raspy, thin. "Every little thing here was Sara. I couldn't even breathe here, kid. It hurt too much."

"You slept at city hall," I say slowly. "You weren't even here when I woke up in the night with nightmares about being alone."

My dad is stricken, and his face is gaunter than I remember it. It gives me pause.

"I was just a man who didn't know what to do," he answers. "I thought you'd be happier without being exposed to my misery day in and day out. I didn't want you to think that I was upset with *you*."

"The message I received is that if you love someone too much, the pain is too great to bear when they leave," I tell him. "I learned not to talk about those things. I learned not to acknowledge it. I eventually learned not to feel it—in fact, to try not to think of it at all."

"I thought that was for the best," Dad says simply.

"But I'm the one who never had a mom who could deliver treats to the class, and I'm the one who didn't have a mom to make sure I had haircuts and checkups, or a mom to take me back-to-school shopping . . ."

"You never went without," my father protests. "Did I let your hair get a bit shaggy sometimes in between haircuts? Maybe so, but I had a lot on my mind, and shaggy hair isn't a crime."

"No, it isn't. But growing up without a mother was hard enough, without also having a father who banned all mention of her."

"I didn't ban all mention of her," he answers gruffly.

"Not verbally," I tell him. "But I learned not to do it. Every time you'd flinch when I'd bring her up, it told me to stop. And eventually, I did."

"Are you saying I damaged you?" my dad asks. "Because again, I'll just say that I did the best I could. There is no handbook telling a widower how to handle a situation like that."

"No, there isn't," I agree. "And back then, there wasn't the internet to give you advice."

"So are you saying you understand?" my dad asks, uncertain.

"I don't know what I'm saying," I admit. "I don't like coming here, Dad. I don't like being reminded."

My father stares at me. Then nods.

"I know. It hasn't escaped my attention that you've used every possible excuse over the years to not come home."

"Do you blame me?" I ask, and there is a flash of pain in my voice that I wish I could hide.

My dad catches it and shakes his head. "How can I?" he answers.

"You can't," I agree. "I've got issues that I've never worked out. In fact, I didn't even know I had them."

"Everyone has issues, kid," he tells me.

I take the photo back and set it up on his desk. My mom smiles at me, her grin broad and happy. She holds me in her arms, and I'm laughing.

"She loved you," my dad says from the doorway. "With all her heart."

"I know," I tell him. "I've never doubted that."

He nods and then leaves. I hear him talking to Izzy a few minutes later, very patient and very kind. My phone buzzes, and when I look, I find a text from Hoff.

Well?

I realize suddenly that I'd never responded at all when the car had arrived. Too much was going on here.

I'm still considering, I answer. The car was a nice touch.

How did you know that I'd like it? I add.

You mentioned it in an interview a couple years ago. When I want something, I do my research.

I put my phone away.

Restlessly, I poke through a stack of bins in the corner. One of them has other old photos and a couple yearbooks. I thumb through them, finding pictures of me baiting my first hook, wearing my first cowboy hat, playing in my first football game. Through everything, even though I didn't have a mom, my dad was certainly there.

Flaws and all.

A random thought occurs to me—he was my age when my mom died; in fact, he was a few years younger. If I were in that position right now, I wouldn't know what to do. At all.

A yellowed bit of newspaper pokes out from beneath a yearbook, and I reach for it. I find a stack of newspaper clippings— all articles in the *Wall Street Journal* featuring me, spanning the past decade.

I swallow hard. I've been hard on him. Too hard.

I get up and walk back to the living room, taking the bin with me. I find my dad doing a puzzle with Izzy.

I sit at the table and riffle through the yearbooks. There's a picture from my sophomore year of him volunteering his time as assistant football coach. He was there for every game.

"Dad," I say out of the blue. "I appreciate you."

"Don't you have anything better to do than get sentimental?" my dad answers gruffly.

I turn the page of the yearbook and find the cheerleading squad, photographed as they were doing drills by the football field.

Noel is wearing a red bow in her red ponytail as she raises her arms in a V.

Behind her, I'm crouched low on the football field, my face sweaty.

There's no way I wouldn't have noticed a girl as pretty as Noel a mere twenty yards away.

I sit back in my chair.

"What's wrong, Jerry?" Izzy asks me, concerned.

I smile at her gently. "Nothing, Izz. I just realized that I did used to know someone. I just don't remember it *at all*."

With a start, I realize that's how Izzy must feel all the time, and my gut contracts.

It must be awful.

And I know, in this moment, that I want to make this memory village happen. Not just to breathe life back into this town, but to help all the Izzys out in the world.

"I'm a hundred percent in, Dad," I tell him. "For the memory village."

"I know, son," he answers.

"I mean it. I want it to happen. Not just for you and this town, but for everyone out there like Izzy who needs it."

"I know, kiddo." He looks up at me. "I knew you'd get here."

"Where?"

"To this moment where you found yourself personally invested."

"And you knew that all along?"

Dad nods. "You're my son. I know you."

I don't know why I feel like tearing up. I turn away and hear my dad chuckling.

I don't trust myself to look, but when he gets up to refill Izzy's ice water, he puts his hand on my shoulder as he walks by.

It says everything that he can't verbalize, and more.

CHAPTER TWENTY-FOUR

Noel

That's never going to fit in this car," I tell the Lowe's worker, a friendly fellow who has just wheeled out two pallets' worth of white Christmas lights.

"You're correct," he agrees, eyeing the small trunk. "I can take it inside while you arrange for other transport. It's no problem."

Not for him.

"Thank you," I tell him. "Do you have trucks I can rent here?"

"We do, but I believe I just heard my manager say they were all gone right now. But I'll run and check for you."

"Thank you."

He leaves, and I call my mother.

"You ordered enough Christmas lights to decorate Fifth Avenue," I tell her. "It won't fit in the car! There's two entire pallets!"

"Lord, Noel, calm down," she says, and I envision her holding the phone away from her ear. "You're shrieking."

"I'm standing at Lowe's with no way to haul two wooden pallets of Christmas lights in the car," I tell her. "So I'm a little frustrated."

"It'll all work out, Noel," she says. "Don't be dramatic."

"Mom, seriously. I'm standing here in the snow and the wind. It would've been nice if you'd told me that all this wouldn't fit in the car that you knew I was driving to pick it up. That's all I'm saying."

"That's fair," she concedes. "You're right. I'm sorry, honey."

"It's okay." I sigh. "I don't mean to be grumpy."

"I know, sweetie. Have you eaten today?"

"Yes," I answer, annoyed. "I'm not hangry, Mom."

"I just thought I'd ask."

"I'm trying to rent a pickup here at Lowe's," I tell her, but as I do, the worker comes back out. He sees I'm on the phone, so he just holds up the thumbs-down signal. "Drat. Nope. They don't have any available right now. Which one of your friends is most likely free to come over with a pickup?"

My mom thinks. "Um, well, we could ask Wyatt or his brother Jeremy. But I think they're on the two-day fishing retreat that Louise was talking about at book club yesterday." She thinks again. "We could ask Tom next door, but I saw him leave in his pickup a little bit ago. I don't know when he'll be back. You know, you could ask Jonah. His dad has one."

"You think he'll want to help us set up for this party?" I ask doubtfully. "You know they don't want us to have it."

"They approved it," Mom says simply.

"That's true. And I'm desperate." I think on it and sigh. "Okay, fine. I'll try Jonah."

I hang up and call him.

He answers on the first ring.

"I don't suppose you'd want to rescue me again?"

He laughs, a husky sound that tightens my chest a bit.

"I'm getting pretty good at this whole white knight thing," he answers. "Whatcha need?"

I try to put the image of him with Heather out of my head. "I'm stranded at Lowe's. My mom sent me to pick up Christmas lights for the party, and she failed to tell me that there were two full pallets of them."

"Whoa," Jonah replies. "Does she intend on lighting up the entire state of Wyoming?"

"It appears that way. Anyway, I was wondering if you could possibly help me out with your dad's truck?"

Jonah pauses, and I rush to add, "But you're not obligated. If you're busy, that's fine."

"It's not that," he says. "I just don't have it right now. Jace took it to pick up grain for the horses, and he's not back yet. If you don't mind, I can call him and have him swing over and pick it up for you."

"Mind? That would be fantastic."

"Okay. I'll try to reach him, then I'll text you to let you know."

"You're going to get the white knight badge," I promise him.

"I'm counting on it!" I almost hear the wink in his voice, and I smile in spite of myself. "Stand by."

He hangs up, and I do stand by. Literally. I stand by the front curb at Lowe's, rubbing my mittened hands together in the cold.

Two minutes later, a text comes in from Jonah.

He's en route. ETA: ten minutes.

OMG, you're a lifesaver, I reply.

Luckily, he was in Cheyenne for the grain already.

I pull my car away from the front curb and park it in a slot before I go inside to buy a thick pair of work gloves. I have a sneaking suspicion that I'll be helping hang these two pallets of lights.

As I browse, I see a poinsettia that my mother would like, with rich full red leaves. I buy it, and they cover it in plastic so the winter wind doesn't shock it.

I return to the doorway just in time to see Judd's old red truck rumble up to the curb. Jace sees me and waves, a big grin on his face.

"I don't think I've seen you when you're not smiling," I greet him. "Are you really this happy all the time?"

"What's not to be happy about?" he asks. "I get to help out a beautiful lady today. I'd call that a good day."

I shake my head. "I'm sorry to ask you to go out of your way. But you truly are a lifesaver."

"Where are the goods?" he asks, opening his door and getting out. "I'll get them loaded."

We head back inside and find them right inside the door, still on the cart.

Jace easily maneuvers the cart, and between the two of us, we manage to get them loaded, although Jace definitely takes the brunt of the weight.

He secures them with a tie-down, then opens the passenger-side door for me.

"Your chariot, madam," he says, offering his hand.

"Oh, it's okay," I tell him. "My car is right over there."

Jace eyes it doubtfully. "Errr, I'm not doubting your driving skills at all, but there's a nasty snowstorm coming in. When's the last time you drove in a blizzard?"

I hesitate.

"That's what I thought." He chuckles. "Leave your car. Ride with me. We can see better in the truck."

"Thank you," I say. I take his hand and get settled with the poinsettia on my lap.

As he pulls out of the lot, I text my mom.

> I found a truck. I'm going to leave the car parked directly outside the garden section and we can come back for it tomorrow. There's a nasty storm coming.

I slip my phone back into my purse.

As we drive toward Winter Falls, we make small talk and listen to Christmas music. I find Jace just as lighthearted and fun as he appears to be. He sings "Jingle Bells" at the top of his lungs and waits for me to join in. When I don't, he starts the song from the beginning.

He's trying to force me into being as happy as he is. It's obnoxious, but also a little endearing.

"Jingle bells, jingle bells," I sing. Jace grins.

"That's the spirit," he encourages me.

"You're just trying to soak up all the Christmas spirit you can before you go back to Scrooge's house." I laugh.

Jace chuckles but then sobers. "He's a really good person," he tells me.

"Judd? Or Jonah?"

"Both," he says. "They're cut from the same cloth. Judd is obviously rougher around the edges and old-school, but they're the same deep down where it counts."

"Is that a good thing?"

"It's the *best* thing." Jace nods.

"Why are you telling me this?"

He shrugs. "I don't know. I just feel like you see this cantankerous side to Judd, and that's not all he is. He's got his reasons for avoiding the holiday."

"So I've heard," I answer. "I get that. I do. It's just not fair to punish an entire town because of an issue *he* has."

"No, it isn't fair," he agrees with me. "But I do think he'll come around. At least a bit. He doesn't want to limit people, Noel. He just doesn't want to face his own pain. I'm surprised you haven't picked up on that by now."

"Are we still talking about Judd?" I ask. "Or Jonah?"

He smiles. "Both."

He turns onto the highway that runs through town. The tires hum as we barrel down the road.

"This old thing feels like a lumber wagon," I remark.

"I hope you weren't partial to your kidneys," he says. "They might bounce out."

I chuckle, then lean my forehead against the cool glass of the passenger-seat window.

The snowy fields blur by as we drive, and for a while, I just enjoy the vastness of the country and how we go for miles without seeing another vehicle.

"It's not like this in New York," I tell Jace. "There's so much open space here."

"I know. Cities make me feel claustrophobic."

"I like both," I decide. "For different reasons. I love the energy of the city and the life. I love the lights. I love the bustle. But here, I love that I can breathe."

He doesn't ask what I mean by that; it seems as though he already knows. He nods.

"That's the perfect way to describe it," he says. *I can breathe here.*"

"O Holy Night" comes on, and he turns it up. "I love this one," he says.

The music is peaceful, and it's perfect with the glistening snow surrounding us.

What happens next seems to happen in slow motion.

With my forehead pressed to the glass, I see a streak of movement, then two large canine bodies running into the road in flashes of gray fur.

Instinctively, Jace hits the brakes, but the bed of the truck breaks away and swings around.

We spin in the road and then we're sliding. Our tires can't find traction, so we skid and skid. We careen into the ditch, then up and into the snow embankment with a hard thud.

My head slams into the glass, which actually cracks.

The silence is loud as we sit still for a moment, dazed. I shake my head, reaching my fingers to touch my injury. My fingers come back bloody.

Jace throws open the glove box and searches, grabbing some clean napkins. He presses them to my wound, then leans into my face.

"Are you okay?" he asks. "God, I'm so sorry." He looks into my eyes and holds up his fingers. "How many fingers do you see?"

"Three. Were those . . . wolves?"

Jace nods. "I think so."

"Are *you* okay?" I ask him, scanning his body.

"I'm fine," he assures me.

"Do you think they're out here watching us?" I ask, eyeing the cracked window.

The wind howls outside the truck, whirling the snow around us. It's slightly eerie, and I picture hungry wolves circling us.

"We're okay," he tells me. "They don't attack humans like that. They're too smart. They only attack what they know they can kill. They're survivors."

"Can we get out of here?" I ask. "Just in case."

"Here goes nothing," he says, nodding. He shifts the truck into four-wheel drive, and to our mutual surprise, we aren't stuck. The tires spin for a second, then slowly pull us out of the ditch. Jace turns it onto the road and crows triumphantly before he stops in the middle of the road.

He grabs my chin and turns my face to look at it.

"I can't tell if you need stitches or not. Head wounds bleed so much. Judd's house is nearby. Can I take you there so we can clean it up and look at it?"

I nod, and all of a sudden, I feel woozy and my teeth begin to chatter.

Jace notices. "You're in shock," he says. "It's normal, don't worry." He pulls me over until my head rests on his shoulder, his arm around my shoulders.

"You're warm," I say, shivering.

He turns the heater on full blast. "We're almost there," he tells me. He drives faster than he should, making the wind whistle through the cracks on the window.

A couple minutes later, we pull into Judd's driveway. Judd and Jonah are outside, messing with something on the porch. I can tell the second Jonah sees me. His eyes fill with concern. He's got the passenger-side door open before the truck even comes to a full stop.

"What happened?" he demands, unfastening my seat belt and helping me from the truck. I stumble, still dizzy. His brow furrows, and he simply scoops me up, heading to the house.

Judd opens the door for him, and Jonah carries me in, depositing me gently onto the leather sofa. A fire is roaring, and he wraps a warm blanket around me, crouching in front of me to examine my wound.

"There's at least one glass sliver in it," he says, peering at it.

"I don't think you need stitches, but, Dad, come see what you think. Dad was a corpsman in the navy," he tells me.

Judd comes to check me over.

"There's definitely glass in it, and we need to clean it out. I don't think it needs stitches, either. But we'll need to watch her for a concussion."

"I'm just going to take her to the ER in Cheyenne," Jonah says, standing up, but his father is already shaking his head.

"You can't. You can't see six inches in front of you out there right now."

Judd sits on his heels in front of me.

"Squeeze both of my hands," he tells me. So I do.

"Good," he encourages me.

He shines a flashlight quickly into each eye.

"She doesn't seem to be concussed," Judd says. "Although she's in mild shock. We need to keep an eye on her, and I'll continue to check for concussion every couple of hours. Help her into the kitchen, Jonah. I'll get the wound cleaned and dressed."

Judd pulls a chair up to the sink and rolls a towel under my neck, as though I were at a salon. He gently flushes the cut until he's sure that every tiny piece of glass is gone. He pats it dry with clean gauze, applies antibiotic ointment, and then covers it with more gauze, then a nonstick bandage.

"I probably look like I have a head wound." I laugh.

"You do have a head wound," Jonah points out.

"Good point," I tell him.

"I'm going to call Rich and Suze to let them know that she'll be safe here tonight," Judd says. "I'll need to wake you up every couple hours tonight, just to be on the safe side."

"Thank you," I answer, and I squeeze his hand.

"Of course. Don't worry about a thing." He looks at Jonah. "There's a heating pad in the top shelf of my closet. Can you get it?"

Jonah leaves immediately.

"I'm sorry about that farm truck," Judd apologizes. "I guess I really *do* need to get a new one. I got rear-ended a few years back, and I never had the airbags reset. So it's my fault you're bleeding right now. I'm sorry."

"It's not your fault," I tell him. "Honestly, the way those wolves came out of nowhere, we're lucky it wasn't worse."

"Wolves?" Judd asks.

"A few wolves ran into the road in front of us," Jace confirms. "Brakes locked up."

"I've seen some tracks around the barn lately—they must be hungry. I'd better keep the horses in the barn at night for now."

Jonah returns with a large heating pad, and they get me situated on the couch, snuggled up with the heating pad and several blankets. He sits next to me and watches me like a hawk, with a gaze so intense, it's almost unnerving.

"I'm fine," I say finally. "Why do you keep looking at me?"

"Just making sure," he answers. "I'm not convinced you don't have a concussion."

"You don't need to sit here and watch me," I tell him. "Seriously. I'm feeling better. See? My teeth aren't chattering anymore."

"Well, that's a good start. I'm sorry this happened in our truck."

"It's not your fault," I answer. "It wasn't Jace's, either."

He glances at my bandage and then stares into my eyes. There's such concern in his, such worry, that it almost takes my breath away.

"You're sure you're okay?" he asks, his voice low.

I nod. "I'm positive."

He pulls me to him, and I don't know when I fall asleep. All I know is that when I do, it's in his arms, tucked against his chest.

CHAPTER TWENTY-FIVE

Jonah

I wake when the gray dawn starts peeking through the window. It's early, probably no later than five A.M. The fire is dying, and Noel is snuggled into me like a bear hibernating for winter.

It's odd, but I feel more comfortable than I've felt in quite a while. Noel is soft against me, and she somehow smells like cashmere.

"How's she doing?" My father's voice is low in the doorway.

"She seems to be okay. I fell asleep with her."

"She needed the warmth," he answers. "She was in shock."

"She seems better now." Her cheeks are flushed with a healthy pink.

"She'll be okay," Dad says. "I'm going to put the coffee on."

I nod, and he leaves.

I tighten my arms around her, enjoying this feeling before she wakes up and it turns awkward.

She feels right in my arms.

She feels like *she belongs there.*

"You smell good," she mumbles into my shirt.

"You're awake," I say, surprised.

"And I wish I weren't," she says. "What time is it? Three?"

"Five," I answer.

Her eyes open. "Your dad called my parents, right?"

I nod. "He did. They know you're safe."

"Thank you so much," she says softly. "For all this."

"Please." I wave it away. "If Jace was a better driver, you wouldn't be in this position."

"I heard that," he calls from the kitchen.

"He's up early," Noel remarks.

"I think his mom was up earlier," I say. "I vaguely remember hearing them talking. I was half asleep still. But she tends to wander in the night. He gets up, puts her back to bed, and then he sometimes can't go back to sleep himself."

"He's a good son," she says. "Jonah?"

"Yes?"

"You can let go of me now."

I've still got her wrapped in my arms. I'm surprised at how reluctant I am to let her go, but I do it.

She sits up, her fingers lightly touching her head. "Ow."

"I'll get you some ibuprofen," I tell her, getting up. "And some coffee."

While I'm in the kitchen, I look out the window to find that the storm has passed, and visibility is clear.

I make a cup of coffee, guess at the amount of cream and sugar to add, and carry it to her, along with two painkillers.

"Breakfast of champions," I say as I hand it to her.

She smiles. She's pale but looks so much better than she did yesterday. She sips at her coffee and pulls her phone out.

"Oh, hey, I've only got three hundred texts from my mom," she says wryly.

"That's okay," I answer. "That means she cares."

"If the number of texts she sent is the barometer, then she cares a LOT."

The moment she starts answering them, her phone rings.

"Hi, Mom," she says without even looking at the caller ID.

"Are you okay?" Susan asks. Noel tries to turn the speakerphone off but gives up.

"I'm fine," she promises. "The Blakes have taken incredibly good care of me."

"I'm sending your dad to come get you right now," Susan says. "You need your own bed."

"It's five A.M.," Noel answers, sighing toward me. "Let the man sleep. I'm sipping on some coffee. Let me wake up a little, please. Besides, I don't have a bed at your house. Elliott took it."

I can't help but laugh at that.

Susan hears. "What's so funny?"

"I think he's amused that a canine stole my bed."

"That's exactly why I'm amused," I confirm.

"Well, I'm glad you all think this is funny," Susan answers. "You could've been killed, Noel."

"We slid into a ditch, Mom," I tell her. "I wasn't going to die."

"I'll send your father over when he's up and about," Susan says.

"Thanks, Mom."

She hangs up and looks at me. "My mother has a way of

making everything sound like it's my fault. I should've reminded her that she's the one who sent me out in a snowstorm."

She chuckles, but I cringe. "That might've pushed her over the edge. She sounded really worried."

"She was. But she always is. She's always worried that I'm going to die somehow in a tragic freak accident."

"I'm glad you didn't die," I tell her seriously. Then I smile.

"Me too," she agrees. "Do you know if my parents' Christmas lights are okay?"

"They are. I'll drop them off at the town square later. Are they planning on lighting up landing strips at the Cheyenne airport with those?"

Noel stands up slowly, assessing her balance. "Hey, I'm pretty good," she decides. "I'm not dizzy at all now."

"That's progress!"

She makes her way to the kitchen then stumbles awkwardly backward, right into me.

"Hmm. You wouldn't be fibbing about not being dizzy, would you?" I ask.

She shakes her head. "No. It's just early, and I'm not properly caffeinated yet."

I carry her cup, and deposit her back at the table, in a chair by the window.

The snow outdoors is drifted into banks, glistening like crushed opals as the sun breaks over the horizon.

"How many inches did we get?" she asks my dad.

He glances through the window. "Looks like ten or so."

She takes another sip of coffee, holding her face in the steam, her eyes closed.

"Where'd Jace go?" she asks curiously, without opening them.

"Probably back to bed," I answer.

"Actually, he's out feeding the horses," my father says. "You might want to help."

I hesitate, and Dad notices.

"It wasn't his fault, and you know it."

"Everyone knows not to hit the brakes when something jumps in front you."

"It's instinct," he says simply. "You did the same thing once."

"I was seventeen," I answer evenly. "I didn't know better."

"Well, he'll know better now, too," Dad points out. "She's okay, Jonah. All's well that ends well."

"Uh-huh," I answer. I bundle up, pausing by the door. "I'll be outside if anyone needs me."

I feel Noel watching me as I trudge through the thigh-high snow and pull the barn door back. I glance up and meet her gaze.

Hers is warm, soft, and . . . I blink.

Knock it off. She wants everything in life that I don't.

I break eye contact and close the door behind me.

I find Jace by the corral out back, stroking Denim's nose. I can see the horses have already been fed. I lean against the fence with him.

"I know you're ticked at me," he says without looking over. "And I feel really stupid. I'm sorry."

"It's fine. My father is right—it was an accident."

"You seem *very* protective of Noel," Jace points out. "I knew you might be interested in her, but I didn't realize that you actually care."

"I know. It's very unlike me," I answer wryly.

"You know what I mean."

"Well, she and I are very different people, and we want different things. So it's a road that would lead nowhere."

"Does that mean I have a chance?" Jace grins and lifts an eyebrow.

"Not even slightly."

He laughs. "You know, people change, Jonah. Maybe if you really examine it, what you used to want isn't what you'd want now."

"That's doubtful," I answer, then change the subject. "Was there ice on the back trough? I think I fixed the heater, but I'm not sure."

Jace nods. "You fixed it. You're turning back into quite the country boy."

"Well, sadly, it's like riding a bike."

We close up the grain bins and make our way back toward the house. As I'm pulling the big door shut, Noel steps from the house with her father. My dad escorts them out and helps Noel into the car. I stay where I am, leaning against the barn, but our eyes meet as the car pulls away.

She holds up her hand.

I hold mine up, too, and smile.

She smiles back.

Then they're gone.

"Who was that, Jerry?" Izzy asks when I reenter the warm house. She stares up at me with her white puff of hair and cloudy eyes.

"A friend, Izz."

"Is that all she is?" my dad asks pointedly before he heads back into the house. I don't have an answer, because all of a sudden, I don't know myself.

I spend the afternoon helping Jace with his financial projections, and by dinnertime, we're satisfied with the numbers.

"This is shaping up nicely," I tell him. "It's looking sound. Have you heard back from your developers with their estimate of the builds?"

"It's an initial estimate," he says, "but yes. They'd need to come here and evaluate in person for more concrete estimates."

"That's fine," I answer. "That's perfect."

"What else do we have left?"

"My legal team is checking into the regulations for memory facilities, and the requirements, et cetera. There's bound to be red tape, but a good project manager will sort through it."

"Do you really think this can happen?"

I nod. "I really don't see why not. And if we can't get it done here in Winter Falls, we'll do it elsewhere. This *will* happen, Jace."

"Thank you," he says simply. "You don't know how much I appreciate you."

"Your mom made my life better during a time when I needed it," I tell him. "This is the least I can do to help pay it forward."

He turns away, and if I'm not mistaken, it's because he's tearing up. I pretend not to notice and instead stoke the fire.

"You're a good friend," he says later when we're both sitting in front of the flames.

"So are you," I reply.

My dad carries a chess game in and sets it in front of us. He walks out and never says a word.

I move a piece, starting the game.

We play the rest of the evening, and I have to admit, I feel more at ease tonight in this small, rustic home than I've ever felt in my penthouse condo in New York City.

CHAPTER TWENTY-SIX

Noel

My mother sticks to my side like glue for the rest of the day, asking me if I'm dizzy every five minutes.

"I don't know if we should take her to Cheyenne to be checked out," she frets near bedtime.

"I don't need a doctor," I tell her. "I can make this choice myself. I'm thirty-seven years old. Judd was a navy corpsman, and he says I'm fine."

"What do you think?" Mom asks my dad, as though I'd not spoken at all.

"She seems okay," Dad muses.

"I'm FINE," I insist. "And the only place I'm going is to bed. It's been a long day."

"I'm keeping Elliott and Moxie in our room tonight so that you are undisturbed," she says.

"Now that, I appreciate," I tell her. "But you'll probably regret it."

"We'll be okay," Dad says.

I soak in a hot bath, then change into clean pajamas.

Elliott comes over and sniffs at my head, delicately, as though he knows I've been injured. He lays his face against my shoulder, and he's such a calm, comforting soul. I scratch behind his ears and then give him a hug good night.

He disappears into my parents' room, and I close the door to mine.

I curl up on the fresh sheets, and even though there's nothing better than crisp, clean bedding, I can't sleep.

I toss and turn. As I do, I catch a whiff of Jonah's cologne in my hair. I grab a tendril and bury my nose in it. I stare out the window.

At some point, I sleep.

When I wake, the room is flooded with light, and Elliott is quietly sitting next to me, observing me while I sleep.

I startle, then relax.

"Are you watching over me, boy?" I ask.

He thumps his tail.

"I'm okay, I promise."

He's not convinced and lightly snuffles my bandage. He sits back and observes, waiting.

"Whatcha need?"

He thumps his tail.

"Did Timmy fall down the well?"

His tail thumps again.

"Do you even know who Lassie is?" I ask.

His tail thumps.

"Okay, I'll get up," I tell him.

I pull my robe on and stick my head out my door.

The kitchen light is on, and I can smell coffee and bacon.

Elliott and I enter the kitchen in time for my dad to toss a piece of bacon to the dog. Elliott neatly catches it in his mouth, a trick that they've clearly been practicing.

"Dad, he's supposed to be losing some weight," I tell him. "Bacon isn't gonna do it."

"I don't give him much," Dad claims, and I sense that isn't true at all.

I'm making a cup of coffee when my phone buzzes in my pocket.

I have some news, Emily texts. Michel has decided that he's not into women right now.

Don't freak out. I'm trying to talk him into at least accompanying you to the party. It's only a week away.

I answer her quickly.

NO. Absolutely not. I didn't want to go with him in the first place.

Noel, you need a date, she tells me. You can't go alone.

I certainly can, I reply. I'm a strong, independent woman.

I'll get him to accompany you.

I AM NOT GOING WITH MICHEL.

OMG, she answers. You don't need to get so testy. All you had to do was say so.

I've said so, I answer. A hundred times. You didn't listen. So listen now. I AM NOT GOING WITH MICHEL.

> For all you know, I'll find my own date.

She sends a crying-laughing emoji.

I think of Jonah and his hazel eyes and the way he'd looked at me with utter concern last night.

I'm not kidding, I tell her.

WHO IS IT, she demands. TELL ME EVERYTHING.

There's nothing to tell. YET. I add a wink emoji and then put my phone away.

I climb back into bed and open my laptop instead, and to my absolute delight, there's an email from Pad.

From: <Padraig.Sinclair@sleighmail.com>
To: <n.turner@parkerhamiltonpublishing.com>
Subject: Now we're cooking with gas!

Dear Noel,

These chapters are flowing out of me like water at this point! I've attached several more for your input. I'm interested in how you think we should wrap up this story. According to my calculations, we're about 3/4 done. I need to start pulling it all together now. Nora and Jack are at the point of no return—will they or won't they?

The stakes are high.

I'm interested in your thoughts!

All best,
Pad

From: <n.turner@parkerhamiltonpublishing.com>
To: <Padraig.Sinclair@sleighmail.com>
Subject: Re: Now we're cooking with gas!

Pad,

My mother won't stop knitting sweaters. I've attached a photo of Elliott's Christmas sweater. He's a good sport and wears it without complaint. He'll have a fully stocked wardrobe by the time we leave here.

You should see how fast he's picking up training. He's smarter than he wants us to realize.

I'm diving into your chapters now!

All best,
Noel

True to my word, I do immediately dive in. Nora and Jack's story line envelops me, and I allow myself to get drawn in.

It's when Nora trips while she's hiking and hits her head that I sit up in bed. Jack takes her back to his house and nurses her back to health.

What a coincidence.

I've been filling Pad in on Elliott's hijinks, but I haven't told him about the car accident and hitting my head.

Jack . . . Jonah.

Nora . . . Noel.

Jett . . . Jace.

"Is he using my life to write his book?" I wonder aloud. I think back to anything that I've told him . . . and I haven't told him much about my personal life.

It's impossible.

It's a coincidence.

"Of course it is," I say, feeling dumb.

I write him another email.

From: <n.turner@parkerhamiltonpublishing.com>
To: <Padraig.Sinclair@sleighmail.com>
Subject: Weird coincidence

Dear Pad,

I must admit, some of the parallels between this story and my own life right now are interesting. It's like you're in my head. We must be vibing on the same frequency or something.

I look forward to seeing how you tie everything up. Will they or won't they?

I'm on the edge of my seat, and that's what every good book should do to a person.

Thank you,
Noel

My mom breezes into my room. "That poinsettia looks so beautiful on the kitchen table, Noel. Thank you again for the thoughtful gift."

"It's just a little thing," I tell her. "I just want you to know that you're pretty special."

She looks surprised. "Well, thank you, honey. That's very sweet." She opens my blinds. "Your father and I are going to the town square to start hanging lights. It was so nice of Jace to drop them off. If you need us, call."

"I'll come help," I offer, standing up. She's already shaking her head.

"No. You need to rest. I want you in tip-top shape for the party."

I sit back down. I recognize the tone in her voice. She's not to be trifled with.

"Okay," I concede. "I'll rest. I don't think it's necessary, but I'll do it. Because you've asked me to."

If she's surprised, she hides it well.

"I'm also going to do a bit of Christmas shopping. So you'll be alone here most of the day. If you need anything, I mean it—call. I'm leaving you some lunch to heat up. All you'll have to do is stick it in the microwave."

"Mom, stop worrying," I tell her. "Thank you for the food. Thank you for the fussing. But seriously. I'm okay. And I can feed myself."

"Well, okay," she says. "Call us if you need us."

She breezes back out, and I comb my hair. I check my phone, half hoping there will be a text from Jonah.

There's not. I swallow the disappointment.

It's fine, I decide. It's fine.

I check my phone again an hour later. Still nothing.

At this point, I'm annoyed. I spent the night in this man's arms the night before last. Doesn't that mean something?

No, it wasn't sexual. But he literally used his own body heat to stop me from shivering. That was intimate. I check my phone an hour later, after I've showered.

This time . . . his name is there.

How are you feeling? he asks. I have a question.

I smile, unable to help myself.

What's the question? I reply.

When can I see you again?

My heart ricochets against my rib cage.

I'm coming into town for supplies, and I thought I'd swing by and check on you. If that's ok.

What a gentleman! I answer. I look forward to seeing you.

That's an understatement.

I do my hair, put on light makeup, and study my bruised-up face in the mirror.

"Okay, you've seen better days," I admit to myself. "But if he closes one eye and looks through his lashes, maybe he won't notice."

I exhale.

My eye has a black rim underneath, and the lump on my forehead is apparent, even through the gauze.

Not five minutes later, there's a knock at the door.

I open it, expecting to find Jonah.

"You made good time—"

It's not Jonah.

Emily stands on the porch, her hair perfectly coiffed, her outfit—slim black pants and a tailored shirt—on point. She definitely came straight from the city.

My mouth drops open, and she grins.

"First," she says, "you look terrible. Did you *literally* get hit by a bus?"

I start to tell her, but she holds up a hand. "You know what, I'll have to take a rain check on that. I need to tell you something."

"Like why you're here?" I prompt.

"Yes."

Suddenly her eyes widen, and she takes a step back. "What in the world . . ."

I feel Elliott's hot breath on my leg before I see him.

"This is Elliott," I introduce him. He stands quietly, a perfect gentleman.

"You were not lying when you said he's a Clydesdale," she decides. "But I need to tell you something. Don't be mad . . . but—"

"Hey, Noel."

Jonah steps onto the porch behind Emily, wearing his gray peacoat and jeans that fit him like they were made for him. He towers over my assistant, and she stares at him in awe.

"Jonah, this is my assistant, Emily. She just turned up on my porch, and I'm waiting for her to tell me why she's here."

She holds out her hand. "And you are?" she asks Jonah.

"He's a friend," I tell her. "Jonah Blake."

She shakes his hand, and he and I both wait, watching her.

"Why you're here," I prompt.

"Yes," she says. "As I was saying, don't kill me, but . . ."

"All good conversations start with that phrase," Jonah says, amused.

"As I was saying," Emily tries again.

"Hey, folks!"

Yet another voice comes from the front walk, and I lean to see around Emily.

Pad stands on the sidewalk, wearing red plaid pants mismatched with a brown-and-green-plaid coat. He has a steamer trunk by his feet and what appears to be a typewriter case on top of that.

"As I was saying." Emily sighs. "I've got Padraig with me."

CHAPTER TWENTY-SEVEN

Jonah

W hat were you thinking?"

Padraig and I sit in the living room, and we can clearly hear the discussion in the dining room, where Noel quizzes her assistant in a raised voice.

"Never *ever* bring an author to my personal home, Emily. This is ridiculously unprofessional."

"It's not unprofessional," Emily argues. "It's unorthodox."

"It's both," Noel answers. "What were you thinking?"

"You need my help with the party," Emily tells her. "And Padraig wanted to be here in Winter Falls. He said that everything you've mentioned has inspired him, and he thinks he can finish his chapters *this week* if he can immerse himself in this town."

"You brought an author to my home," Noel says. *"Emily."*

I pull out my phone and text her.

> It might interest you to know that this gentleman and I can hear every word of your discussion.

I hear her phone ding and then their voices grow hushed. I turn to the man sitting across from me.

"How was your flight?" I ask politely.

Padraig seems unbothered by the ruckus his arrival has brought. Elliott goes back and forth between us, allowing both of us to pet him. He was happy to see the elderly man, but honestly, no happier than he is to see anyone else.

"It was just fine," Padraig says. "I shared cookies with the little boy behind me, so he kindly stopped kicking my seat."

"Your luggage is interesting," I can't help but say, eyeing the steamer trunk by the door. It's covered in old-fashioned travel stickers.

"It's carried me through an interesting life," he agrees.

"We'll have to find you a Winter Falls sticker," I tell him. "If there's room for it."

"I can always make room," he says. "I've been doing it my whole life. When I have the need, space opens up. Like magic."

"Just like that, huh?"

"Just like that," he confirms.

Noel and Emily come out of the dining room, and neither looks worse for the wear. In fact, Emily has her arm around Noel's waist.

"Padraig, I hear you need to be immersed in Winter Falls magic so that you can finish your chapters," Noel says, as though she were on board with the idea the entire time.

"If it's no trouble," Pad says, lifting a bushy white brow.

"It's not," she answers. "I don't have a guest room here, but there is a darling bed-and-breakfast just off Main Street. You can book you a room there and write while you have a view of our little town."

"That sounds perfect," he says in delight. "Would you be so kind as to keep Elliott here with you?"

"Of course," Noel says quickly, perhaps too quickly. "He can stay here as long as you need him to."

At this moment, the kitten we'd found wet and angry in the forest comes sauntering out of the hallway, yawning and stretching, its fur as fluffy as a cotton ball, and wearing a blue Christmas sweater.

"Another one?" Noel says to herself. "She just can't stop herself."

"What's that?" Pad asks.

"My mom has a yarn addiction. This is Elliott's best friend, Moxie."

Pad bends down and scoops the kitten up, scratching beneath her chin.

"Well, now, lookie here," he says softly. Moxie arches under his hand, eating up the attention. "How would you like a little nibble?" He pulls something tiny out of his pocket, and she eats it delicately, then licks her paws.

This, of course, captures Elliott's interest, and he jogs over to investigate.

Pad hadn't forgotten him, and he pulls a large bone out of his trunk.

Elliott's eyes light up, and he can scarcely wait until Pad takes the wrapping off and hands it to him. He scoops it up in his mouth and trots away with it.

Pad rubs his hands together.

"Well, if you can show me to the hotel, I'll be on my way. I don't want to inconvenience anyone."

"You aren't," Noel lies. "I gave Emily the address, and she's going to give you a lift." She shakes his hand. "I'm sorry for the confusion. It was unexpected, but we'll sort it out. I hope you get settled in quickly. I'm excited for the end of your book. You've written it startlingly fast."

"That's what happens when I have great subject matter," he says. "When I have a great story, it flows right out of me."

"I'll see you in a few," Emily tells her, and she picks up Pad's typewriter.

I try to carry his trunk for him, but he declines, and so I watch as he and Emily load up her rental car.

"Well, that was something," I say.

Noel sighs, and plops onto the couch.

"I can't believe she did this. It's not like her at all."

"Well, maybe the book will be worth it."

"I have a gut feeling that it's going to be a bestseller," she says absently. "So . . . it should be. But time will tell."

"What happens if a book doesn't turn out to be a bestseller?" I ask. "Does that make it less of a good story?"

"What an interesting question," she says, cocking her head. "And the answer is no. I don't think it's less of a good story. It simply means that not enough people have found it. I don't publish bad stories, Jonah."

"That's what I figured," I say. "So maybe this will be good. Maybe this will make the story so immersive, the reader will feel like they're literally here, because the writer actually is."

She eyes me suspiciously. "Did Emily get to you?"

I laugh. "No. She did not. I'm just saying, don't automatically discount something because it's not the way you normally do it."

"I mean, would you want a client showing up on your doorstep?" she asks. "What if you don't know him that well? What if he's a crazy person?"

"I think authors are a bit crazy, by trade," I say carefully. "But crazier than normal? I doubt Padraig is. He seems very kind."

She nods. "I think so, too. I'm not actually upset. Anymore."

I smile at that last part.

"It'll be nice to have Emily here to help."

"She seems very devoted to you," I tell her. "She's a good person."

"You gathered that from three seconds?" Noel asks.

I nod. "I'm very good at measuring up a person."

"Everyone says that," she answers.

"True. In fact, I believe you told me the same thing not too long ago."

"True," she acknowledges. "And like you, I'm actually good at it. Emily is a good person. She's my cousin, in fact, so we're pretty close."

She pauses and then looks at me.

"So, you were coming over here for a reason . . ." she prompts me.

"Ah, yes," I answer. "I was."

I don't continue, and she waits.

Then glares.

"And that was for . . ." she prompts again.

"Ah, yes. Before all the hullaballoo I found here?"

"I love that word," she commends me. "And yes."

"Okay, to truly explain, I'll need your cooperation."

She waits, and I turn to face her.

I hold my hands up, signaling for her to place her palms in mine.

She's uncertain but does so anyway. Her hands are slender, her fingers nearly an inch shorter than mine. The heat from her hands is electric, and I feel the effects in my entire body, like my heart is pumping electricity through my veins.

She waits, staring into my eyes.

"Yesterday, when I saw you with your head gashed and bleeding," I begin, "pale as a sheet, I've never felt an instant discomfort like I did then. In that moment."

"I think that's called fear," she offers helpfully.

"Whatever it was . . . I didn't like it, and it made me examine why I'm so affected by you."

"What did you decide?" she asks, interested now.

"I haven't," I admit. "I can't figure it out, and I can't stop thinking about you. So I came here specifically to do this."

In one motion, I curl my fingers around hers and pull her to me, kissing her soundly on the mouth.

Her eyes widen, startled, and she stares into mine before she melts into me, her eyes fluttering closed, a slight sigh escaping her lips. She tastes like fresh air and mint, like strawberries and sunshine.

We finally separate a few minutes later, and I feel almost woozy. Our connection is electric.

"I'm sorry," I manage to say. "I should've asked for permission first."

"I would've granted it," she assures me. "What did that feel like to you: 110 or 220 volts?"

"You nearly electrocuted me," I admit. She grins.

I look into her eyes, and I want to know all her layers. The good ones, the annoying ones.

"I don't know what it is about you," I tell her. "I can't verbalize it, but I feel like *I know you*."

She smiles, and it's beautiful.

I don't love the way I feel right now. I don't love that she might matter to me. When people matter, and you lose them, it's horrible.

"Why do you look terrified?" she asks.

"I don't know," I fib.

"I have something I want to say," Noel tells me. She's so serious that I'm almost nervous.

Will she say we shouldn't see each other?

She cups my face in her hands and pulls me to her for another long kiss.

CHAPTER TWENTY-EIGHT

Noel

I've never kissed someone so soundly in my entire life.

I've never felt the effects from a single kiss in my entire body before.

I've never felt so strangely connected to someone I've known for only a few days.

"I'm experiencing a lot of firsts right now," I say against his lips, my hand on his warm, strong chest. I inhale his heady scent, and it doesn't do much to cool my ardor. I take a deep breath and exhale slowly.

"I find cold showers are effective," he says to me knowingly, his hazel eyes sparkling.

"If you don't need one right now, then I'm going to—"

"Oh, I need one," he assures me. "But we're in your parents' house, and well, I have to say, I feel a bit like a teenager right now."

He chuckles, but I completely agree.

"Me too," I admit. "Now what?"

"You mean, where do we go from here?"

I nod.

He shrugs. "I don't know. But you had some interesting things to say a minute ago. Care to go back to that?"

I hold up my hand. "Want to? Yes. Should we? No. Not here and right now. My parents will be back, and . . ."

"You're right," he agrees. "We should go back to trying to thwart each other's father's campaign."

"It should be illegal to smell as good as you do," I tell him. "It almost renders a person senseless."

"All part of the plan," he says with a wink. "To immobilize with my charm and scent."

"If your business plans are this good, my parents are sunk," I say as I get to my feet.

"I'm not writing Jace's plan," he reminds me. "I'm available to help all of you." He grins devilishly. "Is there anything I can help you with right now?"

He stands up, and we're face-to-face again.

I take a step back so I'm not tempted.

He smirks.

"I'll see you later," he promises. "I just wanted to make sure you're all right today."

I nod. "I'm perfectly fine."

Then he's gone, and I'm alone.

I touch my lips lightly. This day is quickly turning out to be *nothing* like I thought it would.

I feel like a schoolgirl—all I want to do is moon over the handsome, strong man and write his name over and over again in my notebook. It annoys me, so I'm happy when Pad calls and asks me to come read his latest chapter.

"I've been up since four A.M. working on this," he tells me. "It's something I didn't see coming."

Thirty minutes later, Elliott and I find ourselves standing in front of Queen Bee's Bed-and-Breakfast. The bee on the sign is wearing a crown.

Elliott is, of course, wearing a blue sweater with snowflakes on it to match Moxie's. Moxie stayed at home this time, something that neither she nor Elliott was happy about.

"You're not actual siblings," I tell him now. "You do understand that, don't you?"

We greet the owner, Queenie, in the lobby, and she oohs and aahs over Elliott and brings him a piece of turkey.

"You've made a lifelong friend now," I tell her. "So be prepared."

He noses under her hand, encouraging her to continue petting him.

"I love him," she says.

I do, too, I realize with a start.

I have fallen in love with a snorting, snoring, bellowing, huffing, ornery dog who slobbers. A dog who belongs to someone else.

I shake my trepidation away because I know full well that I'll have to give him back at some point, and I'm not going to think about that today.

We knock on Pad's bedroom door, and when he answers, his face lights up in a grin.

"Please, come in. This is a lovely room, and I was just getting ready to have some cookies by the fire as I mull over Nora and Jack."

I sit in one of the chairs, and he offers me a cookie. I decline, but Pad takes mine and gives it to Elliott.

"He's supposed to lose weight," I tell Pad. "The vet said if he doesn't, it will be bad for his joints."

"Did she? Then we'll need to be careful, won't we?" He doesn't look terribly concerned.

Instead, he stares out the window, watching my father climb a ladder to string Christmas lights around the square. "Your parents are certainly working hard," he observes.

I nod. "They won't let me help. I had a little car incident." I touch my head, and Pad chuckles.

"Well, I didn't want to say anything, but I *was* curious."

"It's just a minor scrape," I tell him, settling into the green velvet wingback. "No big deal."

Pad peers at me. "So, as you know, I've been working on how to get stubborn Nora and Jack to realize that they belong together."

I nod, waiting.

"It turns out that Elliott will have a bigger role to play than I thought! I knew he'd be a key player, but this . . . Well, here. See for yourself."

He hands me a sheaf of typewritten pages and sits back, clearly wanting me to read them on the spot.

I willingly oblige, enjoying the warmth of the fire as I scan the pages.

When I get to the fourth page, I gasp and unconsciously hug Elliott to me with one hand.

"You can't," I tell him. "You can't tempt fate by even insinuating that something could happen to him."

"But don't you see? If Elliott gets attacked by wolves, it will bring everyone together, especially Nora and Jack."

I shake my head. "Maybe so, but you can't put that out into the world. The mere thought . . ."

The mere thought makes my chest tight, and I pull Elliott to me while I rest my chin on his head.

"That's precisely what a mother would say." Pad stares at me thoughtfully. "A mother wouldn't risk harm to her child—or her dog child—for anything in the world. Even the thought of it makes her shudder."

That gives me pause.

"I think maybe Elliott is changing me for the better," I decide out loud. "Let's hope it sticks after he goes home to you."

I have a hard time uttering those last few words. Pad looks at me again, and it's like he's looking through my eyes and into my soul.

"Elliott sure has taken to you," Pad says. "I was thinking, what if you were to keep him?"

I gasp, afraid to hope.

"I'm getting older. It would be better for Elliott to have a younger owner, one who can go to obedience lessons with him and go for hikes. Unless you're not up for the responsibility yet," he says. "If not, I completely understand."

"Of course I'd be up for the responsibility," I tell him, and he nods. "I just don't want you to miss him. He brings such joy into my life. I can't imagine you'd want to lose that."

"Oh, darling girl," Pad says. "I want you to keep that joy in yours."

He smiles so sweetly that I don't feel guilty for shrieking, "Yes, I do want him! Thank you! Thank you!" and throwing my arms around Pad's neck.

And squealing like a little girl.

And accidentally kicking Pad when I do a jig around him.

Pad bends and looks Elliott in the eye.

"Be good for your mom, boy. You've got a good one here."

He pats him on the head.

"I won't have him attacked by wolves," Pad tells me before we leave. "Ol' Bess and I will think of something else." He gestures at his typewriter. "She gets agitated if I ignore her ideas, but we'll think of something."

The visual of Pad arguing with his typewriter in the middle of the night makes me smile.

"I can't wait to see what you come up with," I say as he shows us out.

"You'll be the first to know." He winks.

He walks us out to the sidewalk, and all I can think is *I never have to give Elliott back.*

I don't think of the drool, the shenanigans, or the drool.

I think of the way he waits for me when I'm gone, and the way he looks at me when I return.

He offers the purest love of all: he doesn't want anything other than for me to love him back.

He doesn't want to change me.

He's not a red pen.

He's vinyl with all its imperfections.

"Hey, Noel?" Pad's voice beings me back to the moment. He's staring across the square, a thoughtful look in his eyes. "I just had an idea."

CHAPTER TWENTY-NINE

Jonah

I can't remember the last time I felt *this good.*

I drive through town, and it seems like every light turns green, my favorite songs play on the radio, and the road has the perfect amount of grip—not too slippery.

The scene from earlier plays in my head, of Noel and me on the couch, of our hands pressed together, then our lips. I suck in a breath, and smile.

I did not realize this morning that today was going to turn out this way.

I hum as the trees blur past, and I catch a glimpse of gray. I only have a flash of a second to see a fast-moving animal dart out of the ditch. There isn't time to brake, but miraculously, the animal leaps away from my car in the nick of time and continues running across the field on the other side.

My heart pounds.

A fraction of a second saved that wolf's life.

I'm still rattled when I pull into my father's driveway and walk into the house.

Jace is asleep on the couch, probably lulled by the roaring fire. Izzy is sorting buttons on the other sofa, and she smiles at me when I come in.

"Hey, Izz," I greet her.

"Shh," she says. "Jerry's taking a nap."

"Okay," I whisper.

She beams. I take a seat next to her and lean on the arm of the couch.

I see that my father has moved the photo of me and my mother to the mantel. I stare at her smile, and mine, and for a second, I remember being here in this room with her.

She's pulling on her coat and hat and bending to kiss my cheek.

"I'll be right back, Jonah," she says, tweaking my nose. "We just need some red food coloring."

I don't want her to leave, but she shakes her head with a smile. "How can we make candy cane cookies without red, silly?" she asks. "I'll tell you what. You can have one cookie while I'm gone—just one. And when I get back, we'll finish the rest."

The promise of the cookie is enough. I nod.

"I'll be right back, baby," she says. She stands and yells the same to my dad, waves, then closes the door behind her.

I blink, staring at the closed door.

She'd closed it behind her so long ago, that last time I'd seen her. If I shut my eyes, I can still smell her perfume.

"Are you okay, Jonah?" Izzy asks, staring up at me in concern. Real concern.

"Izz?"

"You're shaking," she tells me.

"I was just remembering something sad."

"Oh. Sad memories. Stay away from those. They don't do you any good."

"I don't know that they do someone any good if they're all locked up, either," I answer, not expecting her to understand. I'm surprised when she replies.

"That's a bad deal, too." She nods. "What you need to figure out is how to be okay with whatever happened. The memory itself—*that thing*—it happened a long time ago. That *thing* isn't tormenting us. Our *memory* does."

Her words make perfect sense.

"Of course. I already grieved my mother's death. I can't re-live it over and over. That's like killing her a thousand times."

Izzy nods with a smile.

"And I can't just . . . *not* love someone . . . because I'm afraid of losing them. That's insane. And I'm a smart, *very sane*, man."

Izzy nods again.

I kiss her cheek. "Izzy, you knew exactly what to say to help me. I . . . thank you." It's all I can think of to say.

Izzy beams.

"Have you seen my mother, Jerry?" she asks. "She needs to hem my wedding dress."

I blink. "Um. I haven't seen her today, Izz. But if you stay here sorting these buttons, she'll be able to find you."

That satisfies her, and she returns her attention to the task at hand.

My father comes in the back door, his hands full with a box.

"Whatcha got?" I ask, coming over to see.

He pulls out a pamphlet and waves it.

"Your marketing team is incredible," he tells me. "They created a mock-up pamphlet to hand out after our presentation to the town. And they're putting together a slideshow—all I'll have to do is speak."

He sounds completely bewildered by it all, which makes me laugh.

"They've created a product out of nothing," he continues with awe. "They've made it look like it's already being built and we just need investors. It's truly incredible. We even have a logo!"

"It's the wonder of modern marketing, Dad," I tell him.

He shakes his head. "I just find it impressive that you have a whole team of people *that smart* who do everything you ask them."

His comment makes me feel oddly proud of myself.

"I do," I agree. "I'm lucky."

"So they're getting me set up for the presentation," Dad says. "There's nothing really left for you to do."

"Well, I do need to examine the viability of both business plans," I answer. "And Rich and Susan don't have to give me theirs until tomorrow."

"Well, yes. Except for that."

Jace wakes up and stretches. Then he startles until he sees his mom safe and sound on the sofa.

"She's fine," I tell him. "You must've needed the sleep."

"She's been wandering a lot in the night," my dad says.

"It's hard to keep up with," Jace admits. "I can't be everywhere all the time. It's why I need to get this memory village built as soon as possible. If can't, I worry it will be too late for her. She'll have to go to a nursing home, and that will kill me."

"We won't let that happen," I tell him.

"No, we won't," my dad agrees. "In fact, we have a product." He holds up the pamphlet, and Jace crows, leaping up and over the back of the sofa to get a better look.

"We've got a legitimate product," he says with wonder. I see hope in his eyes, and that's the first time I've really seen it there lately.

My team did that.

It's a good feeling. Usually, at work, I don't get a lot of personal gratification. Being mercenary is helpful on Wall Street, but you don't get to do a lot of soul-searching or purpose-fulfilling.

This feels *really* good.

My phone buzzes in my pocket, and when I see Noel's name, I feel a jolt of electricity.

> Do you think you'd be able to come to Queen Bee's? I have a professional question.

I'm intrigued, I reply. I'll be there in a few.

I don't stop to wonder why she's asking me to come to a bed-and-breakfast. I just know that she asked, and I'm now on my way.

It only takes me a few minutes to get there, of course, and when I do, I find her standing on the sidewalk with Padraig Sinclair, her author, as they examine the building next door.

"Hey," I greet them, patting Elliott's giant head. I notice

Noel's eyes light up when she sees me, which makes my heart swell a size. "You rang?"

She smiles. "Well, Pad has an idea. He wants to buy this building for a bookstore. Whichever way the council votes, a bookstore would fit in. It would be a good investment for him, right?"

I study the brick building in front of me. It looks like it was built at the turn of the nineteenth century or so, and it's solid.

"Either business plan should mean an uptick in traffic to this town," I say. "And if you can buy this building before property values around here start to rise, you could be looking at a pretty good deal. Depending on your business plan."

"Thank you, young man," Pad tells me. "I'm not looking to get rich at my age. All I really want to do is live among my books, write my stories, and be content. I have a nest egg that I can buy the building with, so I really only need to cover the expenses with my monthly income."

"And I have reason to believe he'll have at least a steady moderate income from book royalties," Noel chips in.

"It sounds like you're in a good financial place, then," I tell him. "I can't give you specific advice without specific details, but I think it would be a sound investment, yes."

"Thank you," Noel says, beaming at me. "It's been a wonderful day for good news."

"You look radiant," I tell her, unable to help myself.

"It's been a great day so far," she says, smiling knowingly at me.

I wink.

Pad pretends not to see.

"Well"—she turns to him—"I'll ask my parents, who you should talk to about this building, and then I'll get back to you, and you can take it from there."

He thanks her profusely and returns to his room.

I walk Noel and Elliott around the square to her car.

"Are you that kind to all your authors?" I ask.

"I try to be. But you know, I'm not with them usually. We work from afar, and I see a handful once or twice a year at book conferences. I don't usually have the opportunity to work with someone in this capacity."

"It suits you," I tell her. "You looked absolutely in your element when you were describing what Pad wanted to do."

"I love it when something feels meant to be," she answers, and she pauses next to her car. Neither one of us wants to stop talking.

Behind her, her mother and father work together to assemble a lit snowman, one to match the other five standing around the square.

"I've already tried to help them," she tells me, seeing where my gaze has fallen. "But they won't allow it. I think my mom still thinks I have a concussion."

"It doesn't hurt to be safe," I say, and the rush of concern I feel over her is disproportionate to the moment. *She's okay*, I remind myself, blinking away the memory of the blood on her forehead.

She sighs. "Now you sound like my folks."

I laugh. "They seem like smart people."

"Do you want to get a coffee?" she asks bluntly, taking a step into my personal space and staring up at me.

I breathe out.

"Yes," I tell her, feeling a bit of relief from a stress I didn't know I was carrying. "I do."

I take her arm, and we walk down the street to the Busy Bean.

As we do, Rich turns the power on for the lights that they've strung today. The entire street lights up, and we're suddenly standing in the middle of a winter wonderland. It's magical, even during the day. At night it will be breathtaking.

Noel looks up at me, and we laugh.

"I feel like this might've been a meet-cute scene in a movie," she says.

"Only we met forever ago . . . literally days and days," I tell her. "We're practically related by now."

"Not related." She shakes her head.

I swallow. "No. That would make how I'm feeling right now illegal."

She smiles. "Same."

I open the coffee shop door, and she steps close to me. "Thank you," she says in my ear. Her breath skims my neck, and I shiver.

She winks, holding my gaze.

She knows exactly what she's doing, I realize.

We sit at a bistro table in the corner, next to each other and near a lit Christmas tree. We both order cappuccinos, and when they come, she gets milk foam on her nose. I reach over and wipe it off.

Then I lick my finger.

She meets my gaze again. Her eyes are stormy gray.

"Are you angry?" I whisper.

She shakes her head. "No. Just unsettled."

"I unsettle you?" I fear my grin is ornery.

She shakes her head. "Do I unsettle you?"

"Oh, yes," I admit immediately. "I'm completely unsettled right now."

She smiles, satisfied, and takes a drink.

"Tell me about your job," she says.

"I make people money," I answer.

"Sounds pretty cut-and-dried."

"It is. I used to like it. It's made *me* a lot of money. And yes, that's tacky to say. I only mention it because lately, I've been increasingly feeling like there's got to be more than that in life. You know?"

"More than cutthroat corporate stuff?" she asks. "There absolutely better be."

"Tell me about your job," I request, staring at her then tucking a tendril of her fiery hair behind her ear. She holds my gaze.

"I help people create worlds," she says simply. "Fictional worlds for people's enjoyment. No more, no less."

"That's not true," I tell her. "You give people an escape from reality. There are some hard days out in the world. Reading is a great break from it."

"True," she concedes. "But it won't cure cancer. It won't cure Alzheimer's. It can't help someone like Izzy."

"We can't all exist to cure things like that," I remind her. "We all have a different purpose in life. I can safely tell you that mine is not becoming a biologist who cures cancer."

"No, but you could be the one who *finances* it," she says. And she's not wrong. "That means you're still making an impact."

"And you provide the cancer patient with a break from the chemo when they read another chapter while their treatment flows through their veins."

She blinks. "I guess that's true, yes."

"And you stimulate the minds of children and encourage them to daydream and to write."

That one gives her pause. "Well, some editors do. I don't do children's books. But I like the sentiment."

I smile. "Your job matters. You make the world a more beautiful, multifaceted place. And for people like Izzy? What about books that she read as a child? Don't you think those would bring her comfort now? I do. So you do make an impact, far and wide."

"You are good for my ego," she decides.

"You're good for my . . . everything," I say confidently, not caring a single bit that I'm wearing my heart on my sleeve and that I'm being transparent. "I want to be an open book for you," I tell her. "It's been a problem for me in my past. Not wanting to open up. So I want to be open now. I want to do this right. Whatever you want to know, ask."

"I don't know you well," she says. "But I feel like this is uncharacteristic of you."

"To say the least," I agree. I lean forward and touch my nose to hers. "But so is PDA, and I keep wanting to touch you." I lean closer and run my nose along the line of her neck, up to her ear, where I whisper, "To breathe you in."

She sucks in a breath.

"You're making me feel things I haven't felt before," I tell her. "And you're making me want to be someone I've never been. Is that too blunt to say?"

She shakes her head.

"I don't think I've dated anyone who willingly decided to be transparent," she says slowly. "You're recognizing traits in yourself that need work. That's commendable."

I nod. "See? I'm a good boy."

She rolls her eyes at that one. "That remains to be seen."

CHAPTER THIRTY

Noel

When Jonah walks me to my car, I eye my parents' handi-work. The scene is honestly like something out of a Hallmark movie, and I can't believe they're pulling it off.

"I wonder how much money they spent on all this," I say wryly.

"More than I would've advised," Jonah answers. His head is swiveling as he takes it all in. The hanging ornaments, the lit snowmen, the white lights, the reindeer. "A lot more," he adds.

The next several things happen in blurred succession.

I step into the street.

My foot slides in slush.

A car barrels around the corner.

Jonah reacts like lightning,

yanking me backward toward him,

and I collide with him.

Our legs tangle, and we tumble to the ground.

"That was a bit of overkill," I say, my face in his coat.

When I pull away, he's white as he can be, and if I'm not mistaken, he's actually shaking.

"Jonah," I say, sitting up, my hand on his arm. "I'm fine. Are you okay?"

He sits up, too, and yes, he's shaking.

"I . . . It's weird. In that moment, I was seeing something that I never actually saw. When it happened, I mean. I was only told about it afterward, but a moment ago, I saw the situation unfold but with your face."

"Can you explain a bit more?" I ask, not understanding.

"My mother died at this corner," he says simply. "This very corner. Not far from where we're sitting now."

My breath freezes in my throat.

"It was Christmas Eve. I was four. There was a Christmas Eve party in the town square, because Winter Falls used to throw one every year. My family was there for a while, and then we went home. My mom and I were baking Christmas cookies to leave out for Santa and to hand out to the neighborhood the next day. We ran out of red food coloring."

He pauses, swallows, then continues, his jaw clenching.

"She went to the store."

He exhales.

"She died because she went to the store for red food coloring. To make Christmas cookies for her son to leave out for Santa."

"I . . ."

"People were milling around, and when she stepped out into the street, the way you did just now, someone came around that corner."

"Just like this," I say, gesturing to our situation. "Oh, no," I breathe, and my heart hurts.

"She was supposed to come right back," he says now. "Nolan had to come tell my dad and me."

I think of the crusty police chief, and I feel for him. I wonder how many times he's had to deliver bad news.

"God, that's tragic," I say.

My teeth are beginning to chatter from being cold and wet, and Jonah immediately notices. He gets to his feet and pulls me up. Then he wraps his coat around me.

"No," I try to protest. "I already have a coat."

"Leave it," he says. He helps me into my car, actually checks my seat belt, and then kisses me on the forehead. "Turn the car on, and the heater on high," he instructs. "You'll catch your death."

"I'm not going to catch my death," I tell him. But I do as he says. I even turn my seat warmer on. "Will you get in for a while and talk? I'm not ready to leave you yet."

He hesitates and then nods, walking around to climb into the front seat.

I turn his seat warmer on, too, and grab his hand, rubbing it between mine. He's not wearing gloves, and his knuckles are red from the cold. Something about this powerful, confident man being so vulnerable to me in this moment is enough to make me ache.

I grip his hands tight with mine and stare him in the eye.

"You were a little boy who needed his mom," I tell him. "And I'm so very sorry that she couldn't come home to you."

His hazel eyes gleam, and I see myself in their depths.

"It must've been so hard for you," I say. "I don't want to dredge up old wounds, but it feels like they're strong tonight already."

He nods and breathes out.

"It always gets like this when I come home," he says. "Especially if I come home in winter."

"That's understandable," I tell him. "Everything looks the same and smells the same. Of course it will be a memory trigger."

"It's not fair to my dad," he says. "I see that now. All these years, I invented every excuse possible to not come here, when what I should've done was get myself here and sort out my issues. But of course I couldn't do something sensible like *that*."

I smile. "We never do what we should do for ourselves."

"I'm going to now," he says. "I'm going to figure out how to let this memory slip away. I don't want it to have power over me anymore."

"I love that," I tell him. "Do you have any idea how you'll go about such a small task?"

"That's the hard part."

We laugh softly, happy for a little levity.

"Izzy actually said something insightful to me about this," he says. "We decided that my mother only died once, yet because I haven't let the memory go, she's died a thousand more times in my head."

"Wow," I answer, and I squeeze his hand. "That's powerful."

"Then Izzy had a moment of lucidity, and she said something like . . . and I'm sure I'll mess this up, but she said that what we need to figure out is how to be okay with what happened. The thing happened a long time ago, the damage was already done. Heal from it, and move on."

"Wow," I say again, eloquently.

"It was a profound moment for me," he says. "It broke it down into the simplest of terms . . . that I need to be okay with what happened. My mom is gone. She's not coming back. I cannot change that. The little boy already grew up without her. It's done. It's past time to let it go. If I don't, those issues will continue to taint my present. And my present has recently become something with the potential to be amazing."

I look at him, my eyes wet.

"Your eyes look like the ocean when you cry," he says, and he kisses me, so suddenly, so firmly, that I forget I was crying. "Like stormy seas," he murmurs in my ear.

He nuzzles his face into my neck, and a rush of something so warm, so intense, so fierce flows through me. For the first time in my life, I want to protect someone, I want to shield him, I want to hold my hands out and prevent anything from hurting him.

He's been hurt enough already.

I have the urge to lie with him all night, to shield him with my own body, to protect him while he sleeps.

"I'm feeling things I've never felt before, too," I tell him. "I want to protect you. I want to help you heal. I want to shield you from anything that could ever hurt you again."

"That's impossible, you know," he says, and the way he gazes at me almost feels more intimate than any sexual encounter ever could be. "You can't protect me. But you *can* love me. Someday."

I feel like I love him now. I feel like I've loved him for a thousand years.

"That could be arranged," I say thinly. "It's not outside the realm of possibilities. I mean—"

He kisses me again, and the car windows are fogged up, and my parents are down the street.

But neither of us cares.

The kiss is long, and desperate, yet still sweet, still searching, still . . . pure. It's filled with wonder, and hope, and passion, and curiosity, and magic. It carries the weight of any decision I'll ever make, while feeling as light as a happily ever after.

It makes my lips tingle and my belly yearn.

It fills an emptiness I didn't know I needed filled.

"I have to get out of this car," he says against my lips. "Before we do something indecent in the middle of the Winter Falls town square."

"Can I at least take you to your car?" I ask, against his lips, as well.

"I can't stay in here that long."

He opens the door and throws himself out as though his life depended on it. The cold air pours in and cools my flushed cheeks.

"You look beautiful right now," he says, the light in his eye setting my belly on fire again.

"I'll see you soon," I tell him.

"When?"

"Tomorrow."

"Breakfast? Nell's?"

"It's a date," I tell him.

He leans in and kisses me again, a light brush against my lips.

Then he groans and lingers slightly longer the second time.

"Get out of here," he says, straightening and backing up. "Drive safe."

As I drive away, I see him in my rearview mirror, standing tall and strong, knowing full well that I'll watch him until I can't see him anymore.

When I reach my parents' house, there are two texts waiting for me.

> What time is breakfast tomorrow?

> I need to know how long I have until I see you.

A week ago, I would've thought this was corny. Tonight, it makes me melt.

I float into the house, where I find my mom and Emily putting together giveaway bags for the party. They, of course, include "Vote for Rich" promo items.

I don't care tonight. Tonight, nothing matters but the ethereal way I feel.

Emily immediately knows that there is tea to be spilled.

"Hey, Noel, I need to get your approval for a last-minute cover change," she says.

"Sure," I answer, knowing full well what I'm in for as she pulls me into my bedroom.

"Why are you glowing?"

I show her the last two text messages, and I see her melt, too.

"Who in the— Ohhhhh. How did I not see this? Of course you're falling for Jonah."

"Am I crazy?"

She's already shaking her head. "Nooo. He's. So. Beautiful. And my word, he smells good. I mean, not to make it weird, but I want to swallow him whole. He smells *that* good."

I laugh. "I know what you mean."

"How long has this been going on? Why didn't you tell me?"

"Because it's new. And it's happening so fast. I feel like we've always been together, if that makes any sense. I want to go back and see him right now, even though I only left him four minutes ago."

"You're falling in love," she says excitedly. "*You're in love*, Noel."

"Shh," I caution her. "I don't want my dad to think this changes anything with his campaign."

"Your dad wants you to be happy," she says. "You weirdo. Anyone can see that."

"I just want it to be private right now," I tell her. "So I don't have to define it. I just want to *feel* it."

She nods, a dreamy look on her face. "Your kids will be beautiful."

Kids.

"You know, he mentioned a while back that he never wants kids."

Emily looks at me. "Does that work for you?"

"I don't know. I guess I always envisioned myself having them. I didn't consider any other way."

"Well, before you get too much further into this, you might want to consider that."

"And this is why I don't want to tell people," I announce. "Now reality is setting in."

"You're allowed to feel what you're feeling right now," Emily answers. "Be in this moment. You can enjoy this moment without worrying about the future, you know."

"I know. But is it worth anyone's time to pursue something that won't ultimately work if we don't want the same fundamental things out of life?"

"You just killed your own buzz," she says. "Congratulations."

"I'm serious," I tell her.

"So am I," she answers. "You're your own worst enemy sometimes. Enjoy the clouds and rainbows tonight. You can worry about tomorrow *tomorrow*."

I, of course, can't do that. Because I'm my own worst enemy. "I need to run a quick errand."

"Noel," she says, chasing me out the front door. "I shouldn't have said anything. I'm sure it's nothing. Don't go over there."

"I'll be right back."

"Don't make a mountain out of a molehill," she calls.

I have the strangest compulsion to get this into the open right now. To get it settled. To not waste anyone's time. We all deserve to want what we want. And I can't spend a whole night wondering if a huge thing like children will bring everything to a halt.

If we don't want the same things, that's that. No one can force someone else to want the same things they do.

I drive straight to Judd's, and Jonah must see me arrive. He's at my car door before I can even climb all the way out.

"You read my mind," he says, cupping my face and leaning down to kiss me.

"Wait," I say, and it takes every bit of self-control that I possess. He stares into my eyes questioningly as he presses me against the car, and I am quite aware of what body part is where. "A while back, you told me that you never want kids."

He freezes now and takes a small step back, dropping his hands.

"I did," he says stiffly.

"It's okay if the answer to this question is yes," I tell him. "Did you mean it?"

He's silent, and so am I.

He opens his mouth, then closes it.

"Because here's what *I* think." I take a breath. "Wanting a child needs to be mutual. And it needs to be something that is based upon a decision made after childhood wounds are healed, with an open heart and mind, and without the confines of fear."

He studies me, his eyes glistening.

"What I'm really asking is, could you wait to make that decision until after you've faced your past? Until after you've let the memory slip away? If, at that time, you still don't want children, I'll respect that. I can live without having a child, but I'm not so sure that I want to live without the way you make me feel . . . right now."

He pulls me to him, his arms a tight vise around my chest. "You'd give that up for me?"

"If you give it fair consideration, yes."

"You trust me to be unbiased and fair?"

I smile and look into his eyes. "Yes. I do."

"Then that is exactly what I'll be."

CHAPTER THIRTY-ONE

Jonah

I spend the early morning at city hall, going over Jace's proposal while I wait to meet Noel for breakfast.

"It's sound," I tell him. I lean back in my chair so I can see Nancy. "Have Suze and Rich brought theirs by yet?"

She shakes her head. "But she sent a message that she'd have it here by noon."

"Good."

"I saw you outside with Noel last night," Jace says. "Your dad did, too. I'm sorry, man. I tried to block the window."

"It's okay," I answer. "I'm a grown man." I pause. "But on a scale of one to ten, how mad is he?"

"Oddly enough, not at all."

I lift my brow. "Not at all?"

"No. He said, 'I'll be damned,' and then he went back to bed."

"And he hasn't said a thing to me about it today," I reply.

"Could it be . . . he's letting you make big-boy decisions?" Jace asks with a grin.

I grab him in a light headlock.

"This is a place of business," my father calls from the doorway as he enters. "Not a wrestling match.

"I left the brochures at home," he continues, "and Nancy needs them to put together gift bags for the party tomorrow night."

"You're doing gift bags?"

"Yes. I think the Turners will be, too. Anyway, focus. Can you go get them? They're by the back door. I put them there so I wouldn't forget them."

"Effective," I note. "And yes. I'll go right now."

I trot down the front steps and briefly ponder stopping to see Noel. For just a minute.

My dad pokes his head out. "And no pit stops, please," he says. "Nancy really does need to make these bags. I want her to be able to leave early today."

"It's like you know me," I say. He grins.

I drive home, and the box is right where Dad said it was; in fact, I don't know how he didn't trip on it while he was leaving.

I'm walking back to the car with it when I glance at my dad's shop. It would be a shame to give back that Caterham 7 before I actually drive it.

I hesitate and then march to the garage slot and pull off the slipcover. The car glistens red in the shadows, the open-air top waiting for me to climb inside.

"It'll be a cold ride but worth it," I mutter. I put the box of pamphlets on the passenger seat and carefully back out.

It handles with razor precision. I briefly ponder reconsidering all my recent life decisions, and then sigh.

I stop at the bottom of the driveway and pull out my phone.

Thank you for considering me, I text Huff. But I can't accept at this time. I'll have the car returned to you after Christmas.

I put my phone away and drive toward town.

The wind is loud enough that I barely hear my phone when it rings, and if it wasn't Noel, I wouldn't have answered.

But it is, and I do.

I pull to the side of the road so I can hear.

"Jonah, your dad says you're out driving."

She's upset, I can tell.

"I am. What's wrong?"

"Emily didn't know that Elliott can open the front door and she didn't lock it." She chokes up, pauses, then continues. "He's gone. Can you keep an eye out for him?"

"Oh, no. Yes. I'm on my way back to city hall right now—I'll drive all through town and hunt. Call me when you find him."

"Thanks, Jonah."

I hang up and head for town, scanning the horizon as I go, watching for any sign of the lumbering dog.

"That's one bright spot," I say to myself. "He's hard to miss."

I don't see him on the way in, and I unload the pamphlets.

"Jace, can you take Dad's truck and help us search?" I ask. Jace is already standing up.

"On my way."

My dad throws him the keys without looking up from his desk.

We crisscross through town, slowly trawling over the city lanes and the country roads right outside town.

"Come on, Elliott," I mutter. "Where are you?"

I scan the snowy fields and the slushy streets, and I'm just about to give up when I'm two miles outside town again.

"He didn't come out this far," I decide, and turn back toward town. And that's when I see them.

Across a silvery-white field, a gray wolf runs, his legs sleek and long, his fur shaggy for the winter.

Elliott is chasing him.

"No," I say, rolling down the window. "Elliott!" I call as loudly as I can. It's not loud enough. I turn the car toward them and power through the ditch, pushing through snow.

"Come on, baby," I urge the car. "You can do it."

The sheer power of the engine keeps us from getting stuck, and I keep my eyes on Elliott. I honk and honk, trying to scare the wolf away, but neither of them flinches.

Elliott catches the wolf, pulling it down by its leg.

"No," I scream—flooring the accelerator. I lay on the horn and shine my headlights directly in their eyes. Elliott and the wolf roll around and around, flecks of blood flying into the snow, until I skid to a stop in the fray.

There's a thud, and the wolf runs back into the shadows.

The thud was Elliott making impact with my car.

"No, no, no." I lunge out of the car and find that he's still alive, still breathing, although he's very still and whimpering. I know I don't have much time.

Somehow, I manage to heft him and pull him into the compact sports car, wedging him into the front seat. I wipe my hair out of my eyes, and Elliott's blood smears on my face.

I leap into the car and hit the gas. As I drive, I call Noel.

"Call Avery," I tell her. "I've got Elliott, but he needs a vet. It's bad, Noel. Let her know we're on our way and to be ready."

I hang up and step on the accelerator until I'm practically standing on it. The engine screams as we race toward town. I slide into Avery's drive a few minutes later, and when I do, she, Noel, Emily, and Jace are waiting.

"Jace, give me a hand."

As we carefully lift the injured dog from the car, Noel slaps her hand over her mouth, and tears stream down her cheeks.

"Carry him inside," Avery says, all business now as she runs ahead to open the doors.

Jace and I lay him on an exam table, and Avery ushers us out. "You'll only be in the way."

We stare at each other in the waiting room, and I'm covered in Elliott's blood.

"I'm sorry, Noel," I tell her. "I was trying to get to him. He was chasing a wolf across a field. I honked and yelled, but nothing worked. I skidded into them."

"You hit him?" she asks, stunned.

I'm stunned, too. "I did. I didn't mean to. I was sliding. I . . . I'm sorry."

A tear slides down her cheek. "I know it's not your fault," she says. "And I'm not mad. If you hadn't been there, God knows what would've happened. I just need a minute to process this."

I nod, not knowing what else to say. Whatever my intentions were, Elliott is still not in a good way.

We take turns pacing, then sitting, then pacing.

Jace calls the Turners to keep them informed, and my dad even calls to check on Elliott.

It's two long hours before Avery emerges, her face tired and her arms smeared with blood.

"He's okay," she says. "At least for now."

We all exhale, but she cautions us. "These first twenty-four hours will be the most important. I've sewed him up, but he's not out of the woods."

"Can I sleep here with him tonight?" Noel asks, her tear-streaked face upturned. There's no way Avery could say no to that face, and she doesn't. She nods.

"Of course. I'll bring you some extra blankets, and I have a cot in the back. You can drag it in here. He'll be sedated."

Noel nods, and I pull her to me. Her shoulders shake, and I stroke her back.

"Emily, could you bring Noel an overnight bag? Maybe a toothbrush and a nightgown?"

"Of course."

"Jace, I'm going to stay here with Noel. Can you drive the car back to my dad's? Put it in the garage." It's got blood smeared all over it, but I'll deal with that later.

"Of course," he answers. Given the circumstances, he's not even excited to drive it.

I sit Noel down on the cot, and Avery brings her a cup of chamomile tea.

"You're okay," she murmurs, her arms around Noel's shoulders. "You're okay."

"Thank you for everything," Noel sniffs, wiping her nose. "You've been amazing. You've kept him alive."

"Can you get some men together to go find those wolves?" Emily asks before she leaves. "Is that what you do out here in the great outdoors?"

"No," I answer. "The wolves aren't doing anything wrong. More and more of their home has been taken by housing developments. They just want to survive like everything else."

"You're saying this is the circle of life?" Emily asks dubiously.

I shake my head. "It's just the way things are. I'm the one who hit him. The wolf was just trying to run away."

"You mean Elliott was the instigator?" Noel asks now, her cheeks tearstained. "That dog is afraid of the dark. And owls. And other dogs. What got into him?"

"I don't know," I answer honestly.

"I'll update her parents and bring her back a bag," Emily says.

Avery looks at me. "I'll be in my apartment upstairs if you need anything."

"Thank you," I tell her. "For everything."

"I'll be down in a few hours to check on him."

She leaves, and I creep back into Elliott's room, where Noel has already dragged the cot right up next to Elliott's crate. She's stroking his paw through the bars, humming a tune without words.

It hurts my heart.

A lump forms in my throat that I can't swallow and *this right here*, *this* is what I've been hiding from all these years. This helpless feeling of watching someone you love slip away and there's nothing you can do to stop it.

This realization should make me want to run far away from

Noel, so far away that if something happens to her, I won't be around to experience it.

But somehow, the thought of being away from her for even a moment hurts even more.

I wrap my arms around her and hold her tightly until Emily returns with pajamas, a robe, a toothbrush, and a fresh outfit for tomorrow.

"Your mom wanted to come, but she was exhausted from working on the square all day, so I told her you were covered here," Emily says.

"Thank you," Noel tells her. "Go home and get some sleep. We'll let you know if anything changes."

Emily is uncertain and looks at me.

"I won't leave her side, Emily."

She nods. "Okay. I'll be back first thing."

She kisses Noel on the cheek and leaves.

Noel changes out of her clothes, bundles up in her pj's and robe, and washes her face before she returns to hold Elliott's paw and stroke his ear.

"He's such a good dog," she tells me. "I know he's mischievous and he gets into everything, but he's got so much character, and he just loves everyone. This isn't fair, Jonah."

"It's not," I agree. "But I think he's going to pull through. He's the biggest, strongest dog I know."

She actually smiles a little. "That's true."

She hums until she falls asleep, and then she sleeps with his paw in her hand.

I watch her sleep for the longest time, and my mind drifts to other things—specifically, our parents' opposing stances. If this election ends badly, our parents will never stand by silently while Noel and I have a relationship.

Unless I can think of something, *some way*, to end this without anyone getting hurt.

And then, just like that, something occurs to me.

Something potentially genius.

CHAPTER THIRTY-TWO

Noel

When I wake, light is pouring in a window, and large soulful eyes are staring directly into mine.

I startle, gasp, and sit up.

Elliott thumps his tail.

"You're awake," I breathe. Jonah sits up. "He's awake," I say needlessly.

I pat his paw, stroke his ear, and wait for Jonah to get Avery.

She performs her exam and then smiles. "It's looking good."

Elliott lifts his giant head and touches my nose with his.

I sob into his fur, and Jonah rubs my back, unsure of what to do. But just having him here is more than enough.

"I'm going to keep him sedated today," Avery says as she injects something into Elliott's IV, "so that we make sure his injuries continue to heal. We can't risk him hurting himself. So he'll be sleeping all day. I know you have a big night to prepare for."

I nod. I don't want to leave, but I know that Jonah will stay with me as long as I'm here, and I know he needs to be at that party.

"We have to prepare," I tell him, squaring my shoulders. "I'll just check on him several times."

He gives me a small smile. "Are you sure? We can scrap it all and just stay here with him."

"I can't do that to my dad, and you can't do it to yours. Or this town," I add. "You heard Avery. He'll be sleeping all day."

"If you're sure," he says.

I nod. "I am."

"Noel?" His voice is soft, and I pause. "Do you forgive me?"

"This wasn't your fault, Jonah. Not really. I don't know what we're going to do about that car, though. There's an Elliott-sized dent in the hood and blood all over the inside." My voice trembles, and he hugs me.

"Don't even think about that. I'll handle it."

"You know what's weird?" I say as Jonah pulls on his coat. "Pad wrote a chapter where Elliott gets attacked by a wolf. He told me he was going to change it."

Jonah examines my face. "This wasn't his doing, Noel."

I laugh a little. "I know. I just . . . I told him to change it so he doesn't tempt fate."

"This was just a random, weird accident," he says. "It's my fault. Not Pad's."

I nod, even though my instincts don't quite agree.

I change my clothes and promise Avery that I'll be back later, and then Jonah takes me to my parents' house. Mom hugs me in the kitchen, and my dad is already talking about the walks he'll take Elliott on to recover from his injuries.

I cry in the shower, even though I know it's silly. The danger is past. My emotions, however, don't realize that.

I cry when I'm applying my makeup.

I cry when I'm blow-drying my hair.

"Get it all out," my dad says, coming in to give me a hug. "Yesterday was terrifying. You have every right to be emotional."

I cry for a few minutes more, and it's a relief to cry on my dad's shoulder while he tells me that everything will be okay.

Emily and my mom bustle about, preparing things for the party, preparing things for the presentations afterward. My dad practices his presentation, and I call Avery four times. Each time, she tells me that Elliott is fine. That he's still asleep. That he's still alive.

Each time, I cry.

My mom leaves another sweater for Elliott on my bed.

I cry.

By four o'clock, when we head over to the town square for final preparations, I don't have any tears left. My tear ducts are empty, and oddly enough, I feel done with the weeping.

I lift my chin and put my game face on. Elliott needs strong vibes, positive energy. So that's what I'll give him.

When we arrive, we drop supplies off at city hall, then we head to the square, where the live band is warming up and the lights are merrily shining. I'm dressed in a sparkly black party dress, and my hair is twisted in an elegant chignon. Drink tables are set up with steaming cider, both alcoholic and non, and Christmas cookies are arranged artfully. My parents have rented large patio heaters to keep it comfortable.

"Those were my idea," Emily tells me.

"Thank you," I answer. She beams.

The band starts playing Christmas carols, and the transformation into a picture-perfect movie setting is complete.

Townspeople arrive and mingle, and I watch for Jonah. He left earlier to get his dad, and he hasn't yet returned.

Everyone is dressed for a party. It's nice to see the stress fade away from people's faces, if only for one night. They laugh, they dance, they chat.

Jonah arrives with his father, while Nancy, Jace, and Izzy hand out gift bags.

The party is a wild success. In the middle of "Rockin' Around the Christmas Tree," Jonah's dad takes the stage.

"It's time for the town council meeting. If you care to attend, you are welcome. It's in the city hall. Happy holidays, everyone."

Everyone stares.

Jonah's father hasn't even *acknowledged* the holidays in thirty-three years.

Almost everyone walks to the city hall, and at seven on the dot, Fred Reid, Heather's dad and president of the council, begins the meeting.

"We'll hear both business proposals," he announces. "And then we'll vote as a community. This will not be up to the council alone—we want everyone's voice to matter."

He turns to my dad to invite him to the stage, but to my surprise, Jonah steps up.

"Do you mind if I deviate from the agenda?" he asks. "As the independent financial analyst, I've had the opportunity to examine both proposals, and I have a solution that might be a better fit. A compromise, if you will."

Fred eyes Jonah. "Judd or Rich, do you object?"

"We can hear him out," Judd says, but his expression is guarded. It's clear he has no idea what Jonah is up to, and neither do I.

Jonah takes the podium, and he signals the slideshow to begin.

"My dad reminded me the other day that my marketing and product teams are amazing," he says. "And then I started wondering . . . What if I use their skills for *good*? I asked them to deliver this product, and they've definitely delivered."

He clicks a remote, and mocked-up photos of "Winter Falls Christmas Memory Village" rotate through the presentation. Retro buildings, like in Jace's plan, but with a Christmas theme, like in Dad's. It's a village that's surrounded by brick walls so that memory residents can't wander away but that is also a year-round Christmas village where folks can come to visit any time for sleigh rides, hot cider, and Christmas shopping. Residents get to experience the magic of Christmas every day—because what could possibly be better than Christmas every day when your memories are failing and you're scared?

The idea of merging the two villages is brilliant.

It makes complete sense.

"So in summary," Jonah wraps up, "I think that with this plan, both parties—the Turners and my father—can be satisfied, and the town of Winter Falls will find itself in a win-win situation, with a world-class memory treatment village and a year-round Christmas tourist destination."

"But your father doesn't want Christmas year-round," my dad protests. "He doesn't want it at all, in fact."

"Dad?" Jonah turns to his father, and they lock eyes. It's very, very apparent that Judd hadn't known anything about this. He searches Jonah's face, searching for something. "We have to let it go, Dad," he says. "It's time. Life needs to go on . . . for everyone."

The room is silent. And then . . . Judd nods.

The room erupts into cheers.

"With this turn of events, there is no need to have an emergency mayoral election," my dad announces.

There is more cheering and shouting and celebrating.

Jonah finds me in the melee.

"You sly dog," I say to him. "A heads-up would've been nice."

"I thought of it last night, while I was watching you sleep with Elliott. I knew that we could compromise, just like you'd compromised your lifestyle for this dog that you love now. So I called in a favor with my marketing team, and they worked all day to deliver this."

"It's perfect," I tell him. "You're a genius."

"I am, aren't I?" He grins.

"I'm going to go text Avery, but I'll be right back."

He nods, and I slip away. While I'm standing to the side texting the vet, Jace comes over to me. "Have you seen my mom?"

I shake my head. "Not since she was handing out gift bags."

"She's gone."

My dad turns to us. "She was looking at Christmas lights with Judd a little bit ago."

Sure enough, we find her sitting with Judd in the town square, mesmerized by the Christmas lights.

"Look at the snowmen, Jerry," she says to Jonah's father. "Have you ever seen anything like it?"

"No, I haven't," Judd says. Izzy keeps hold of his elbow, and for the first time in thirty-three years, Jonah's father attends a Christmas party. He tends to Izzy, taking her to get hot cider and a slice of red-and-green cake.

I'm hunting for Jonah again when I notice Padraig sitting outside the B&B and in front of his future bookstore. He's got a red-plaid blanket wrapped around his shoulders, and I bring him a cup of hot cider.

"Thank you," he says, taking the cup. "It seems everything has worked out amazingly well."

"So far," I tell him. "And Elliott is stable. Avery thinks he's going to fully recover."

"That's the best news I've had all day," he says with a grin.

"Me too." I look at him. "How are the last few chapters coming along?"

"They're finished," he says, rubbing his hands together. "I sent them to you yesterday morning."

"Oh! I'm sorry. I didn't see them," I answer, disappointed. "I could've read them today! How did you end it?"

"I think . . . I think you should read them yourself. To get the full effect."

"I can't wait," I tell him honestly. "I'll read them in the morning—as a Christmas gift to myself."

Jonah comes to find me, and he grabs my hand, pulling me

back to the party, looping me around to dance. He wraps his arm around my waist. I breathe him in.

"I can't believe you fixed everything like this," I tell him finally. "This is impressive."

"There's only one question left," he says. "What now?"

I look up at him, and he's solemn.

"Noel, when I came here, I was annoyed. I didn't want to be here, but I didn't really want to be at home in New York, either. I wanted something, but I wasn't sure what. I was empty, but I wasn't sure why. Then, a competitor—someone I've respected for years—offered me a job in London."

My heart stops. "London?"

He nods. "And two weeks ago, I might've taken it. But now?"

I wait.

"Now, I can't."

"Why?" I ask.

"Because you're here. Because my dad is here. Because my life is here. Only I wasn't really *living* much before. I just did a lot of *working*. I'd like to try really living. Now. With you."

"What are you saying?" I ask. I can't seem to suck in a breath.

"I'm saying that I don't know where we should live. I don't know what we should do. But I am saying that I want to be with you. Every day. Beginning right now."

Everyone around us bursts into applause, and I hadn't even known people were listening.

He pulls me to him and stares into my eyes.

He waits.

And then . . . I say . . . "Yes."

The crowd goes wild.

CHAPTER THIRTY-THREE

Noel

Christmas Morning

The last gift has my name on it.

I carefully open the beautiful wrapping and pull out Pad's manuscript, complete with the final chapter.

"He brought it early this morning," my mom says. "He said he'd already emailed the ending to you but that he wanted you to have the whole book typewritten. The original."

I clutch it to my chest.

"It's a perfect gift," I say happily. Emily tries to steal it so that she can read it first, but I tuck it safely into the waistband of my pj's.

It's not until after our breakfast feast that I steal away to wait for Jonah to arrive, and as I do, I pull out the manuscript.

A Christmas Wish

I skim through the chapters I've already read until I come to the last two chapters, where once again, the author shifts to a third-person POV. It takes me a moment to acclimate, because he's changed the name of the town to Winter Falls, which makes sense since he's based his book upon it. It doesn't take me long to get pulled in once again, and with a start, I realize that Pad also changed the names of the characters.

As Elliott nudged open the back door, Moxie followed him, and they made their way to unexpected freedom.

They trotted to the end of the driveway but stopped there in their tracks.

A large gray wolf sat staring back at them, his yellow gaze hungry as it zeroed in on the small kitten in front of him. His lip drew back to reveal large teeth as he leaped to his feet.

Moxie spun and ran back to the house, while Elliott lunged to intervene. In a moment of rare ferocity born from the need to protect his friend, Elliott chased the wolf out of town and across the countryside. . . .

My breath freezes in my throat as I skim through a retelling of the night when we waited to see if Elliott would survive. *This chapter was written before the event.* I keep skimming, past where Jonah proposes to me to Christmas morning.

. . . Christmas morning in Winter Falls was one for the books.

The Turners celebrated in a larger-than-life way, which of course was no surprise. The surprise was that Judd and Jonah

Blake celebrated for the first time in thirty-three years as they took Izzy to church to sing.

Plans for the Winter Falls Christmas Memory Village were underway, and the townspeople had hope that something good was coming for the first time in a long while.

Jonah and Noel were in love, everyone around could see it, could feel it, and they loved it. It was something else— something to believe in.

Elliott healed from his injuries and lived to carry out many more adventures, with his trusty little cat Moxie riding sidecar in his candy saddle. When Mrs. Turner had made it, she hadn't realized at the time that she was designing feline transportation.

Jonah and Noel returned to New York City after the holiday and Jonah attended the New Year's Eve party for Lillianna Cox with Noel. They were a sensation, and there was talk right then and there that Noel had the job of editor in chief in the bag.

The problem was . . . she no longer wanted it.

She wanted to edit and she wanted to get back to the story, back to the author. She didn't want anything to do with the executive-level stuff that came with the EIC job. She had to save her time for the Winter Falls Christmas Memory Village, since she and Jonah were going to become personal investors.

They would go on to live part-time in the city, and part-time under the big Wyoming skies.

Elliott and Moxie loved their life. They loved being jet-setting pets and they kept the doorman Matthew wrapped around their paws. He kept dog treats in his left pocket and cat

*treats in his right, and you'd better believe that they remem-
bered which pocket was which.*

*As far as the Turners, they were living out their dream.
They were surrounded by Christmas every day for the rest of
their lives, in the town that they loved, and with the daughter
and son-in-law whom they loved more than anything.*

*Izzy and Judd became best friends, and he found quite a bit
of wisdom in her lucid moments.*

*The memory village became known throughout the coun-
try for its cutting-edge techniques and for the happiness of its
residents. (Ten out of ten residents would recommend it to a
friend.)*

*And Padraig, well, he lives above the bookstore and makes
himself available to other folks in Winter Falls who might want
to change their stories. All they need is a magic snow globe to
wish upon, and an enchanted typewriter to write their story.*

That's when I stop reading, pull on my boots, and run into
town, through the town square, into Queen Bee's, and up to
Pad's room.

On Christmas morning.

In my pajamas.

I'm breathless when he answers.

"Noel, what a nice surprise," he greets me. "I wasn't expecting you until later. You skipped to the end, didn't you?"

"Was this always about me?" I hold up the manuscript.
"You've changed the names of the characters and pulled Izzy
and Judd into it. Was this always about us?"

He stares at me.

"Pad, did I wish into a snow globe that my life would be different?" I ask him, knowing full well that I sound nuts.

Padraig touches his nose and shakes his head. "Noel, does that sound like something you would do?"

"It doesn't sound like the me in this moment, because I wouldn't change a thing about my life right now. But did I before? Has my life changed and I don't know it?"

Pad smiles at me kindly. "Dear girl, do you love your life now?"

I nod. "I do."

"Then do you really want to question it?" he asks. "I mean, does it really matter?"

I think about that. And then slowly, I shake my head.

"I guess it doesn't."

"Merry Christmas, Noel."

"Merry Christmas, Pad." I walk toward the door and then pause. "Pad, your last chapter. Is that what will happen?"

He smiles again and chuckles, with his hand pressed to his belly. "What do you think, Noel? Do you think I can see into the future?"

I look at him carefully, into his faded eyes and kindly face. And then I honestly say, "I don't know what to think anymore, Pad."

"It's okay, though, don't you think?" he asks. "Time will tell. It always does."

"I'm glad I met you, Pad," I tell him with a smile.

He smiles back. "Me too, Noel."

When I make it back to my parents' house, Jonah is there waiting for me, and just like Pad's typewriter had written, he, Judd, and Jace had taken Izzy to church to sing this morning.

When he can steal a second alone with me, Jonah pulls me into my dad's den.

"I wanted to give you your gift in private," he says with a strange look in his eyes.

I smile and reach for him, but he pulls away to reach into his pocket.

He pulls out a box.

Inside, there is a simple princess-cut diamond. "It was my mother's," he says. "I was wondering . . . if you'd . . ."

"Yes. I would be honored to wear her ring." I throw my arms around his neck and inhale him. I run my hands over his back and pull him close.

"Yes," I say again for good measure. "Absolutely yes."

He kisses me and grins against my lips.

"I love you," he says, unafraid.

"I love you, too."

He kisses me, once, twice, three times.

"I'll be a good husband," he promises.

"I know you will," I answer.

He runs his nose along my neck until he gets to my ear. He whispers into it, "Will you be a good wife?"

"Every day," I answer. Then I bite his earlobe.

"It will always be interesting," he says.

"That, I can agree upon."

It's not until later, after everyone has gone home and my

parents have gone to bed and Emily is asleep on the sofa, that I pull Pad's final chapter back out.

Lying in bed, I finish it.

Jonah did let the bad memories slip away. Bit by bit, until they were gone. And once they were exorcised, he opened his heart to things he never had before.

One year later, their son, Ethan, was born, and two years later, their daughter, Kate. Elliott was their nanny dog, a role that was grossly underpaid but came with bonuses in sticky hugs and Kool-Aid grins.

Jonah and Noel decided to be like Wyatt and Josephine Earp, who promised to never be apart for longer than a day. Bit by bit, year by year, they built a life bigger, better, and more loving than they'd ever dreamed possible.

The little boy who was too afraid to love had found more love than he knew what to do with.

I suck in a breath and hold the pages against my chest.

What if . . . could it be . . .

"Please," I say aloud. "Please."

I fall asleep with that wish upon my lips.

Across town, moonlight shines into a window, falling upon a snow globe sitting on a stack of books.

The glittery snow stirs, lifting into the liquid, surrounding the glass family in a flurry that lasts several minutes before once again settling into motionless silence.

ACKNOWLEDGMENTS

I'd love to thank everyone who trusts me to deliver a story worthy of your time—my readers, editors, agent. My husband, my family.

A story goes through many stages before it lands in your hands—the idea needs to be cultivated, the red pen needs to be used, covers need to be designed, marketing happens . . . It takes a village, and I appreciate everyone in mine.

Thank you.

Truly.

ABOUT THE AUTHOR

COURTNEY COLE is a *New York Times* bestselling author who loves eating her emotions for breakfast. She also loves witty banter, cashmere socks, and walking along the beach at midnight. Speaking of midnight, she also loves decorating for Christmas at 12:01 A.M. on November 1. She believes that blond hair dye and red lipstick can change your life, and a well-timed smile can change the world. Learn more about Courtney and her books at courtneycolecreates.com.

ALSO BY
COURTNEY COLE

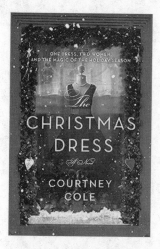

"A very heartwarming, touching story about the magic of true love, family, and friendship."

—HARLEQUINJUNKIE

From *New York Times* bestselling author Courtney Cole, the magic of the Christmas season sends a woman back in time to the 1940s where she meets her own grandmother and learns the true meaning of family and the holiday.